SMART
WOMEN

"Blume's sensitivity to a child's viewpoint elevates this book . . . the children are splendid in their richness."

—The New York Times Book Review

SMART
WOMEN . . .

"is filled with good insights and great, quotable one-liners . . . Men are always asking what women like and don't like, want and don't want. Why don't they read Judy Blume and find out?"

—Washington Post

SMART
WOMEN

"Real people experiencing real crises . . . Ms. Blume has an emollient style which, while realistic on detail, also exudes good feeling . . ."

—John Barkham Reviews

Books by Judy Blume

Forever . . .
Smart Women
Wifey

Published by POCKET BOOKS

SMART WOMEN

JUDY BLUME

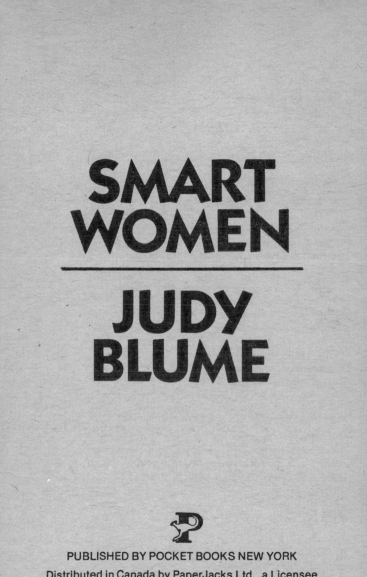

PUBLISHED BY POCKET BOOKS NEW YORK

Distributed in Canada by PaperJacks Ltd., a Licensee
of the trademarks of Simon & Schuster, Inc.

The author gratefully acknowledges permission from Holt, Rine-
hart and Winston, Publishers, the Estate of Robert Frost, and
Jonathan Cape Ltd. to quote from "Stopping by Woods on a
Snowy Evening" from *The Poetry of Robert Frost*, edited by
Edward Connery Lathem. Copyright 1923, © 1969 by Holt,
Rinehart and Winston. Copyright 1951 by Robert Frost.

POCKET BOOKS, a division of Simon & Schuster, Inc.
1230 Avenue of the Americas, New York, N.Y. 10020
In Canada distributed by PaperJacks Ltd.,
330 Steelcase Road, Markham, Ontario

Published by arrangement with G. P. Putnam's Sons
Library of Congress Catalog Card Number: 83-15958

ISBN: 0-671-50268-9

First Pocket Books printing March, 1985

10 9 8 7 6 5 4 3 2 1

POCKET and colophon are registered trademarks
of Simon & Schuster, Inc.

Printed in Canada

*To the smart women in my life . . .
my friends*

PART
ONE

1

MARGO SLID OPEN THE GLASS DOOR LEADING TO THE PATIO outside her bedroom. She set the Jacuzzi pump for twenty minutes, tested the temperature of the water with her left foot, tossed her robe onto the redwood platform, then slowly lowered herself into the hot tub, allowing the swirling water to surround her body.

The late August night air was clear and crisp. The mountains were lit by an almost full moon. The only sounds were Margo's own breathing and the gentle gurgling of the water in the tub. She inhaled deeply to get the full aroma of the cedar as it steamed up, closed her eyes, and felt the tensions of the day disappear.

"Margo . . ."

The voice, coming out of the stillness of the night, startled her. She looked around, but all she saw were the barrels of overgrown petunias and geraniums surrounding the hot tub. She never remembered to pick off the dead flowers, but that didn't stop them from flourishing.

"Over here . . ." the voice said.

He was standing on the other side of her weathered wood fence. She could barely see him.

"What are you doing?" she asked sharply.

"Just wondering if you'd like to have a drink. I'm Andrew Broder. I'm staying in the house next door."

"I know who you are," Margo snapped. "Didn't anyone ever tell you it's impolite to spy on your neighbor?"

"I'm not spying," he said.

"And that eleven is too late to come over for a drink?"

"Is it?" he asked.

"Yes, it is."

"I'm a night person," he said. "It feels early to me."

"Well, it's not. Some of us have to get up and go to work in the morning." She expected him to apologize and then to leave. She looked away. Certainly she was curious about him but no more so than any of her friends' ex-husbands. Last Saturday she had seen him struggling with grocery bags. As he had walked from his truck to his house one had torn and everything had come crashing out, including a carton of eggs. Margo had watched from her upstairs deck, where she'd been reading. He'd stood there quietly, shaking his head and muttering. Then he'd cleaned up the mess, climbed back into his truck, and an hour later had returned with two more bags of groceries.

And on Sunday she'd heard him laughing with his daughter, Sara. She'd thought how nice it is for a father to enjoy his kid that way. And then she'd felt a pang because she

4

never heard her kids laughing with Freddy any more. She didn't even know if they did laugh together.

"Look," he said, and Margo realized that he was still standing by the fence. "Francine said that . . ."

"Francine?"

"I guess you call her B.B. . . . she said that if I needed to borrow sugar I could ask you."

"Is that what you want then, sugar at eleven o'clock at night?"

"No," he said. "I told you, I thought we could have a drink." He held up a bottle.

"What is it?" Margo asked. "It's dark. I can't see that far."

"Courvoisier. I've got the glasses too."

Margo laughed. "You're certainly prepared, aren't you?"

"I try to be."

"The gate's unlatched," she said.

And then another voice went off in her head. *Margo, Margo . . . what are you doing?*

I'm not doing anything.

Bullshit.

Look, he's not a killer, he's not a rapist, I know that much.

You know more than that. You know why you shouldn't let him in.

It's just for a drink.

I've heard that before.

I'm just being neighborly.

Some people never learn.

He opened the gate and walked across the small yard to

5

the hot tub. He sat down at the edge and poured them each a drink. "To neighbors," he said, lifting his glass.

"It's dangerous to drink in a hot tub," Margo told him. "The alcohol does something . . . it can kill you." She dipped her tongue into the glass, tasting the brandy, then set it down. Her body was submerged in the foaming water and the steam had made her black hair curl and mat around her face.

"You look different up close," he said.

"Up close?"

"I've seen you a few times, walking from your car to your house."

"Oh." So, he'd been watching her too.

"You look like the girl on the Sun Maid Raisin box."

"I'm hardly a girl."

"Her older sister then."

"Is that supposed to be a compliment?"

"I like raisins," he said.

Margo tried to remember how the girl on the raisin box looked, but all she could picture was a floppy red bonnet.

"I've never been in a hot tub," he said. "What's it like?"

"Hot," she told him. "Some people can't take it."

"I'd like to give it a try," he said.

"There are several hot tub clubs in town, but Boulder Springs is the best. You should call in advance. They get booked up."

"I was thinking more of now," he said.

"Now? In my hot tub?"

"I wouldn't mind," he said, pulling his sweatshirt over his head.

"Hey . . . wait a minute . . ."

He kicked off his sandals, loosened his belt buckle, and dropped his jeans. He wore bikini underpants. Margo was suspicious of men who wore boxer shorts. Freddy had worn boxer shorts, had insisted that they be ironed. "Wait a minute . . ." she said again, as he stepped out of his underwear. She hadn't looked directly at him as he had undressed, but she'd seen enough to know that he was tall and lean and very appealing. She'd seen that while she'd been watching him last weekend. She'd seen that while he'd been fully dressed. "What do you think you're doing?"

He slid into the tub, facing her. "I thought you said *okay* . . ."

"No, I didn't say that."

"You want me to get out?"

"I didn't want you to get *in.*"

"Oh, I misunderstood."

"Yes, you did."

"But now that I'm here, is it okay? Can I try it for a few minutes?"

"I suppose a few minutes can't hurt."

When the Jacuzzi timer went off he climbed out and reset it for another twenty minutes. But before it went off again he told her he was feeling light-headed. Margo urged him to get out quickly, before he fainted. He did, and just in time. As it was she had to wrap a blanket around him, revive him with a glass of Gatorade, and help him back to his place. It wasn't easy getting him up the steep flight of outside stairs leading to the apartment over the garage.

"I warned you," she said, as he slumped onto the sofa in his living room.

7

"It was worth it," he told her.

"You'd better take a couple of aspirin and get some sleep."

"Can I try it again tomorrow?" he asked.

"I don't think so. It doesn't seem to agree with you."

"I'll get used to it."

"I've got two kids, you know."

"I've got one."

"Mine are teenagers."

"Mine's twelve."

"Mine have been away all summer, visiting their father. They're coming home tomorrow."

"I'd like to meet them."

"Don't be too sure."

"You're very defensive about them, aren't you?"

"Me, defensive about my children?"

"You have beautiful breasts," he said.

Margo looked down and flushed. Her robe was open to the waist. She pulled it closed. "Another piece of useful information," she said. "Hot tubbing is not a sexual experience."

"I'll try to remember that," he said.

"Goodnight," she told him.

"Goodnight, Margo."

The next afternoon, while Margo was driving to Denver to meet her children at the airport, she thought about last night and her strange encounter with Andrew Broder. She never should have let him into her hot tub. It was going to be tricky living next door to him for the next three months now.

Her impulsive behavior, though she was well aware of it, continued to cause her problems.

Didn't I warn you?

Okay . . . okay, so you warned me.

Margo knew that B.B. was divorced, but unlike other divorced women, B.B. never complained about her former husband. Never said a word about how cheap he was or how miserable a father. Never talked about how he ran around with girls young enough to be his daughter or the fact that he had no sense of humor or that he was colder than a fish. Never laughed bitterly about the lack of style in his lovemaking. B.B. never shared the details of how or why her marriage to Andrew had failed and Margo didn't feel close enough to ask. Until last May, until the day that B.B. had called Andrew a fucking bastard, Margo had never even heard B.B. say his name.

It had probably been a mistake to arrange for him to rent the apartment in the Hathaway house. B.B. should not have asked for her help in finding him a place to live. But what's done is done, Margo thought.

She glanced at herself in the rearview mirror, wondering what her children would think of her new layered haircut. For years she had worn her dark hair shoulder length, parted in the middle, and blown dry, but this summer she had felt ready for a change.

"Look," Stan, the hair stylist, had said, assessing her, "you might as well take advantage of what you've got . . . good skin, nice eyes, and naturally wavy hair."

That's it? Margo had thought. *After forty years that's what it comes down to?*

After her haircut she had vowed to let her hair grow back

and never cut it again. But now she had to admit, it did show off her eyes.

"We should have named her Hazel," her father used to joke, "for those big eyes."

"Who knew she was going to have such eyes," her mother would say.

"You have unbelievably ugly eyes," James had said, making her laugh. James had been her first lover and something about Andrew Broder reminded her of him. It could have been the way he looked directly at her or the way he laughed, heartily, without holding back.

Margo had met James when she was seventeen. He was a tall, lanky college freshman, wildly funny, yet sweet and tender, a perfect combination. It was his wry sense of humor that kept them going during their first awkward attempts at making love and from then on their lovemaking was filled as much with fun and laughter as with passion, which wasn't all that bad, Margo realized later. In fact, there was a lot to be said for it.

James had died of pancreatic cancer two and a half years after they met. She had not even known that he was sick. Her mother had come across the obituary. *James Schoenfeld, twenty, following a brief illness.* Even though Margo and James weren't going together anymore, hadn't seen each other for sixteen months, his death had so affected her that she had not made love again until she and Freddy were married.

At the time Margo could not stop thinking about the night she and James had broken up. She could not stop thinking about how she had flirted with another boy at the fraternity party, had actually slipped him a piece of paper with her phone number on it. James had consoled himself by chug-a-lugging a six-pack of Miller's. Then he'd passed out on the floor. Margo had had no choice but to let the other boy, Roger, drive her home. The next afternoon James had come over, looking pale and acting sheepish, and he had apologized for his behavior. They'd gone for a walk to the pond, but she had not let him kiss her. "It's over," she'd said. "I'm not going to see you anymore."

"Why?" he'd asked. "That's all I want to know. Why?"

"I don't know," she'd said. "It's just something that I feel . . . or don't feel . . ."

James had turned and walked straight into the pond, fully dressed, his hands over his head. She had stood on the grassy bank, yelling and screaming and laughing until tears stung her eyes. Maybe she did love him, she'd thought. But there were so many boys to love. She wasn't ready to love just one.

Her mother urged her not to confuse sadness with guilt. It was not her fault that James had died. Her father cradled her in his arms, stroking her hair. Her sisters, one older, one younger, stood in the doorway to her bedroom, silent.

Margo went to the funeral by herself. After paying her respects to James's parents and his brother she asked who the small, long-haired girl was, the one who was weeping hysterically, and his brother said, "That's Rachel. She and James were going together."

Margo nodded and bit her lip. James had replaced her. Well, what had she expected? She approached Rachel. "I'm Margo," she said. "I just wanted to tell you how sorry I am."

Rachel stopped crying and looked at Margo. "He told me

about you," she said. "About how you were his first girlfriend. It was a long time ago, wasn't it?"

Not so long, Margo thought.

"We were pinned," Rachel said. On Rachel's black dress was the Phi Ep pin that Margo had once dreamed of wearing.

She still had dreams about James. James walking into the pond. She would call, "Come back, James. Let's start over . . ." but it was always too late. She would awaken with tears on her cheeks.

Freddy had been as different from James as any young man Margo had met. Perhaps that was why she had married him.

She had been married to Freddy for fourteen years and had never been unfaithful, although she had certainly thought about it. After Freddy, there was Leonard, and after Leonard, her boss, Michael Benson. Then, a series of brief affairs, some lasting months, some weeks, some just the night. There had been twelve of these men, from a physiology professor at Colorado University, to a Buddhist at Naropa, to more than one construction worker. And then, this summer, for five days, there had been Eric.

Margo kept a list of her lovers at the office, in her top desk drawer, the one that locked. She wondered if other women did the same. She wondered what her children would think if she died suddenly and they had to go through her papers. There were seventeen names on her list. Seventeen men. Not so many lovers for a divorced woman of forty, she thought. She knew some women who barhopped every weekend, picking up men for the night. They could wind up with fifty lovers in a year. She'd been divorced for five years. Multiply that by fifty and she could have had two hundred and fifty lovers by now. She laughed aloud at the idea of two hundred and fifty lovers. It seemed to her both wildly funny and grotesque, and then, terribly sad and she bit her lip to keep from crying, the idea was so depressing.

She switched on the car radio and rolled down her window. A piece of brush blew across the highway, rested briefly on the hood of her car, then flew off. The end of summer, Margo thought.

It had been a full summer. She'd worked long hours on a new project with Michael Benson, a complex of solar condominiums in town. She'd taken only one break, a week in Chaco Canyon, where she had gone to be alone, completely and absolutely alone for the first time in her life. It was to be a test of self. To prove—she wasn't sure—that she could survive on her own, she supposed. But on her second day out she had met Eric, twenty years old and irresistible. Eric, she decided later, was to be the last of her impulsive sexual encounters. Because afterwards she always felt empty. Empty, lonely, and afraid.

She would wait the next time she felt tempted and make an effort instead to find a steady man. In the meantime she would concentrate on her work, which was going well, and on her kids, who were coming home.

She had been up early this morning to cook their favorite dish, a tangy chicken in rum sauce. She hoped it would be a happy homecoming, hoped the new school year would be an improvement over the last one. She was going to try. She was going to try to give them more time, more understanding, to be there when they needed to talk, to be less judgmental, to be the warm and gentle earth mother she had always wanted to be, yet never seemed able to pull off. This would be her last chance with Stuart. He would graduate next spring, then go off to college.

And with Michelle, she didn't know. She didn't think she could take another year of hostility. Maybe when the plane landed she would find that Michelle was not on it. That Michelle had stayed in New York with Freddy and Aliza. What would she do then? Jump on the next plane to New York and drag Michelle back? She wasn't sure. If only Michelle could understand that you don't quit just because of rough times. That you work through your problems not by shutting out the people who love you most, but by letting them in to help and comfort you.

Margo turned off the Valley Highway, then followed the signs to the airport. She was twenty minutes early. Good. She'd have time for a quick cup of coffee before the plane landed. Time to relax for a moment before her reentry into motherhood.

Later that night, after the welcome home dinner, Margo showered and put on the robe that her friend Clare had given to her last week for her fortieth birthday. God, the feel of the silk against her nakedness. Yards and yards of pure silk, the color of a young girl's blush.

"When you put it on in the morning you're supposed to glow," Clare had said. "That's what the saleswoman told me, anyway. So what do you think?"

"I think it's not the kind of robe you put on in the morning," Margo had said, "unless it's the morning after . . ."

They had laughed over that.

There were rumors around town that Clare was part Navajo, rumors that Clare enjoyed more than anyone. And when she played it to the hilt she did look like some gigantic, exotic half-breed, with her dark, silver-streaked hair, two slashes of color accenting her high cheekbones, deeply tanned skin, and ropes of turquoise and coral wrapped around her neck. Had Margo met Clare ten years earlier she might not have taken the time to get to know her. She might have put Clare down as an oil heiress from West Texas, with an accent so offensive you couldn't possibly get past the first sentence.

"When I celebrated my fortieth birthday, last year," Clare had said, "I bought myself a sheer black nightgown and a feather boa."

Margo was reminded that she still had a drawerful of sheer black things, left over from her time with Leonard, but she hadn't worn them lately. Hadn't even thought about them. Too bad.

Leonard had been one of the reasons Margo had left New York three years ago. She'd been running away from a no-win affair with him, running away from Freddy and his new bride, and finally, running away from herself, hoping to find a new self in the mountains, and if not exactly finding one, then creating one.

She'd decided on Boulder because of her interest in solar design and was lucky enough to land a job with a small architectural firm, Benson and Gould, based on her port-folio, a letter of recommendation from her boss in New York, and an interview that had gone very well. Later, she'd found out that Gould was spending more than half his time in the Bahamas, that Benson had a neurotic fear of responsibility, and that they had been overjoyed when she'd accepted their job offer.

Margo moved to Boulder in mid-August and, with her half of the cash from the sale of the co-op on Central Park West, bought a house on a dirt road, tucked away against the mountainside. A funky, upside-down kind of house, with the kitchen and living room on the second floor, to take advantage of the view of the Flatirons, and the bedrooms on the first, with a hot tub outside the master, which is what really sold her. The realtor, a woman called B.B., assured Margo that the house could only go up in value.

Two months after Margo moved in, B.B. introduced her to Clare, who was looking for an architect to renovate her gallery.

Now Margo walked down the hall to say goodnight to her children. Michelle was sitting up in bed reading *Lady Chatterley's Lover.* "How do you like it?" Margo asked.

"I'm only reading it because I have to . . . it's on my summer reading list," Michelle said defensively.

Margo laughed. "Not the book . . . this . . ." She twirled around the room, showing off the silk robe, keeping time to the music coming from Michelle's stereo. It sounded like Joan Armatrading, but Margo couldn't be sure. Michelle was very into female vocalists singing about the female experience.

"God, Mother . . . what *is* that thing you're wearing?"

"It's a robe. Clare gave it to me for my birthday. Isn't it gorgeous?"

"It's a weird gift for one divorced woman to give to another. She could have given you a painting from her gallery. We have a lot of bare white walls.''

"I think she wanted to make it a personal gift.''

"Yeah . . . well, it's personal all right.''

"So how do you like it?''

"It's okay, I suppose, if you're into silks and satins.''

"I meant the book.''

Michelle looked up at Margo, her mouth set defiantly, ready to do battle. "I told you . . . it's assigned reading.''

"I know that. But you can still either like it or not like it.'' Margo warned herself to stop. This conversation was going no place.

Michelle closed the book and rested it on her lap. She gave Margo a hostile look. "It's an interesting book . . . in an old-fashioned way.''

In an old-fashioned way, Margo thought. That was hard to take. She remembered when she'd read *Lady Chatterley*. She had been in college and she'd found the sex scenes so steamy she'd locked herself in the hall bathroom and stood under the shower for an hour. "D. H. Lawrence lived in the southwest . . . in Taos. Did you know that?''

"Of course I know that, Mother. But this particular book is set in England.''

"Yes,'' Margo said, "I know.'' She approached the bed and tried to drop a kiss on Michelle's cheek, but Michelle squirmed away.

"Please, Mother . . . don't be disgusting.''

"Goodnight,'' Margo said, trying to sound pleasant, trying not to let Michelle see that she was getting to her.

"Goodnight,'' Michelle answered, opening her book

again. "And Mother . . . you really should do something about your breath. Have you tried Lavoris?"

"I had chili for lunch."

"Well, you don't have to advertise."

Margo sighed and left the room.

She did not understand how or why Michelle had turned into this impossible creature. Margo would never voluntarily live with such an angry, critical person. Never. But when it was your own child you had no choice. So she kept on trying, kept hoping for the best, kept waiting for the sweetness to come back.

She passed the bathroom that separated her children's bedrooms and stopped in front of Stuart's closed door. She knocked.

"Yeah?" Stuart called over the latest album from the Police.

"Just wanted to say goodnight," Margo said.

"Yeah . . . okay . . . goodnight . . ."

Margo had been speechless when she had first seen Stuart at the airport that afternoon. It wasn't just the haircut, but the clothes. A Polo shirt, a sweater tied over his shoulders, a tennis racquet in one hand, a canvas duffel in the other. He looked as if he'd stepped right out of some Ralph Lauren ad in the Sunday *Times*. She'd had to suppress a giggle. She wasn't sure if she was glad or sorry that her son had turned into a preppie over the summer.

"Where'd you get all the new clothes?" Margo had asked him, driving back from Denver.

"Dad took him shopping . . . to East Hampton," Michelle said.

"I can talk for myself, Mouth," Stuart said. "And I don't

18

think there's anything wrong with taking a little pride in the way you look. Even Mother has a new haircut."

"I noticed," Michelle said.

Before Margo had a chance to ask Michelle what she thought of it, Stuart said, "I want to get my college applications in early. Dad said he'll take a week off in October and we'll do the tour and interviews together."

Margo felt a pang. She'd always thought she would be the one to take him to his college interviews. She had saved a week of vacation for just that purpose.

"I'm thinking of applying to Amherst, early decision."

"Why Amherst?" Margo asked.

"You know Dad's friend, Wally Lewis?"

"Yes."

"He went there . . . and he said he made contacts at school that have lasted a lifetime."

Margo felt nauseated. This was too much. "Really, Stuart," she said, "you're beginning to sound exactly like your father."

"What's wrong with that?" Stuart asked. "He *is* my male role model, you know. Besides, it's time to think about my future. I've grown up a lot this summer, Mother."

Margo went upstairs to the kitchen, and poured herself a glass of brandy. She wished she didn't feel so alone. She wished she had an ally in her own home. "Here's to you, kid," she said, toasting herself. "You're going to need it."

2

WHAT A CASE HER MOTHER WAS, RUNNING AROUND IN that robe that looked as if it belonged on some ancient movie star, Michelle thought. And expecting Michelle to admire it or something. God! Michelle did not understand what was wrong with her mother. But ever since last winter she had been impossible. Whatever Michelle said Margo took in the wrong way. So naturally she wasn't going to tell Margo the truth about the robe.

On the plane, flying home today, Michelle had hoped that this school year would be better. She had vowed to try—no more towels on the bathroom floor, no more unwashed dishes left in the sink, no more sarcasm. She had hoped that Margo would like her better this year and treat her as a human being, recognizing the fact that she had feelings too. But after just a few hours together they were right back to where they had left off before the summer.

Michelle tried to pinpoint the exact time of the change, but she couldn't. It wasn't the end of one of her mother's love affairs, which was always an intense time around the house, with Margo weeping all over the place, then putting on a big, phony smile for the sake of the children. Also, at the end of an affair Margo tended to appreciate her kids more and to show them a lot of attention and affection.

Like after Leonard.

Leonard had been her mother's first boyfriend after the divorce. The only trouble was, he was married, with three kids, two girls and a boy—Anya, Deirdre, and Stefan. Dumb, asshole names. They used to phone all the time. His wife, Gabrielle, put them up to it. They used to phone and cry and say, *Please give us back our Daddy.* They said it to Michelle and she was only eleven then. How was she supposed to understand what was going on? His kids were younger. They called every week, sometimes twice a week. *Please give us back our Daddy. We miss him. We need him.* Michelle would have been glad to give him back. But he wasn't living with them. He had a place on Gramercy Park. *Your Daddy doesn't live here,* she told his kids. *Call him at his office.*

One time his wife, Gabrielle, came to their apartment, took a gun out of her purse, waved it around, and threatened to kill Margo. It turned out that the gun, which had scared the shit out of them, wasn't real. But it had looked real. And that had been it. The next day Margo decided to leave New York and move to Boulder.

Leonard came out to Colorado one time. *Just passing through,* he had said. *On my way to San Francisco. Just wondered how you were getting along?* They were getting along just fine, thank you, Michelle thought. And that had been the last they'd seen of Leonard.

No, it wasn't the end of an affair. Besides, Michelle kept mental notes of who her mother was sleeping with, so that she would be prepared in case of a disaster, but for the past school year there hadn't been anyone special. No one bringing his kids over for Sunday supper, no hour-long phone calls in the middle of the night, no one appearing in the kitchen unexpectedly in the morning. As far as Michelle could tell, her mother had just been sleeping around this year and not that often either. So it wasn't sex. And it wasn't money or work either. There was a time, right after the divorce, when money and work were Margo's number one problems, but not now.

Michelle rolled over in bed and felt the beginnings of a lump in her throat. She was scared out of her mind that if she couldn't make peace with Margo, Margo would ship her to New York, to Freddy and his Sabra wife. Well, let Margo try it. Michelle would run away. Then Margo would be sorry she'd been such a bitch lately.

She hated it when people told her she looked just like her mother. People were always telling kids they looked just like this parent or that one. It was all such bullshit! If Michelle could look like anyone she knew it would not be her mother, it would be B.B., this big time realtor in Boulder. When B.B. walked into a room, people noticed. Michelle wished that people would notice her that way. A lot of the time Michelle felt invisible.

When they had first moved to town Michelle used to babysit for B.B.'s bratty kid, Sara. B.B. was going out with this movie producer from L.A. and they had some of the most intense fights. They would come storming into the house around midnight and B.B.'s face would be all puffy from crying and twice she had black eyes and she would race into her room and slam the door and then he—his name was Mitch—would pay Michelle and drive her home and he never said anything, except goodnight and thank you very much and B.B. will phone you to make arrangements for next weekend. He wore brown loafers without socks winter and summer and left his shirt unbuttoned so that you could see the hair on his chest, which was black and curly and extremely disgusting.

Michelle had never told her mother about B.B. and Mitch and their fights. She was afraid that if Margo knew she wouldn't let Michelle sit for them anymore. And she never told B.B. or Mitch about the time that Sara bit her on the shoulder because she made Sara turn off the TV and go to bed. And everyone knows the human bite is far more dangerous than the bite of an animal.

Michelle saw B.B. driving around town all the time. She drove a BMW 528i. She had dark red hair, like an Irish setter's, hanging down to her shoulders. Her skin was very white and she was tall and thin and Michelle wondered if maybe she was anorexic, like Katie Adriano, this girl in her class who was always vomiting. Probably B.B. wasn't because she ate out a lot and anorexics don't like restaurants.

B.B. had a slight overbite, but on her it looked good. Michelle knew about teeth because her father was a dentist. Frederic Sampson, D.D.S.—a Professional Corporation. Michelle liked the idea of her father being a professional corporation. It made her feel secure, as if her father owned General Motors or something.

But she hated her father for having insisted that she spend another summer at Camp Mindowaskin. "You have to keep in touch with your own kind," he had told her. "You can't grow up thinking everyone is like . . ."

"Like what?" Michelle had asked.

"Like the people in Boulder."

"What's wrong with the people in Boulder?"

"Nothing is wrong with them, exactly . . . but there's more to life than . . ."

"Than what?"

Her father had sighed heavily.

Her experience as a camp waitress had been a disaster. This was her last summer there, no matter what. She was going to be seventeen, for God's sake. She was old enough to make her own decisions about how to spend her summer. And she was sick of those little bitches calling her The Pioneer just because she lived in Colorado. She might have turned out like them if her parents hadn't been divorced and her mother hadn't moved her away.

And it wasn't any better after camp, when she went out to Bridgehampton to spend two weeks with her father and Aliza. Two weeks of being talked at by her father, when all she wanted was for him to love her the way she was. At dinner the conversations centered around tennis and why, after nine years at camp, Michelle still couldn't serve. *Oh, love me, Daddy . . . please love me . . . never mind my serve. Tell me that you're proud that I'm your daughter. That I'm just right . . . that no matter what you'll always love me . . .*

But that was not the way it was. He loved Aliza now. He was interested in Stuart and his college applications, but not in Michelle. She was nothing to him. Nothing but a pain in the ass. She reminded him of Margo. She heard him say so to his friend, Dr. Fritz. "Every time I look at her," he'd said, "I see Margo."

"You've got to fight those feelings, Freddy," Dr. Fritz had told him.

"I'm trying," her father had said. "But it's not easy."

Michelle had been eleven when her parents were divorced. At the time she had wanted to die. But she got over it. Then, less than two years later, her mother had told her they were moving away.

"Moving where?" Michelle asked.

"To Colorado," her mother answered.

"Colorado?"

"Yes . . . to Boulder."

"Boulder . . . you mean where Mork and Mindy live?"

"Mork and Mindy who?" her mother said.

Michelle had laughed. Her mother was so out of it.

All her friends in New York thought she was really lucky to be moving to the town where Mork and Mindy lived. They said maybe she'd get a job working on their show. They said maybe she'd even get to be a regular and then they'd be able to see her on TV every week. She promised to get Mork's and Mindy's autographs for every one of them.

But when they got to Boulder, Michelle found out that Mork and Mindy hardly ever came to town. They filmed most of their shows in California. She didn't blame them. Boulder was a big zero. It was just this little college town in the middle of nowhere. It couldn't compare to New York

City. And Michelle hated her mother for ruining her life. But she got over that too. And now she even liked it here, especially in winter, when the mountains were covered with snow.

That robe her mother was wearing tonight was such a joke! The idea of it made Michelle laugh into her pillow. But then the lump in her throat started again and this time it wouldn't go away, no matter how hard Michelle swallowed. She didn't understand the lump in her throat any better than she understood her mother. She didn't understand why she cried herself to sleep every night either.

3

B.B. CONCENTRATED ON THE SOUND OF HER BREATHING and the rhythm of her feet as she ran along the road. She did three miles each morning before breakfast. Then she showered, dressed, and was at her office by nine. She ran not just for the physical exercise, but to clear her head. It was a time for solving problems, a time for making decisions. Her body was as trim and firm as it had been when she was twenty, but she felt better now. She supposed one day she would have to face growing old, the way her mother was facing it now, but it seemed very far away. She breathed deeply, reminding herself not to gulp air. Sometimes she gulped and became bloated. She checked her watch as she rounded the corner. She'd gone two in eighteen-four. Not bad, B.B., she told herself.

She hadn't always been called B.B. She'd been named Francine Eloise Brady by her Jewish mother and her Irish father in Miami, in 1940. All her life she had been Francie to her family and friends and Francine to everyone else. Then she married Andrew and had taken his name—Broder. She thought she would be married for the rest of her life, but in twelve years it was over.

She left Miami a month before the divorce was final. She left with Sara, who was six years old, with two suitcases, and with thirty-two thousand dollars in cash, which she had earned selling real estate. She left in the Buick at four in the morning and drove west, away from Florida, away from the ocean, away from reminders that she'd once had another life, a life she could not get back.

She headed for Colorado because the year before she had seen an article in *Architectural Digest* about restored Victorian homes in Boulder. She remembered the color of the sky and the snowcapped mountains in the distance, which seemed as far from anything she had known as possible. When she arrived she checked into the Boulderado Hotel and two days later she bought her own small Victorian house on Highland. A week after that she went to work for the agency through whom she'd bought the house. And after a year she had opened her own agency. *Francine Brady Broder—Elegant Homes*. People around town began to call her B.B. because of her double last names. She didn't mind. She thought it had a snappy sound to it.

She ran up her driveway and paused at the car, checking her pulse. Lucy came up to her and licked her legs. B.B. patted Lucy on the head, then went inside to the kitchen.

"Hi, Mom . . . table's all set," Sara said. "Did you have a good run?"

"Yes, I could have kept going. I didn't even feel tired."

"Did you know that female athletes sometimes have trouble getting pregnant?"

"Really?" B.B. said, washing her hands at the kitchen sink.

"Yes," Sara said, popping an English muffin into the toaster. "I read about it. They get too thin and their periods stop. All that exercise isn't good for their reproductive organs." Sara drained her glass of orange juice and poured another. "So you should be careful, just in case."

"In case what?"

"In case you want to have more children."

"I'm forty, Sara. I'm not about to have any more children."

"You never know," Sara said. "Jennifer's mother is forty-one and she just had a baby."

"Well, I'm not going to have any more babies."

"Okay . . . fine. I just thought you should know."

"Thanks for the warning. Do you want scrambled eggs or fried?"

"Fried . . . so the yolks don't run."

"Hand me the frying pan, would you?" B.B. said, putting up the kettle.

"Do you remember your first day of junior high, Mom?" Sara asked.

"Yes . . . I was so scared I couldn't eat a bite of breakfast and my mother made me carry a buttered roll in my book bag. I flushed it down the toilet in the Girls' Room."

Sara laughed. "I'm not that scared. Besides, all my friends from Mapleton will be with me and Jennifer's in my homeroom."

29

"You're braver than I was."

After breakfast B.B. brushed Sara's hair, which was thick and honey-colored, like Andrew's. "A braid or a ponytail?" B.B. asked.

"A braid," Sara said.

When B.B. finished her hair, Sara collected her new notebook and pencils. They walked to the front door together. "Goodbye . . ." B.B. said, "I love you."

"And I love you," Sara answered.

"For how long?" B.B. asked.

"For always and forever."

"That's how long I'll love you too."

B.B. gave Sara a hug, then went back to the kitchen and put the breakfast dishes in the sink to soak.

Until last spring B.B.'s life in Boulder, aside from Mitch, had been peaceful and rewarding. Then, in May, the letter from Andrew had come. B.B. had arrived at her office a few minutes later than usual that day because she had taken extra time dressing. She had invited Clare and Margo to join her for lunch at The James to discuss an intriguing real estate deal. A twenty acre parcel of land outside of town had come on the market and if she could interest Clare in putting up half the cash, she was ready to make an offer. It was the perfect site for passive-solar cluster housing, a concept she knew appealed to Margo. She was prepared to offer Margo a piece of the action in exchange for her architectural services. She admired Margo's work. It had a class feeling, even when it was just a remodeled garage.

Miranda, B.B.'s secretary, had brought in the morning mail before noon and B.B., thumbing through it, had stopped when she'd come to the letter from Andrew, marked personal.

They never wrote. All communication between them regarding Sara was handled through his attorney in Miami and hers in Boulder. So what was this?

She slit the letter open with a silver and turquoise opener, a gift from a satisfied client. She read it quickly the first time, then slowly, to make sure she understood.

Dear Francine,
I plan to spend the next school year in Boulder, writing another book. That way Sara and I can have more time together, which we are both looking forward to.

I expect to leave here the second week in August and to drive cross-country, arriving in Boulder somewhere around the 20th. I hope that we can work out the arrangements easily when I arrive. I will need to find a small apartment or house, with enough room for Sara. If you have any suggestions I would be grateful.

Yours,
Andrew

She felt herself grow hot, then cold. A pounding began in her temples. And although she rarely sweat, she felt a dampness under her arms.

She stood and walked around her office, watering her African violets, straightening the Fritz Scholder posters on the walls. She went back to her desk and read the letter a third time. She lifted the phone to call her lawyer, then changed her mind and hung up. She folded the letter and dropped it into her purse. She could not believe that he was serious.

She took five shallow breaths and did a Lion, one of the Yoga exercises she learned last year. Then she grabbed her purse and went to meet Margo and Clare at The James.

4

MARGO HAD BEEN SURPRISED BY B.B.'S INVITATION TO lunch last spring. Margo and B.B. were not close. Margo could never get beneath the surface, could never connect with B.B.'s feelings, so she had settled for a friendly relationship rather than a true friendship. Clare was really the link between Margo and B.B. and while the three of them lunched together every now and then it was always informal and arrangements were made at the last minute.

It had been a soft May day, a perfect day to eat outdoors and as they were seated at a table in the courtyard of the restaurant Margo caught the scent of lilacs. They were served by a waitress who was both pleasant and efficient, a welcome change from the sullen crowd usually employed by The James.

B.B. explained why she had asked them to join her as soon as their salads were served and Margo was flattered that B.B.

had chosen her to design the cluster housing and grateful for the opportunity to participate in the joint business venture. If the deal took off it could mean big money. Margo got by on her salary and commissions, had even managed to save a little, but she wasn't exactly rolling in it. Freddy's child support payments helped, but she couldn't count on them after the kids went off to college, nor did she want to.

Several times during lunch B.B. put her hand to her head and closed her eyes, but Margo did not find that unusual. B.B. often seemed to be someplace else, even when she was talking to you, even when it was business.

They lingered over their coffee until B.B. checked her watch and said, "I've got to get back to the office." She paid the check and the three of them walked out of the restaurant. But before they reached the corner B.B. put her hand to her head again and swooned, as if she were about to keel over. Too much wine, Margo thought.

"Are you all right?" Clare asked, grabbing her.

"No," B.B. said quietly. And then she broke away from Clare and flung her purse into the street, shouting, "No, goddamn it, I am not all right!" The contents of her purse spilled out, a bottle of Opium smashing at Margo's feet, lipsticks rolling under cars, a hairbrush, a notebook, a pocket calculator, an envelope, all scattered on the ground. "I wish he were dead!" B.B. yelled.

"Who?" Margo and Clare asked at the same time.

"My ex-husband, the fucking bastard!"

Margo was stunned. Until that day she had never seen B.B. react emotionally to anything. And that was the first she had heard of Andrew Broder.

* * *

34

Five days later Clare had called Margo, asking if she knew how to make chicken soup, because B.B. had not eaten anything but tea and Jell-O since climbing into bed on the afternoon of their lunch.

"She says the only thing she wants to eat is the kind of chicken soup her mother used to make when she was a little girl. Jewish chicken soup. She says her father told her it would cure anything except warts and he wasn't sure it wouldn't cure those too. Do you know how to make it, Margo?"

"I haven't made chicken soup in years," Margo said, "but I could call my mother. I think the secret is in the kind of chicken you use."

"Let's try it," Clare said. "Otherwise I'm afraid she's going to wind up in the hospital."

That night Margo phoned her mother in New York. Her mother was on her way to the ballet at Lincoln Center, but she was delighted that Margo wanted to make chicken soup and she explained how to do it, step by step, reminding Margo to use only a pullet, enough dill, and not to forget the parsnip.

On Saturday morning Margo shopped early. She came home and set the ingredients on her kitchen counter. The house was quiet. Stuart was at work, churning out ice cream, and Michelle was still asleep. Margo washed her hands at the kitchen sink, dried them with a paper towel, rolled up her sleeves, and soon the aroma of her childhood filled the house.

When Michelle came up to the kitchen, rubbing the sleep from her eyes, she sniffed around and asked, "What *are* you doing, Mother?"

"Making chicken soup."

"Chicken soup?"

"Yes. B.B. isn't feeling well. It's for her."

"You never make soup for me when I'm not feeling well."

"I thought you don't like homemade chicken soup, Michelle. I thought you said the little particles of fat floating on top make you nauseous. That's why you always ask for Lipton's when you're sick."

"I like it fine when it's cooked with rice," Michelle said. "The way Grandma used to make it."

"Which Grandma?" Margo said. "Grandma Sampson or Grandma Belle?"

"Grandma Belle," Michelle said. "Grandma Sampson used to make vegetable soup for me and she always strained it so I wouldn't gag on the vegetables."

"Oh, that's right," Margo said and she laughed. "So what's wrong with B.B.?"

"She's depressed. Her former husband is coming to town unexpectedly."

"You mean the Brat's father?"

"Sara's not a brat, Michelle."

"You don't know because you never babysat her."

"Well, that's true. But she's older now."

"I doubt that makes much difference."

"Michelle, you're so hard on people. Why can't you give them a chance?"

"Me . . . hard? Come off it, Mother." She grabbed a carrot from the refrigerator and stalked out of the kitchen.

"Is that all you're having for breakfast?" Margo called.

"Carrots are extremely nutritious."

Late that afternoon Margo tasted the soup. She wasn't sure if she had put in enough dill, but it certainly wasn't bad. She was pleased. She had sworn off everyday cooking when she'd left Freddy, but now she found that cooking could be fun if nobody pressured her. And her kids had learned to cook too.

That night Margo and Clare arrived at B.B.'s house with supper. Margo brought the chicken soup and Clare brought a salad, a french bread, and a bottle of white wine. B.B. was sitting up in bed, wearing a white eyelet robe, her hair pulled back and tied with a ribbon. She looked as fragile and beautiful as Camille on her death bed. She made Margo feel shlumpy in her jeans and plaid shirt. Everything in B.B.'s house was as white and delicate as she was. There were fresh flowers in every room, even the bathrooms. Her house made Margo want to go home to clean, scrub, and redecorate.

B.B. laughed over the chicken soup. "It's delicious," she said. "It's just like my mother's." She finished her first bowl and asked for another. "I'm going to get out of bed tomorrow," she told them. "And on Monday I'm going back to the office. I may even go to see Thorny Abrams . . . just for advice."

Thorny Abrams was one of Boulder's many shrinks. Margo had worked on a solar addition to his house last year. His wife, Marybeth, could never make up her mind about anything, so plans for the addition had to be reworked seven times. Thorny would say, *It's up to Marybeth*. Marybeth would look forlorn and say, *You know I can't make decisions, Thorny*.

"And Richard Haver is looking into the law for me,"

B.B. continued. "It may be that I don't have to let Andrew have Sara at all. We've got an agreement, you know . . . and it calls for two weeks at Christmas, Easter vacation, and one month every summer. That's it. So if he comes to town and isn't allowed to see Sara, then surely he won't stay." She looked from Margo to Clare. "I mean, why would he stay under those circumstances?"

A week after that B.B. had phoned Margo, asking her to meet for a drink after work at the Boulderado.

"I'll get right to the point," B.B. said as soon as they had ordered Perriers. "Do you know if the Hathaway apartment is available?"

"I haven't seen anyone in it lately," Margo told her. "They usually rent it to university people for the summer."

"I'd like you to find out if it is available," B.B. said, "and if it is, I'd like you to secure it in the name of Andrew Broder, for three months beginning the third week in August, at say three hundred and fifty dollars a month."

"You're going to find him a place to live?" Margo asked.

"I've decided that's the best way to deal with it," B.B. said.

"It sounds tricky to me. Are you sure you want to get involved? Why don't you let him find his own place?"

"Because if Sara's going to spend any time with him I want her in a decent neighborhood. If I leave it up to him he'll rent some place off Twenty-eighth Street."

"But you're in the business . . . surely you could . . ."

"Do it for me, Margo . . . please . . ."

"Okay. If you're sure that's what you want."

"It is . . . yes . . . it's what I have to do."

38

Margo knew that there were times when you could feel so desperate that just making a plan helped. It gave you a feeling of control. Following her separation from Freddy, Margo had experienced that kind of despair, until she'd mapped out a plan for the next year in her life, and then, even though she eventually changed her mind, that sinking feeling disappeared. So that evening before dinner Margo called on her neighbor, Martin Hathaway, to see about the apartment.

"What were you doing talking to Mr. Hathaway, Mother?" Michelle asked later at the dinner table.

"Do I need an excuse to talk to Mr. Hathaway?" Margo said. God, she sounded as hostile as Michelle. If you lived with it long enough it became contagious.

"I thought you said he was a sniveling old fart," Michelle said.

"Did I say that?" Margo asked, trying to laugh.

"On several occasions," Michelle said. "And it's true, Mother . . . he is a sniveling old fart."

"I was discussing the apartment over his garage," Margo said.

"What about it?"

"Well . . . B.B.'s ex-husband is coming to town . . . I told you that, didn't I?"

"Yeah . . . so?"

"So, she's trying to find him a place to stay."

"Go on . . ."

"She asked me to find out about renting the Hathaway apartment for him."

"For how long?" Michelle asked.

"About three months."

"Let me get this straight," Michelle said, holding her fork in the air. "You're saying that B.B.'s ex-husband is going to live here . . . next door to us?"

"Yes," Margo said.

"God, Mother!" Michelle said, plunking her fork down on the table. She stood up, grabbed a deviled egg and shouted, "I just can't believe you!" She shoved the egg into her mouth, charged out of the room, and stomped down the stairs.

Margo stood up and called after her. "Why don't you ever say what you mean, Michelle? Why won't you communicate?"

But Michelle did not answer. Margo sat back down at the table, feeling very tired. "Why won't she communicate?" Margo asked Stuart. "Why won't either of you communicate?"

"Give me a break, Mom," Stuart said. "I'm eating my supper."

5

Probably Sara should have told her mother about Daddy's plan to come to Boulder. Then Mom wouldn't have been so surprised by his letter. On the day that the letter arrived Clare had been at the house when Sara got home from school.

"Where's Mom?" Sara had asked.

"She's in bed," Clare said.

"What's wrong . . . is she sick?"

"She's having a bit of a crisis," Clare said.

At first Sara hadn't understood because Clare was talking very West Texas and when she did every word melted together, making it sound as if Mom had a *Bitova Cry Cyst*, which sounded serious. "What should we do . . . should we call a doctor?"

"No," Clare said. "There's not much you can do. It takes time, that's all."

"It's not catching, is it?" Sara asked.

"No," Clare said.

"That's what I thought," Sara said. "How long do you think it will last?"

"It has to run its course," Clare told her. "Don't worry. She's going to be fine."

That afternoon Sara heard her mother crying and saying things like *He has no right . . . he can't do this to me.* And then, *I've always known I couldn't trust him and this proves it, doesn't it?* So Sara knew the crisis had to do with her father.

She called Jennifer for advice, but Jennifer told her to just stay out of it. That parents have to learn to solve their own problems. Then Jennifer reminded her to eat lightly because of Arts Night. Sara and Jennifer were both in the dance program at school.

Sara was disappointed when her mother said she couldn't get out of bed to go to Arts Night and disappointed again when Clare said that she wouldn't be able to take her either because she had to go to some business dinner in Denver. So Clare asked Margo Sampson if she could take her and Margo said yes. Sara did not want to go to Arts Night with Margo. She hardly knew Margo. She would rather have gone with Jennifer's family, but everything was arranged before she had a chance to say a word. Margo came by with her kids, Stuart and Michelle, and took Sara to Beau Jo's for pizza. Stuart ate a whole pizza by himself, with pepperoni and extra cheese. Margo, Michelle and Sara shared a large vegie supreme with whole wheat crust. Sara picked the onions and the mushrooms off her slice and Michelle picked off the olives. Margo said, "Maybe vegie supreme was the wrong choice."

When Sara was younger and Michelle babysat her, Michelle never let Sara stay up late like babysitters are supposed to do. Sara's first babysitting job was coming up soon and she was going to be really nice and let the kid stay up as late as he wanted, even if he fell asleep on the floor.

Sara didn't finish her pizza. She was afraid she'd get gas.

When Sara came home from Arts Night she tiptoed into her mother's room. Her mother was asleep. Her mother's necklace, the one that Clare had given to her for her fortieth birthday, lay on the bedside table. It spelled out FRIENDSHIP in tiny gold letters. Sara thought it was very pretty.

Mom opened her eyes. "How was Arts Night?"

"Pretty good," Sara said. Her mother's eyes were all puffy from crying and her face had red blotches on it. "Are you feeling any better?"

"A little . . . but my head still hurts."

"Do you want a cold cloth?"

"That would be nice."

Sara went to her mother's bathroom and held a blue washcloth under the faucet until it felt very cold. Then she squeezed it out and brought it to her mother. Mom lay back against the pillows and Sara placed the cloth on her forehead. "Better?"

"Much."

Sara sat on the edge of the bed holding her mother's hand. She loved the feel of her mother's hands. Her skin was so soft and her fingers were long and thin, with perfectly polished nails. She wore two delicate gold rings, one on the ring finger of her right hand and one on the middle finger next to it.

As Sara tiptoed out of her mother's room she saw the letter from her father lying face up on the dresser. She read it quickly, while pretending to be arranging Mom's perfume bottles in a row. It was a friendly letter. It didn't say anything bad.

Mom's crisis lasted five days and when she finally got out of bed and went back to work she was really tense. When Mom got tense she yelled at Sara. Then Sara would start biting her nails, which only made her mother yell some more. For weeks after that Sara's stomach felt queasy and she took Pepto-Bismol every day. She was glad when it was time to leave for summer camp. She figured that by August her mother would be used to the idea of having her father in town.

6

ANDREW HAD CALLED B.B. ON AUGUST 20 TO SAY THAT HE was in Hays, Kansas, and expected to arrive in Boulder by eight P.M. It had been six years since she had heard his voice. Six years since they had seen each other. She was a wreck all day, knowing that he was on his way. She gulped too many vitamin C's and washed them down with too much cranberry juice. Her stomach tied into hard little knots, giving her spasms of pain. She had just rye toast and camomile tea for supper. Then she showered and tried to get dressed, but she couldn't decide what to wear. So she sat on the edge of her bed in her robe for an hour, gnawing on the insides of her cheeks, until they were swollen and sore.

Finally, she got off her bed and dressed in jeans, sandals, and a baggy white sweater. She let her hair hang loose. She wore no makeup. What did she care how she looked to him anyway?

It was a matter of pride, she decided, spraying her wrists and the back of her neck with Opium, out of habit. She wanted him to be sorry he'd lost her. She wanted him to love her still, to desire her, so that she could reject him again. Punish him. Cause him pain. The way he had caused her pain. Damn him! She had worked it out so carefully. She had convinced herself that she would never have to see him again. At least not until Sara graduated from high school or college or got married. And each of those events were years away. One of them might be dead by then.

Once last spring, after a lengthy session with her lawyer, who had told her that legally she could not keep Andrew out of town, she had become so filled with rage that she had gone to her room after dinner and had screamed, surprising herself as well as Sara.

Sara had rushed into her room, her face ashen. "Mom . . . Mom, what's wrong?"

"Get out!" B.B. had yelled.

"Is it about Daddy coming to live in Boulder?"

"He's trying to ruin my life!" B.B. had cried. She'd picked up a shoe and hurled it across the room. It smashed the little stained glass window above her desk. "That goddamned father of yours is trying to ruin my life!"

"No, he's not Mom . . . really, he's not . . ."

"Oh, what do you know?" B.B. had cried. "You're just a baby."

Now Andrew was on his way and there was nothing B.B. could do about it. She walked through her house, adjusting the pillows on the sofas, picking a wilted flower out of the arrangement on the piano, running her fingers along the oak dining table. Everything looked perfect. Everything was in order. She'd done a good job. And she'd done it on her own. She didn't need anything from him.

She opened the front door and stepped outside. The sky was cloud-covered and the wind was picking up. There was a rumble of thunder in the distance and flashes of lightning over the mountains. She sat on her front porch swing, with Lucy at her side, swallowing hard each time she heard a car.

And then a battered Datsun pickup, the color of infant diarrhea, pulled into her driveway. He never did have any taste. He parked and got out of the truck. Lucy stood and began to bark. B.B. hushed her. He had grown a beard, darker than his sun-streaked hair, which was shaggy now. He was wearing jeans, a gray sweatshirt, and running shoes. During their marriage she had selected his clothes. He'd had nine cashmere sweaters with a color coordinated shirt for each. He was the best-dressed reporter on the Miami *Herald*. She used to stand inside his closet, surrounded by his things— shoes lined up, jackets and trousers carefully arranged, ties hanging in a row—and she would get this warm, safe feeling. He was her man. Now he looked like some aging hippie. The kind of man Margo went out with. Boulder was full of them.

"Hello, Francine," Andrew said.

At the sound of his voice, she felt the tea and toast come up, up from her stomach to the very edge of her throat. She had to fight to get it back down.

"I'm known as B.B. here," she told him. "For Brady Broder."

"I'll try to remember," he said.

She did not look directly at him.

47

"You're looking good," he said. "I like your hair that way."

"Thank you," she said. "You're looking . . . different."

He laughed and ran his hand through his hair. His laugh used to be enough to make her laugh.

"Is Sara asleep yet?" he asked.

"She's spending the night at a friend's."

"Oh. I guess I thought she'd be here. You did tell her I was coming tonight, didn't you?"

"No, as a matter of fact, I didn't. I thought it made more sense to wait." She was pleased at how steady her voice sounded. Pleased and surprised.

He paused, kicking a stone away from his foot. "Okay. I'll see her tomorrow then."

"Tomorrow she's going to Denver to do some back-to-school shopping."

He didn't say anything.

She did not take her hand away from Lucy's head. At that moment Lucy was her security, her connection to reality.

"Well," he said. "I guess that will give me a chance to settle in."

She thought she saw a tightening of that vein in his forehead, the one that stood out when he was angry or thinking hard. She had planned to invite him in, to offer him a drink, to show off the lovely home she'd made for Sara. But now she wanted to get this over with as quickly as possible. "Shall I show you the way to your place?" she asked.

"I'd appreciate that."

She stood up. Lucy walked down the steps with her and began to sniff him.

48

He let Lucy smell his hand, then he patted her on the back. "Nice collie."

"Her name is Lucy."

"I know."

"You know?"

"From Sara."

"Of course," she said. "From Sara." She hated the idea of Sara talking with Andrew. Telling him about her dog, about her life in Boulder. What else did he know? What else did they talk about behind her back?

"You can follow me," she told him. "It's just a few blocks."

"Okay."

She got into her BMW. She held onto the steering wheel tightly, trying to steady her hands. She started the car, then began to count backwards from one hundred, in Spanish. *Ciento, noventa y nueve, noventa y ocho.* Often, when she couldn't fall asleep at night, that's what she'd do. Usually it calmed her. She kept sight of him in her rearview mirror and drove slowly, up to Fourth, left on Pearl, right on Sixth, across Arapahoe, up the hill to Euclid, right on Aurora to the Dead End sign, then up the dirt road to a driveway shared by Margo and the Hathaways. It was just a mile and a half from her house.

He parked alongside her car. "I've got the keys right here," she said, fishing them out of her canvas bag. He followed her up the outside stairs leading to the apartment over the garage. But at the door she had trouble getting the key into the lock, her hands were shaking so badly.

"Here . . . let me . . ." he said, his fingers brushing hers.

"No! I can do it. Just give me a minute."

"Okay. Sure. Just trying to help."

"I don't need your help," she told him. She managed to unlock the door. She stepped inside and switched on a light in the living room. He was right behind her. "This is it," she said. "Living room, bedroom, bath, and kitchen."

"It looks fine," he said. "Exactly what I'd hoped for. Thanks for finding it for me."

"They keep it up nicely," she told him. "It's just been painted and the sofa's been recovered. We got them down to three-fifty a month. You've got a three month lease." She sounded professional now, the reassuring realtor.

"Renewable?"

"You'll have to discuss that with the Hathaways. I didn't draw up the contract myself." God, what gall, she thought. A renewable lease. Did he think she would go out of her way to make sure he could hang around? In three months she wanted him out of town, out of her life. She walked across the room. "Here are the keys," she told him, dropping them on the dining table. "I'm sure you want to get unpacked and I've got to run anyway. If you need anything, like a cup of sugar, my friend Margo lives next door."

"I wish you'd stay for a while," he said. "We've got to talk."

"I don't want to talk," she told him.

"Look, Francie . . . I just want you to understand that I'm not trying to hurt you by being here."

She choked up and turned away from him.

"I'm here for just one reason," he continued, ". . . to be near Sara. That's all there is to it."

"Maybe for you," she managed to say. "Maybe that's

all there is to it for you. But what about me? Did you stop to think about me?"

"Yes, I did."

"I'll bet," she said.

"You never did have much faith in me, did you?" he asked.

"With good reason."

He grabbed her roughly, forcing her to face him. "I've spent six years paying for what may or may not have been my fault. I'll never get over it completely. But I've learned to deal with it . . . with my guilt . . . with your hate . . . with losing Bobby . . . and then you, taking Sara away. Six years is enough."

"Enough for you," she said.

"Enough for any of us," he said softly.

He held her for a moment, the way he used to, and when she looked up at him, her eyes filled with tears, he kissed her. Afraid of what might happen if she let herself respond, she broke away and wiped her mouth with the back of her hand. "What are you doing?" Her voice was hoarse. "What do you want?"

"I don't know," he said. "Seeing you again . . . remembering . . . I just don't know."

He walked across the room, his hands brushing his hair away from his face. She leaned back against the empty bookcase. Neither one spoke.

Finally, he broke the silence. "Can I have Sara this weekend?"

"You can have her on Sunday from ten until six."

"That's not much of a weekend."

"It's enough for now."

He sighed. "Look . . . either we're going to work this out by ourselves, sensibly, or we're going to work it out through our lawyers, and if necessary, through the courts."

"I can't believe you're standing here saying these things. That after six years you think you can walk into my life and destroy everything I've put together."

"You haven't given me any choice."

"You haven't changed. You're as selfish and irresponsible as you always were."

"And you're just as inflexible."

She strode across the room to the door, opened it, paused, then turned back to him. "One thing . . . don't expect anything from me while you're in town. As far as I'm concerned you don't exist!"

"That's right . . . bury your head in the sand the way you always have . . ."

She ran to her car. A flash of lightning lit up the sky, followed by a roar of thunder. She turned on the ignition, raced the engine, and tore out of the driveway, tires screeching. It began to rain heavily, then to hail, pounding the roof of her car. But she hardly noticed for the pounding inside her head.

Men, B.B. thought. You had to learn to use them the way they used you, the way they had been taught to use you. She'd learned that a long time ago. She'd learned that when she was fourteen and her father had died of a heart attack in the bed of a stock clerk from his store. She was a redhead, like B.B., and young, with two babies and no husband in sight. She was Irish, like him. Kathleen Dooley. Her father had been screwing Kathleen Dooley for more than six months when he died. But B.B. didn't know it at the time.

Her mother did though. After the funeral her mother had confided that she'd known it all along. "It was the Irish in him," her mother had said. "He couldn't help himself. He loved us, Francie, more than anything, but some men, especially the Irish, have it in their genes. They can't resist, even when they want to. They're like male dogs, chasing a bitch in heat."

Francine tried to picture her father as a dog, chasing Kathleen Dooley into the stockroom of the store, Brady Army Surplus, barking his head off, nipping at her legs.

"I want you to know, Francie," her mother continued, "that I forgave your father. The first time it happened he came home and cried in my arms. I told him, *I don't want to know about it, Dennis. You have to work late one or two nights a week . . . it's okay . . . just spare me the details.* And then I put it out of my mind. That's what you have to do when things get unpleasant. You have to put them out of your mind. You have to concentrate on other things. And then you don't feel unhappy or angry."

"You weren't angry that he was fooling around?" Francine asked.

"He should have died in his own bed. That's all I'm angry about."

"I'd have been angry," Francine said.

Her mother shrugged. "Marry Jewish. That's my advice. They make the best husbands. Look at Aunt Sylvie . . . look at all the happiness she has with Uncle Morris. A beautiful home, you could call it an estate and not be exaggerating . . . furs, even down here in Miami, where you don't need them . . . jewels . . . cruises every year . . . and for their children, only the best. So remember Francie, when the time comes, be smart. It's just as easy to fall in love with a nice Jewish boy, one with a future, one who'll take care of you."

"Maybe I won't get married at all."

"Bite your tongue," her mother said. "Of course you will. Learn from my mistakes and learn from Kathleen Dooley too. She wasn't so dumb. Use what God gave you to get what you want, but try not to hurt anybody along the way."

So Francine had used what God had given her. Her beauty. She knew she could have any boy she wanted. Just like that! Because boys were stupid and all they cared about was how you looked. In high school she had more boyfriends than anyone else. She was popular with a capital P, her mother told Aunt Sylvie, and Aunt Sylvie said, "Sure, why not? With that Irish nose and red hair . . . she looks like a shiksa. Momma would roll over in her grave if she could see her."

After high school Francine enrolled at Miami U. She spent her first two years living at home and commuting, but then her mother urged her to move into a dormitory to get a taste of college life, and so she did. That very same year she met Andrew Broder, a graduate student in journalism from Hackensack, New Jersey. She liked his seriousness, his shyness, his sense of humor, and the fact that he was exactly one head taller than she was so that when he held her in his arms her lips came up to his neck.

He was awed by her beauty and she used it to tantalize him because this was the man she was going to marry. It took her a while to convince him that he wanted to get married. But finally one balmy night she climbed into his bed, naked, and she let him touch her all over. She let him hold her close and rub up against her until he came, leaving her thigh wet and sticky.

They were married a week after she graduated, on the grounds of Aunt Sylvie and Uncle Morris's estate, under a chuppa covered with roses. She wore a white batiste cotton dress, nipped in at the waist, with a square neck, and a wide-brimmed garden hat instead of a veil, and she carried a single white rose.

Before the ceremony Uncle Morris took her into the house, into his private den, and slipped an envelope into the bosom of her dress, inside her strapless bra. "Twenty-five hundred smackers," he told her, his hot pudgy fingers squeezing her small left tit.

"Thank you, Uncle Morris," she said politely.

"You're a gorgeous girl, you know that, Francine?"

"Thank you, Uncle Morris."

"I wouldn't mind shtupping you myself. You know what I mean?"

"I know that you're teasing me, Uncle Morris."

"Teasing, shmeasing . . . don't be too sure. Look, if he doesn't come through, this guy you're marrying . . . come and see me. Understand?"

"I'm not sure . . . but thank you very much for your generous gift and for giving us the wedding." She pecked his cheek, then ran out of his den, her heart pounding. He had felt her up! Uncle Morris had felt her up on her wedding day.

Sex. That's what they were all after. You had to give it to them though. At first, just enough to keep them interested. Then, enough to make them think you really enjoyed it. You had to, otherwise they wouldn't marry you. And once you were married, you had to keep doing it, twice a week, at least.

But that part, the doing it part, wasn't nearly as nice as the hugging and kissing, Francine discovered on her honeymoon. Andrew seemed to think it was though, so she never told him what she thought. He would moan at the end, then collapse on top of her, as if he were dead. At first, she worried that Andrew would die the way her father had, but as the week went on, she saw that it was nothing more serious than exhaustion. "Oh, Francie . . . my beautiful darling . . . you're so wonderful . . ." he would whisper.

For the next two years they lived in Georgia at Fort Benning and she got a job working as a receptionist in a real estate office. The business fascinated her and she began to study for her broker's license.

They continued to have sex twice a week. On Wednesdays and Saturdays. It hardly took any time at all. She still preferred the kissing and the hugging, but the trouble was, if she started kissing Andrew, he got it all wrong and thought she wanted more, thought she wanted to do it. And she didn't know how to tell him she didn't. So she stopped kissing and fooling around, waiting for him to take the initiative. That way she always knew how it was going to end.

After two years they went back to Miami and he got a job on the *Herald* and she passed the Florida realtor's exam and went to work for Pride Properties. She took six months off when Bobby was born and four when Sara was born and when she went back the second time she was named second vice-president in charge of residential properties.

By then Andrew had his own byline and was talking about

taking a leave of absence. She tried to convince him not to do it. They had too many responsibilities.

"Fuck responsibilities! Let's blow it off and go to Fiji."

"Andrew, sometimes you scare me with your crazy ideas."

"Then New York," he'd said. "Let's go to New York for a year."

"It gets cold in New York," she'd told him. "This is the best place to raise children. They can be outside all year round."

"I'm going out of my mind here, Francie," he'd said. "I've got to have a change."

"This just isn't the right time for a change, Andrew. Take up tennis or something. You'll feel better."

Instead of tennis, Andrew bought a little sailboat, spending most of his weekends out on the bay, teaching Bobby to sail. Which would have been fine, except that now he wanted sex more often, and in different positions, and with the lights on. She went along with some of it. She had no choice. She didn't want to leave him, or worse yet, for him to leave her. His need for constant excitement worsened. He was no longer satisfied with a nice vacation in Jamaica, lolling about on the beach. He wanted to raft rivers, to explore jungles, to live on the edge. She tried to remain calm.

"It's just a mid-life crisis," her mother had told her.

"But he's only thirty-four," Francine had said.

"So, he's an early bird. Just as well to get it out of the way now . . . one less worry for later."

Oh, why did he have to go and ruin things? Why couldn't he just have continued to be a good husband, going to work, playing with the kids, not getting in the way?

The year Francine was named first vice-president of Pride Properties, Aunt Sylvie died of stomach cancer and a year later, right after the unveiling, Uncle Morris married her mother. "I'm happy as a lark, Francie," her mother said. "All in all, I think Aunt Sylvie would be pleased, don't you? And if she wouldn't, what can I say? Life is for the living."

Andrew began to talk about taking a leave from the paper to write a book.

"What kind of book?" Francine asked.

"I don't know yet."

"When you know we'll discuss it," she told him.

But they never got around to discussing it because two months later Bobby was killed.

7

SARA WAS HELPING HER FATHER CLEAN OUT HIS TRUCK. IT was a mess from his long drive cross-country. Her father chewed pack after pack of gum on the road. He said it helped him to stay awake. So his truck was full of Juicy Fruit wrappers and when you were riding in it, with the windows open, the wrappers blew all over the place.

Sara's mother still hadn't accepted the idea of Daddy living in Boulder. If she had she wouldn't be making such a big thing out of Sara seeing him. And Sara wouldn't have to sneak over to his place, the way she had today. She would just be able to say, *I'll be at Daddy's after school. I'll be home by six.*

And then Mom would say, *Okay, Sweetie . . . see you then.*

Daddy's place wasn't much—just this little apartment over Mr. Hathaway's garage, at the end of a long dirt road, which was bumpy and eroded from the summer rains and hard to manage on her bicycle. Twice she had fallen off and scraped her knees.

Sara was helping him fix up the apartment, trying to make it feel more like a home. Last Sunday they had shopped for a cast iron frying pan because her father said it was impossible to cook eggs evenly without one. They had also bought some plants and three posters. Daddy had hung Sara's favorite poster, three coyotes wearing roller skates, over the sofa in the living room. The sofa pulled out into a bed and that's where Sara was going to sleep when she had overnights. Daddy promised that soon she would come for the whole weekend. But for now she should just be patient and not discuss the subject with her mother.

Sara was allowed to visit her father only on Sundays, from ten until six. But what her mother didn't know wouldn't hurt her. Besides, that was such a dumb rule. For the first time in six years her father was living nearby. And until next week, when school started full time, she had every afternoon free and her father did too. So why shouldn't they spend their time together? After all, that had been the whole idea.

Sara's father had come up with the plan last April, while Sara was visiting over spring break. They were sailing in Biscayne Bay that day and Daddy seemed really lonely. "I wish I could see you more often," he had said.

"I wish I could see you too."

"I wish you could live with me for a while."

"That would be nice."

"Really?" Daddy asked. "You mean it?"

"Well, sure . . . but I can't."

"Why not?"

"I can't leave Mom . . . she needs me." Sara hoped that her father wouldn't say that he needed her too, because then she wouldn't know what to do.

Her father understood. And that was when the idea first hit him. Since Sara couldn't leave Boulder to be with him, he would come there to be with her. And that way she would be able to see him whenever she wanted. At the time it had seemed like a very good idea.

Later, Sara wasn't so sure.

Sara's parents never talked on the phone or wrote letters, like some of Sara's friends' parents who were divorced. But they never fought either, which Jennifer said was the pits. Jennifer's parents were always fighting about money and visiting rights and each other's lovers, especially since Jennifer's mother had a new baby from her lover.

Sara's mother didn't have a lover now, but she used to have one named Mitch. He had made her mother cry all the time. Sara had hated him.

Sara had this fantasy that when her parents saw each other again they would realize that they still loved each other and would get married a second time. Then both her parents would live not only in the same town but in the same house. That could happen. Jennifer knew this family who had been divorced for seven years and then the parents got married again. But Jennifer wasn't sure that was a good idea because if they didn't get along the second time you had to go through a whole other divorce.

Sara had been only six when her parents were divorced. Before the divorce they'd lived in a big house in Florida.

Sara had a room with a door to the patio so she could wake up early and go swimming in the pool. Except she wasn't allowed in unless someone was there to watch, even though she was a really good swimmer. But it was silly to think that just because someone was watching you were going to be okay. Even if it was Daddy. Because Bobby had been with Daddy when the accident happened.

There were no pictures of Bobby in their house. It was as if there never was a Bobby. Sara said that she was an only child. That's the way her mother wanted it. Sometimes she felt like saying, *I had a brother, but he died.* But she didn't say it. It would have upset her mother too much. Besides, it all happened a long time ago.

Sara had a picture of the four of them. Mom, Daddy, Bobby, and herself, but she kept it hidden away under the false bottom of her jewelry box. Bobby was only ten when he died, younger than Sara was now. If he were still alive Bobby would be a teenager. Sara wondered what it would be like to have a teenaged brother. Would they be friends or would they fight all the time?

When Daddy's book was published he sent her a copy. Inside he had written, *To my darling Sara, I hope some day you will understand. I love you very much, Daddy.* Sara was just nine when the book was published and she didn't understand all of it, except that it was about a family something like theirs, but not exactly. And in it there was an accident and the youngest child was killed. A boy. Daddy called him David. On the back of the book there was a picture of Daddy before he grew his beard. He was sitting on the sea wall wearing his favorite jacket, the denim one with the torn pocket.

Sara's mother caught her reading the book one time and threatened to take it away from her, but Sara had cried, so her mother let her keep it. She told Sara that she never wanted to see it again. So Sara kept it hidden in the bottom of her closet, in her game box.

Sara was still stuffing the gum wrappers from her father's truck into a trash bag when a blue Subaru drove down the dirt road and pulled into the driveway. Sara was really surprised when Margo and her kids got out. She wondered what they were doing here.

Her father, who was hosing out the back of the truck, stopped when the car pulled into the driveway and called, "Hello . . ."

"Oh, hello," Margo said.

"Who is that?" Sara heard Michelle ask Margo.

"Andrew Broder," Margo told her.

"B.B.'s husband?" Michelle asked.

"Former husband," Margo said.

Daddy walked over to their car. Sara climbed out of the truck and followed him.

"How are you today?" he asked Margo. Sara was surprised that her father knew Margo.

"Okay . . . how about you?" Margo said to her father.

"Much better," her father said.

What did he mean? Sara wondered. Had he been sick?

"Were you sick?" Michelle asked.

"No," Sara's father said, laughing. "I passed out in the hot tub a few nights ago."

The hot tub? Sara thought. What hot tub?

"Our hot tub?" Michelle asked him.

"Yes," her father said. "I guess the heat was too much for me."

"Andrew," Margo said, "I'd like you to meet my children, Stuart and Michelle. Kids, this is Andrew Broder."

Her father wiped his hands on his jeans, then he and Stuart shook hands. Michelle kept her hands in her pocket.

Then her father turned to her. "And this is my daughter, Sara."

"We already know each other, Daddy," Sara said, embarrassed.

"Oh, right," her father said. "I forgot . . . it's a small town."

"I used to babysit Sara," Michelle said.

"A long time ago," Sara said, to set the record straight. "When I was just a little kid."

"You mean a little brat," Michelle said.

"You weren't the greatest babysitter," Sara said.

Then Margo laughed a little and said, "Well, Sara . . . how was your summer?"

"Very nice. I went to camp near San Diego."

"Yes, I know," Margo said. "Your mother told me you were going."

"And I started junior high this year," Sara said, more to Michelle and Stuart than to Margo.

"Wow . . . junior high," Michelle said.

"Which school . . . Casey?" Stuart asked.

"Yes."

"Watch out for Mr. Loring. I've heard he fails half his class every year just for smiling."

"Really?" Sara asked. "For smiling?"

Michelle snorted. "I'm going inside."

"Same here," Stuart said. "Nice to meet you, Mr. Broder."

"Andrew," Sara's father said.

"Andrew," Stuart repeated, shaking her father's hand again.

"I'll be in in a minute," Margo called after her kids.

Then Margo and her father just stood there, looking at each other. "Well . . ." Margo finally said, "those are my kids."

Sara did not move.

"How about a movie tonight?" her father said to Margo.

"No, not tonight," Margo said.

"Tomorrow night?"

"I don't know," Margo said. "We'll see." She looked over at Sara.

"Maybe I could go with you, Daddy. I could ask Mom . . ."

"That would be nice," her father said. "Say, could you run inside and get me that vinyl spray cleaner for the front seat of the truck?"

"Now?" Sara asked.

"Yes, now."

Sara knew he was trying to get rid of her. What did he have to say to Margo that he couldn't say in front of her.

"Please . . ." he said.

"Okay . . . okay . . ." Sara said and she ran up the path leading to the Hathaway house. Probably her father wanted to tell Margo something about how Sara wasn't supposed to be visiting today and that Margo shouldn't mention it to Mom.

When Sara returned with the vinyl cleaner her father and

Margo were standing close, talking. When they saw her, they stopped.

"I've got to go in now," Margo said. "But maybe I will go to the movies with you some night . . . if something good is playing."

"Let me know when you think something good is playing," her father said.

"*Return of Frankenstein* is at the Fox," Sara said.

Margo started to laugh. Then her father laughed too.

Sara didn't see what was so funny, especially since *Return of Frankenstein* was a really scary movie.

8

B.B.'s OFFICE WAS IN A STATELY FEDERAL HOUSE ON Spruce. She had restored it over the past few years and had rented the second floor to a State Farm insurance agent. The house itself was listed in the guidebooks as an historic site, dating back to 1877, and B.B. was as proud of it as she was of her home.

But now it was being painted inside. The painter had convinced B.B. to go with an oil rather than a waterbase paint. It would last longer and look richer, he'd said. She had gone along with him and that had turned out to be a mistake. The strong odor was causing everyone in the office to feel headachey and nauseous and her secretary, Miranda, could not stop wheezing. B.B. assured them all, as well as the insurance agent upstairs, that the painting would be finished by Friday and that she, personally, would make sure the house was aired out all weekend so that on Monday, when they came back to work, the odor of the paint would be gone.

It had also been a mistake to agree to have the house painted during the first week of school. She should have arranged to keep her afternoons free, to make plans with Sara to go into Denver to the museum, or shop—anything. She did not like the idea of Sara hanging out after school. Now that she had started junior high B.B. would have to keep a careful eye on her. Sara would be exposed to drugs, to sex, to kids without values. And it was up to B.B. to make sure that Sara did not stray. It made her dizzy to think of all the problems that lay ahead.

She picked up a WonderRoast chicken on her way home from the office and was preparing butternut squash when Sara came in. "Where have you been?" she asked. "It's after six."

"Out . . . riding my bike with some of the kids from school. What's for dinner?"

"Chicken and squash."

"Butternut?"

"Yes."

"Mashed?"

"Yes . . . the way I always make it . . . with cinnamon."

They sat down to dinner a few minutes later. "Um . . . it's good," Sara said.

"I'm glad you like it."

They ate quietly for a while. B.B. was distracted, thinking about the office. Perhaps she should have gone with strong colors in the reception area instead of off-white.

Then Sara said, "I didn't know Margo lives next door to Daddy. I was really surprised when I saw her there."

"You saw Margo?"

"Yes."

"When?"

"This afternoon."

B.B. lay down her fork. "What were you doing over there this afternoon?"

"Oh . . . I . . ." Sara's cheeks turned red and she began to chew on her fingernails.

Caught in the act, B.B. thought.

"I forgot my library book when I was there on Sunday and I was afraid it would be overdue so I rode my bike over to get it, but I didn't stay."

"I don't want you doing that again," B.B. said. "Do you understand? You are never to go over there without my permission."

"But Mom . . . I was only there for five minutes, maybe less."

"I'm warning you, Sara. If I find out that you've disobeyed me you're going to be grounded. And then you won't be allowed to see your father at all." B.B. did not want to punish Sara for Andrew's foolishness, but what choice did she have? If she didn't hold the reins tightly who knew where it all might end. "And you are never to lie to me again."

"I didn't lie."

"You did and we both know it. You didn't leave your library book over there."

"I'm sorry. It's just that for the rest of this week we get

out of school at noon so I have all this free time and so does Daddy.''

"Use that time to get your room in order."

"It is in order."

"Go over your clothes and pull out everything that doesn't fit. I'll give you a box to stack them in."

"Okay."

B.B. got up to clear away the dinner plates. "So . . . did you introduce your father to Margo?"

"They already knew each other."

"Oh?"

"Daddy said something about passing out in Margo's hot tub."

"Really?"

"Something like that."

"Are you sure?"

"Not exactly."

Sara must be mistaken, B.B. thought as she washed the dishes. Children were always putting two and two together and coming up with five. But she would give Margo a call and ask her to keep an eye on things. Margo could be on the lookout for Sara sneaking over to Andrew's and it wouldn't hurt to ask her to keep an eye on Andrew too. Anything B.B. could get on him, any leverage to use in court, if it went so far, would help.

But when B.B. phoned Margo and asked her to do just that, just a simple favor, Margo turned cold and said, "You're asking me to spy on him?"

"Not spy. Just to keep an eye on things, especially Sara."

"I can't do that," Margo said.

"What do you mean, you can't?"

"It wouldn't be right. I wish you'd stop putting me in the middle."

"How have I put you in the middle?"

"By moving him in next door to me in the first place. And now, asking me to watch him. I don't want to watch him. I don't want to know any more about him than I already do."

"What do you know?"

"Nothing. Very little. He seems like a nice man. That's all."

"I hear he's already been in your hot tub," B.B. said softly, hoping that Margo would deny it and ask where she had gotten such a foolish idea.

"It was nothing," Margo said.

So, it was true. B.B. did not respond.

"Look," Margo continued, after a moment of silence, "I'm sorry I can't help you out. Try to understand."

"Of course," B.B. said coldly. "See you in Jazzercise." She put the phone back on the hook. God, you couldn't trust anyone, could you? She wondered if they'd worn bathing suits.

9

MARGO FOUND HERSELF THINKING ABOUT ANDREW BRO-
der, found herself standing on her deck watching for his
truck or hoping she might run into him on the Mall. If she
did she'd say *Oh, hello . . . would you like to get a cup of
coffee?* And he'd say, *Sounds good to me,* and they would
walk over to Pearl's and sit at the outdoor cafe and order
espressos. She would be wearing her heathery pink poncho
and he would say, *I like the way you look in that. It brings
out the color in your cheeks.*

Fool, she told herself. Find another fantasy.

She wished that B.B. hadn't called, asking her to keep an
eye on Andrew. When she'd told B.B. to stop putting her in
the middle, B.B. had been pissed. Margo had heard it in her
voice.

On Monday morning, at the office, Margo finished up the
preliminary sketches for the cluster housing project and de-

cided to drop them at B.B.'s office on her way to lunch. She told Barbara, the receptionist at Benson and Gould, she'd be back by one-thirty and if Michael phoned from Vail she had information for him on those Trocal windows. Then, as an afterthought, she picked up the phone on Barbara's desk and called home. The phone rang twice before Mrs. Herrera answered. "Mrs. Margo Sampson's residence . . ."

"Hello, Mrs. Herrera . . . it's me," Margo said.

Mrs. Herrera had been cleaning for Margo since Margo had come to town. She cleaned for B.B. on Tuesdays and Fridays and for another friend on Wednesdays. Today, Mrs. Herrera complained that with Stuart and Michelle back the house was a mess and it was going to take her at least two extra hours to clean it properly and was Margo willing to pay?

Margo told Mrs. Herrera that she was.

"Because I don't do this for fun," Mrs. Herrera said.

"I understand," Margo said.

"And last week I left you a list and you didn't buy one thing on it. How am I supposed to clean if you don't buy the supplies?"

"I'm sorry . . . I forgot."

"Mrs. B.B. buys two of everything so we never run out."

"You'll have all the supplies you need next week. I promise."

Margo hung up the phone and smiled at Barbara, who relished the weekly conversations with Mrs. Herrera. "I shouldn't have called home," Margo said.

"She would have called here if you hadn't."

"That's true." Margo slung her leather bag over her shoulder, waved at Barbara, and left.

Benson and Gould's offices were in a handsome red brick building on Chestnut, converted in 1973 from an old warehouse by Jeffrey Gould, before he discovered the Bahamas. When Michael Benson and Margo had been lovers they used to stay at the office until Barbara and Jeffrey had gone, lock the doors, and make love on the floor. Then Margo would go home and prepare dinner for her children. It had been a pleasant arrangement while it lasted. Twice married and twice divorced, with two sets of children, Michael was terrified of personal responsibilities, a trait that sometimes carried over into his professional life. By the time Margo introduced him to her children her feelings for him had fizzled anyway, so she was not hurt at his suggestion that they find other lovers and become friends.

Outside, the temperature was still in the eighties and Margo would not have minded if the weather stayed this way all year long. She walked a few blocks to Spruce, to B.B.'s office.

"She's already left for lunch," Miranda said, when Margo asked for B.B. "She's at The James, with clients. She should be back in an hour."

"I'll just leave these with you," Margo said, placing the folder on Miranda's desk.

"I'm sure she wouldn't mind if you dropped in and gave them to her yourself. She'd probably welcome the interruption. These clients are bo-ring." Miranda fanned the air in front of her face to make her point. Miranda had come to work for B.B. fresh out of C.U. two years ago and now she dressed like B.B., wore her hair like B.B., and was even beginning to sound like B.B.

"I'm in a hurry myself," Margo said. "So just give them to her when she gets back."

"Okay," Miranda said. "Sure."

Margo walked from B.B.'s office to the Mall. Before she'd arrived in Boulder her idea of a Mall was Saks, Bonwit's, and Bloomingdale's strung out around a huge concrete parking area, either in New Jersey or Long Island, and swamped with career shoppers, like her sister, Bethany. In Boulder, which had once been a supply center for the mining towns in the mountains, the Mall was an area of renovated buildings, some dating back to the late 1800s, housing shops, restaurants, and galleries. The streets were cobblestone and closed to traffic. Some of the old-timers complained that it was too tourist oriented, but Margo disagreed. It provided a downtown shopping area for the locals and made it fun to work in the neighborhood.

She went into the New York Deli, ordered two pastrami sandwiches on rye—you had to specify here or you might get it on whole wheat or, worse yet, white bread—and two iced coffees to go. Then she waited outside, lifting her face to the sun. When her order was ready she crossed the Mall and walked to the corner, to Clare's gallery. The gallery represented Margo's most creative renovation in Boulder. She had left as much of the original bank building intact as she could, including the tellers' windows, the winding staircase and the balcony, which had become a sculpture gallery.

Clare had come to Boulder like Margo, following her divorce from Robin Carleton-Robbins, a West Texas banker who had run off to the Amazon or someplace like that— Clare wasn't sure, it might have been the Nile—with one of his tellers. She was very young, Clare said, and smelled like doughnuts. Clare had come to Boulder with her daughter, Puffin, a classmate of Margo's children, and her millions, some of which she used to open her gallery, one of the few in town that was not a front for drug traffic. *Strictly legitimate*, Clare would say, proudly. *I don't wash anybody's money*. And she had never eaten a doughnut again and swore she never would.

At first Margo found it odd that a woman whose husband had run off with a bank teller would choose a bank building for her gallery. One day during the construction phase Margo had mentioned that to Clare and Clare had laughed her big, booming laugh and had replied, "It is odd, isn't it?"

Margo pushed open the heavy glass door to the gallery. "Lunch . . ." she announced.

"Be right with you," Clare called. "Just let me wash up. Have a look at the balcony while you're waiting."

Clare's fall show had opened on Labor Day weekend. It featured artists of the Southwest. The walls were hung with R.C. Gormans, Doug Wests, and Celia Ramseys. Margo went through the gallery to the vault, which served as Clare's office space. She dropped the lunch bag on Clare's desk, then ran upstairs where Clare's assistant, Joe, was setting up a barnyard exhibit of carved wooden animals. "They're wonderful," Margo said, eyeing a brown pig complete with teeth. "How much does that one go for?"

"Ninety-five," Joe said, "but if you're interested . . ."

"I know . . ." Margo said.

Clare would be leaving for Europe day after tomorrow. She went every September, after the fall show opened, and it was always a lonely time in Margo's life. The last time she and Clare had had a good talk had been on Margo's fortieth birthday. Clare had taken her to dinner at John's French Restaurant, had presented her with the silk robe, and had ordered champagne. Over dessert, a decadent hazelnut cake, Margo had confessed that what she wanted most for her fortieth birthday was a steady man. "One who'll be there in the morning," she'd said, feeling giddy from the champagne.

"I wouldn't mind one myself," Clare said, "but they're not easy to find and if we should happen to find them, then we won't be this close anymore."

"That's bullshit," Margo said, draining her champagne glass. "Why should we have to choose between a man and a friend?"

"I don't know. I suppose because it's hard to keep that kind of intimacy going with more than one person at a time. While I was married to Robin I never had friends . . . real friends . . . did you?"

"I had friends," Margo said, "but I never confided in them until my marriage fell apart."

"You see?"

"But it doesn't have to be that way." Margo poured herself another glass of champagne. She knew she was going to be sick, but she didn't care.

Clare came into her office and stretched out on the sofa. Margo handed her a sandwich and said, "I'm crazy about that pig . . . the one with the teeth."

"He's yours."

"I want to *buy* him."

"Consider it done."

"For a fair price."

"Of course."

"Michelle's always campaigning for a pet. Maybe this will satisfy her."

Clare laughed.

"I'm going to miss you," Margo said. "Who's going to listen to me while you're gone? Who's going to laugh at my jokes?"

"I'll be back in three weeks."

"Three weeks is a long time."

"I keep telling you . . . you should come with me."

"I will, one of these days."

"Keep in touch with B.B.," Clare said. "I'm worried about her . . . about how she's handling having her ex in town."

"She'll adjust," Margo said. "She'll have to."

Clare sighed. "That's what life is, isn't it . . . a series of adjustments."

"Did I tell you, I met him?"

"No . . . what's he like?"

"Friendly . . . seems nice enough . . ."

"Who knows, maybe he and B.B. will get back together."

"I doubt it," Margo said.

"Why? Didn't you ever think of getting back together with Freddy?"

"In the beginning, sure . . . during the hard times. I thought about how easy life could be if I didn't fight it. But I wasn't ready to give up. And I wasn't sure he'd want me back . . ."

"They all do . . . eventually."

"I don't think so. Anyway, I'm glad I held out. I would

never have forgiven myself for running back just because it was safe. And I haven't been tempted in years. Besides, he's married, so I don't have to think about it." She balled up her sandwich bag and tossed it across the room into Clare's trash basket.

"I think about it sometimes," Clare said.

"About what?"

"About going back to Robin. We've been separated for four years and we're no closer to a divorce now than we were when he ran off with the Doughnut. It's hard for the wealthy to divorce," Clare said, laughing into her iced coffee. "There's all that money to divvy up, all that property . . . it could take years . . . maybe it's not worth it." She lowered her voice. "He's back."

"Robin?"

"Yes . . . he's in Dallas."

"Why didn't you tell me?"

"I didn't know until yesterday. He called. He wants to see me."

"What about the Doughnut?"

"That's over. It only lasted six months. He's been living in Cuernavaca, alone. A mid-life crisis, he says."

"God," Margo said, "I am so sick of men and their mid-life crises. What about us? When do we get ours?"

"I suspect we've already had them."

"Are you going to see him?"

"I don't know. I'll think about it while I'm in Paris."

"Don't do anything you're going to regret," Margo said.

Clare laughed. "If I didn't do anything I was going to regret I'd never do anything . . . and you know it."

"I want you to be happy," Margo said. "I don't want to see you hurt."

"You sound like a mother."

"I am a mother."

"I know," Clare said, "but not mine."

Margo left the gallery at one-fifteen and was rushing back to the office when someone called her name. She stopped. It was Andrew Broder, standing in front of the Boulder Bookstore, loaded down with packages. "Hello," he said. "How are you?"

"Okay . . . how about you?"

"I've become a shopper . . . as you can see. Do you have time for a cup of coffee?"

"I'm on my way back to the office," she told him. "But I'd love to, some other time."

"It's a deal," he said, shifting the packages in his arms.

Fantasy into reality, she thought, walking away. *Too bad it's too warm for my heathery pink poncho.* She started to laugh. She was still laughing when she got back to her office.

10

B.B. DID NOT GET OUT OF BED ON THE FOLLOWING SUNDAY morning. She lay under the covers in her rumpled nightgown, sleeping fitfully, floating in and out of dreams. She had told herself that she needed to catch up on her sleep, but she knew that she wasn't getting out of bed because there was no reason to, since Sara had gone off with Andrew for the day. She had watched from her bedroom window as Sara had raced out of the house at nine, carrying her Monopoly game. She had watched as they had driven off together in Andrew's ugly truck. It was a warm, sunny early September day and as she dozed B.B. heard children's voices laughing. But they were not the voices of her children.

At five, jolted awake by some inner alarm, B.B. jumped up and out of bed, took a shower, and dressed carefully so that when Sara came home she would be ready to take her out to dinner. She was sitting at the kitchen table, sipping tomato juice and reading the Sunday *Camera,* when Andrew pulled into the driveway. He and Sara got out of the truck and walked to the back door together.

B.B. hugged Sara and said, "Hi, Sweetie . . . I missed you. All set for dinner at Rudi's?" She ignored Andrew.

"I already ate," Sara said. "Daddy made hamburgers and french fries."

"You already had dinner?" B.B. asked.

"Yes, so I'm not hungry . . . maybe just some ice cream later." Sara stood on tiptoe and kissed Andrew. "Bye, Dad . . . see you next week."

"The reason I wanted her back at six," B.B. said to Andrew, speaking slowly and softly, trying not to show the anger she was feeling, "was so I could take her out to dinner."

"I didn't know," Andrew said.

"Sara should have told you," B.B. said.

"But Mom . . ." Sara said, "you didn't say we were going out tonight."

"You should have known," B.B. said. "We always go to Rudi's on Sunday nights, don't we?"

"But Mom . . ."

"I don't want to hear another word about it," she said, her voice becoming harsh. "Just go to your room."

Sara's eyes filled with tears and she turned and ran down the hallway.

"Aren't you being tough on her?" Andrew asked.

"Don't tell me how to handle my daughter," B.B. said, slamming the door in his face.

B.B. went to her room, took off her clothes, got back into bed, and didn't get up until the next morning, not realizing until she began to run that she hadn't eaten anything yesterday and now she was so weak she could only go a mile.

This was no good. None of it was any good. She could feel herself losing control. Her hair was shedding in the shower. The bottoms of her feet alternately itched, then burned. She continued to lose weight.

The weight loss had started over the summer. She had assumed it was the worry of Andrew coming to town. She had always had trouble eating during times of stress. For weeks she had lived on only farina and dried apricots. To clear her mind she had started to run four, five, sometimes six miles a day. With Sara away at camp she had thrown herself completely into business matters and community projects. But instead of her usually innovative ideas, she drew blanks at meeting after meeting. People asked her if she was feeling all right.

In mid-July she had taken a week off to go out to San Diego to visit Sara at camp. She stayed at La Costa, sure that a week of pampering would relax her. On her first day there she took a tennis lesson from a craggy faced but still handsome pro who told her she was the most gorgeous thing he'd seen all summer. He was impressed by her sure, firm strokes as well. They spent the night together, but he was a disappointing lover, fast and hard, with no interest in foreplay. Afterwards he said, "Nice, babe . . ." the same way he'd said it on the court. Then he rolled over and was out cold, snoring and farting in his sleep. She was relieved when at five A.M., he left.

The next night, her fortieth birthday, she dressed in white chiffon and had dinner by herself in the main dining room. When she was a child birthday parties meant black patent leather shoes, ribbons in her hair, and Dixie Cups and then, when she opened her Dixie and licked the ice cream off the inside of the lid, she would find a movie star's picture. One time she had found Lassie's picture and all the other children at the party begged her to trade with them, but she wouldn't. So they'd teased her, calling her Skinny and Red and Freckle-face, and she had cried, but she hadn't given up Lassie's picture.

After dinner she went back to her room and sat on the edge of her bed for a long time, feeling lonely and depressed, wanting to talk to someone, but not knowing who. She picked up the phone and thought about calling her mother, but she knew that as soon as she heard her mother's voice she would start to cry and then there would be questions. So she did not call her mother. She knew a million people, but she had so few friends. Clare was one of the few people she felt close to. With Clare she didn't have to say what was on her mind because Clare sensed it. She wished there were more people like Clare. She would have called Clare tonight but Clare was away too, visiting her mother on Padre Island. Should she call Margo? No, Margo wasn't really a friend. Margo was just someone she sometimes saw for lunch. She reached for the plaque Sara had made for her at camp. *Superwoman*, it said. Was that really how Sara saw her, as a superwoman? And if she was, then how come she felt so small, so insignificant now?

She supposed she could call Mitch, just for old times' sake. Maybe she would even invite him down for the weekend. After all, this was her birthday. She owed herself one. She picked up the phone and dialed his old number.

He answered on the third ring. "B.B.," he said, "wonderful to hear your voice again."

"I'm in San Diego . . . at La Costa . . ."

"Wonderful place, San Diego . . ."

"I thought you might drive down for dinner over the weekend . . . we could catch up on what's been happening . . ."

"Love to," he said, "but I'm all tied up. I'm doing a series, you know."

"I didn't know."

"Yes, one of the top twelve."

"That's great."

There was a long pause.

"And I'm living with someone . . . but surely you knew that."

"No, I didn't."

"Yes. She's a producer too. We have a lot in common. It's working out."

"I'm glad for you," she told him. And suddenly she remembered that the last time they'd been together she'd wound up with a black eye and a strained ligament in her left leg.

She hung up the phone, feeling humiliated, rolled over onto her stomach, held the bed pillow tightly, and wept.

After, she went to the bathroom and washed her face. It was puffy and splotched. *Look at you,* she said to her reflection. *Forty years old . . . half your life, maybe more than half, gone. Look at those lines around your eyes, around your mouth. You're aging, Francine. Oh sure, from a distance you could still pass for twenty-five, but up close, for-*

get it. You're not fooling anyone. Aging, she thought, was the least fair fact of life.

She took off her white chiffon dress. It was a mess now, wrinkled and without shape. She'd kept it tucked away for too many years. She'd bought it for a cruise she and Andrew had taken to celebrate their tenth anniversary. But Andrew had acted sullen and bored on the cruise, so she had flirted with the ship's captain, letting him breathe into her ear on the dance floor, which had infuriated Andrew.

When they'd returned to their cabin, Andrew had practically torn the dress off her, pushing her down on the lower berth, standing over her showing off his erection and telling her exactly what he was going to do with it. But as soon as he entered her he'd lost it, and blaming her, calling her the ultimate C.T., he had run out of the cabin, still zipping up his pants. He'd returned at dawn to apologize, telling her that he'd been drunk and had been sick all night. *Forgive me, Francie,* he'd said. *It's just this goddamned cruise . . . I can't take being cooped up this way.* She had told her that it didn't matter, that she'd already mended her dress. But when he'd tried to crawl into the berth with her, when he'd tried to hold her, to kiss her, she had turned away and pretended to be asleep.

She should have gotten rid of the dress a long time ago, she thought, tossing it into the wastebasket.

How was it possible, she wondered, as she got into bed, that it was working between Mitch and the producer when she had tried so hard to make it work with him and couldn't? She had thought they would marry and move to Beverly Hills where she would find them a big, wonderful house with possibilities. She would open a branch of Brady Broder—Elegant Homes. Sara would go to school with all the right kids. She and Mitch would be part of a tight little social group of producers, directors, writers, and actors. They would all tell her that with her looks she should have been on the screen. She would just pooh-pooh them, take Mitch's arm, smile up at him and he would feel unbelievably lucky to have her for his wife.

But Mitch never asked her to marry him. And she never asked him. Instead, his moodiness turned ugly. She could never figure out his hostile behavior. He was hostile even when they were making love. He would accuse her of either coming on too strong or not strong enough. She had tried so hard to get it right. To do all the things he said he liked in bed. She had studied sex manuals in order to please him. But nothing was enough. He became increasingly critical. Yet she was sure, if she was sweet enough, understanding enough, it would be all right.

He said she drove him to it, to his hostile, abusive behavior. To their battles. He said she was too controlling, too demanding. But what had she ever demanded? She couldn't think of a thing. Okay, so she liked making plans. And she had a lot of plans for them. But that had nothing to do with control or demands.

Why had she phoned him tonight? What had she hoped to hear? That he missed her? That he wanted her? That he had changed his ways? *Fool,* she told herself. *Goddamned fool!* She should have called her mother instead.

The next morning she went to the pool to swim laps. She was getting anxious about being away from the office. Maybe she would cut her week short and leave the next day. At home, surrounded by her things, by the routine of her life, she would feel better. And in just three weeks Sara would return and she would have a reason for living again.

She was in the middle of the pool when she collided with another swimmer. He had been swimming underwater and she hadn't seen him coming. He had kicked her in the head.

"I'm terribly sorry," he said, coming to the surface, sputtering. "Are you all right?"

"Yes, I think so. Are you?"

"I'm fine."

They swam across the pool to the ladder and climbed out. She felt slightly dizzy for a minute and he helped her to her lounge chair. "I'm a doctor," he said. "Let me have a look." He took her pulse, turned her head from side to side, then up and down, and pronounced her healthy. "But we should keep an eye on you today . . . to make sure."

He pulled his lounge chair next to hers. His name was Lewis Branscomb. He was a cardiologist from Minneapolis, a widower, fifty-seven, with two grown children and two grandchildren. He was balding and not terribly attractive, but he seemed to be in good shape. By the time they ordered lunch she decided that he was not unattractive either. And she had always enjoyed doctors. They had a certain self-assuredness that she liked. She knew, before they finished lunch, that he would fall for her and she didn't discourage him.

They spent that night together, and the next, and he extended his stay for the coming weekend. He was good for her bruised ego. He was good for her state of mind. He was sweet and predictable and in bed he expected very little of her. Not like Mitch, who had insisted that she suck on him endlessly, until she was sure her jaw would dislocate.

SMART WOMEN

Lewis told her that he had never had such exciting sex. That just watching her undress was enough to make him feel nineteen again.

"I can't stand the idea of losing you," Lewis said on their last night together. "Come with me to Minneapolis."

"I can't," she told him.

"Why not?"

"It's too cold there."

"I'd keep you warm."

"You're sweet, Lewis . . . but, no."

"I'll come to Boulder, then."

"Come for a visit in the fall, when the aspens turn color."

"What am I supposed to do until then?"

She didn't answer.

"If you marry me," he said, "you can call yourself Triple B."

She laughed. "That's not a good enough reason to get married."

"I'll try to think of a better one."

The next day, as they said goodbye, he gave her a gold bracelet, expensive and elegant. She liked this man. He had style. She liked the idea of having a lover far away. She could not handle someone new and nearby in her life right now.

She did not tell him that Andrew was coming to town.

Lewis phoned her in Boulder several times a week. He sent her cards with absurd messages, books he thought she might enjoy, cassettes, flowers. He had already booked a room at the Boulderado for the first week in October. He was anxious to meet her little girl, to see how she lived, to be with her again.

She did not tell him about Bobby.

He missed her terribly, he said. There was no one else for him. There never would be. And somehow he was going to convince her of this.

She did not tell him, when he phoned on Monday, that she had lain in bed the night before thinking about death, imagining herself hanging from a rope, or with her wrists slit and bleeding, or with half her head blown away by a bullet.

11

MARGO HAD CALLED PUFFIN TWICE SINCE CLARE LEFT FOR Europe and both times Puffin assured her that she was fine. Clare's cousin from Padre Island stayed with Puffin every year while Clare traveled. Margo wanted to have Puffin over for dinner so she asked Michelle and Stuart to choose a night that was good for them.

Michelle said, "Oh, Mother , . . do we have to have her over for dinner? She's such a pissy kid."

"Maybe she's changed over the summer," Margo said. "You never know."

"She's lost about twenty pounds," Stuart said. "I saw her at school yesterday. She's very together looking."

"Well," Margo said, "Thursday or Friday would be best for me. Let me know in the morning. I'm going to the movies tonight."

"What are you going to see?" Michelle said.

"Apocalypse Now."

"I hear it sucks," Michelle said.

"I'm going anyway. I'll be back by eleven."

Margo went downstairs. She brushed her teeth, changed her shirt, tossed a sweater over her shoulders, then picked up the phone and dialed Andrew Broder's number.

He answered on the first ring.

She thought about hanging up when he did.

He said hello twice before she responded. "Hello . . . it's Margo."

"Margo?" he said, as if he had never heard the name.

"Margo . . . from next door."

"Oh, that Margo."

Very funny, she thought. "I'm going to the movies tonight . . . to see *Apocalypse Now* . . ."

"Mixed reviews," he said.

"I'm going anyway. I like Martin Sheen."

"Not Brando?"

"Brando too. It starts at seven-thirty. I'm leaving in five minutes. If you decide to come meet me outside." Before he had a chance to say anything else she hung up. She shouldn't have called. She brushed her hair and glossed her lips.

When she got to her car, he was sitting inside it. "I decided to come along," he told her.

"Good," she said, as if they had just closed a business deal. She fished her glasses out of her bag, put them on, and drove to the Fox.

"I like the way you look in glasses," Andrew said.

"I'm nearsighted," Margo explained. "I need them for driving and movies."

"But not for making love?"

She looked over at him. "Don't you ever think of anything else?"

"Yes, sure . . . all the time," he said. "I didn't mean anything personal. I was just wondering."

"Just for the record," she said, "I don't wear them when I'm making love."

"Some people do, you know . . . but I guess they're farsighted."

"I haven't ever thought about it," Margo said.

"I guess it's because I write," he told her. "An offbeat subject like that could make an interesting article. I could sell it to the *Optician's Quarterly.*"

"Is there such a magazine?" she asked.

He laughed. "I don't know. There might be."

She laughed too. It was hard to be angry at him.

The movie was long and tedious. After an hour Andrew pulled two small boxes of raisins out of his pocket. He passed one box to her. She hadn't eaten raisins in years, not since she'd been sixteen and somewhat anemic. "Either iron tonic or a box of raisins a day," her mother had said. "Which will it be?"

"Raisins," Margo had answered. But after a week just looking at the red box had been enough to gag her. "I'll take the tonic," she'd cried to her mother one morning. "I never want to see another raisin!"

Andrew reached for her hand. His warm fingers wrapped around hers as if they always held hands, as if they went to the movies regularly. And later, when she felt herself about to doze off, her head went automatically to his shoulder. He gave her cheek a quick, gentle caress and his fingers brushed her hair. In the darkened theater they shared a smile.

Afterwards, she drove home.

"You're supposed to ask me in for coffee," he said, when they pulled up in front of her house.

"Really?"

"Yes, it's in the Rule Book."

"Okay. Would you like to come in for a cup of coffee?"

"Yes," he said. "I'd like that."

"My children will probably still be up."

"That's fine."

"Just warning you."

"Stop apologizing for them, will you?"

"I'll try."

Michelle was already asleep, but Stuart was in the kitchen making himself a peanut butter sandwich.

"It's great on rye bread with lettuce and mayonnaise," Andrew told him.

"You've got to be kidding," Stuart said.

"No, you should try it."

"I like it this way, on gross white bread with grape jelly."

"Andrew went to the movies with me," Margo said, feeling an explanation was in order.

"Yeah?" Stuart said, as if he couldn't have cared less. "So how was it?"

"Long," Margo said.

"Your mother found it pretentious," Andrew said.

"Not all of it," Margo explained, as she put up the kettle. "I was moved by some of it . . . but the ending was . . . I don't know . . . I just couldn't get into it . . ."

"That's because you were asleep," Andrew said.

"No shit," Stuart said, laughing. "She really fell *asleep?*"

Margo felt self-conscious. She busied herself pulling out mugs and plates and slicing up a loaf of banana bread.

"So how do you like Boulder?" Stuart asked Andrew.

"Hard to say . . . so far it seems okay. I'm going to be starting work on a new book soon. It should be a good place to write."

"What kind of book?" Stuart said.

"Nonfiction."

"What subject?"

"An in-depth study of Florida's correctional system."

"You mean prisons?"

Why didn't Stuart just shut up and go to bed? Margo thought.

"Yes, but Florida's not unique," Andrew said, as if he needed to make Stuart understand. "The rest of the country has the same problems."

"No shit," Stuart said. Then he turned to her. "Say, Mother . . . Dad called. Michelle left one of her bathing suits at the beach house. Aliza just found it behind the bed. She said it was mildewed so she's throwing it out."

"Okay. Anyone else?"

"Yeah . . . some guy named Eric called. Said you met him over the summer in Chaco Canyon and he just wanted to say hello. He didn't leave a number. Said he'd call again sometime when he's in the neighborhood."

Eric. That was all she needed now. "Okay . . . thanks."

"Well . . ." Stuart said, balancing his sandwich and a glass of milk in one hand, "I'm going to bed. Goodnight."

"Goodnight," Margo said, relieved. "See you in the morning."

"Goodnight," Andrew said.

Margo loaded a tray with the coffee pot, the mugs and the dishes, the banana bread.

"Can I give you a hand with that?" Andrew asked.

"Yes, sure . . ." she said. He carried the tray into the living room and set it down on the coffee table. She turned the stereo to KBOD, classical, then joined Andrew on the sofa in front of the fireplace. It was too warm for a fire now, but in a month or so they'd have one every night. Oh, it would be so nice to share life again. To share it with a steady man. One who didn't get up to go racing home at two A.M. One who slept with his arms around her every night.

Stop it! she warned herself.

"Nice kid," Andrew said, bringing Margo back to reality.

"What?"

"Stuart . . . seems like a nice kid."

"Last year at this time he would have just grunted at you. Now he reminds me of Freddy."

"His father?"

"Yes."

"Sounds like the standard fear of every ex-wife."

"And ex-husband?"

"With us it was different."

She waited to hear more, not sure that she wanted to know how it was between him and B.B., not sure that she didn't.

Instead he said, "Tell me about your work."

"There's not that much to tell," she said. She didn't want to talk about her work tonight. She wanted the magic of the darkened movie theater. "I'm an architect," she said, "with a special interest in solar design."

"Where'd you go to school?"

"The first time, Boston U. . . . fine arts. I was an art teacher for a while, at Walden, in New York."

"So what happened?"

"I don't know. After ten years and two kids of my own I wanted a change. So I took a leave and went to Pratt. When I got my degree I went to work for a small firm in the city. Then, after Freddy and I split up, I decided to try Boulder. And here I am."

"How long have you been divorced?"

"Five years. How about you?"

"Six. You didn't know that?"

"No, why should I?"

"I don't know. I assumed since you and Francine are friends . . ."

"Look, we're friendly, but we're not real friends. There's a big difference." Margo poured each of them a second cup of coffee. She wanted them to hurry up and get this business out of the way. Every time you met a new man it was the same thing. Tell me about your work. Where did you go to school. Divorce details. Problems with children. Every time. What a pain. "Just to set the record straight," she said, "I don't know anything about you, except that you write."

"What do you want to know?" he asked, not giving her a chance to finish. She was about to tell him that she didn't care. That he seemed like a nice person, an interesting person, a very attractive person and that under different circumstances . . .

"I was a reporter on the Miami *Herald* for a long time and

then I quit," he said. "I went to live in Israel for a year, on a kibbutz, but it wasn't what I'd expected. And then I came home and wrote a book. That was a couple of years ago and since then I've been writing freelance articles, mostly investigative reporting. I like the way your mouth curls up. You're very pretty, you know that?"

"Please."

"Please what?"

"It's better if we don't get personal, I think."

"Why is it better?"

"You know."

"I don't."

"I'll write you a letter about it, okay?"

"Sure, okay. You want my address?"

"I know where you live."

"But I pick up my mail. My box number is three-five-nine."

"Three-five-nine," she said. "I'll remember that. I'd like to read your book."

"I'll bring you a copy."

"Okay. But right now I've got to go to bed. I get up early."

He stood up. "When are you going to have me over for dinner? That's what you're supposed to do when someone new moves into the neighborhood."

"Is that in the Rule Book too?"

"Absolutely," he said. "Page forty-two."

"I see."

"Of course, I could have you over too. I make a mean spinach lasagna, an outstanding chicken curry, and I'm working on a stuffed zucchini."

"Sounds delicious."

"So . . . when?"

"When, what?"

"When should we get together for dinner?"

"I'll have to think about it."

"I swim every afternoon at the University pool. Would you like to join me some day?"

"I'm not much of a swimmer. I get water up my nose."

"I'll get you nose clips."

"Then I'd look like a frog."

"What's wrong with frogs?"

"They're green and slimy."

"You're right," he said.

She walked him down the stairs and to the front door.

"I'm reading Proust," he said. *"The Captive."*

"I never got past the endless minutiae of *Swann's Way.*"

"So you're not a romantic," he said.

"Says who?"

"If you were you'd like Proust."

"Not necessarily," she said, opening the front door. They stepped outside into the darkness. She kept forgetting to replace the burned-out bulb in the hanging lamp next to the door. "Why are you telling me all of this anyway?"

"I want you to know me, I guess. I want you to like me."

"I do like you. Now go home."

"How about a soak first?"

"No, not tonight."

"When?"

"I don't know. Maybe never."

"That would be a real shame."

She shrugged.

"Margo . . . I'd like to kiss you goodnight."

"No," she said.

"Can I shake your hand then?"

She put her hand out. He took it. His touch sent tingles up her arm, weakened her legs, sent a flash between them.

Adolescent. Romantic imbecile.

"Goodnight, Margo," he said.

"Goodnight, Andrew." She pulled her hand away just in time. In another second she'd have been in his arms, her mouth on his. Instead, she turned and walked back into the house, closing the door behind her.

Just like Leonard, the voice inside her head said as she was brushing her teeth.

Are you crazy? she argued. *He's nothing like Leonard.*

The same tingles . . .

That's just physical attraction. She spit out toothpaste.

You're telling me?

So I admit it. I'm attracted to him. But he's nice too.

You didn't think Leonard was nice?

Yes, I did . . . in the beginning . . . but it turned out he was neurotic.

And how do you know this one isn't?

I don't. How could I? We hardly know each other.

Ah ha! That's exactly what I've been trying to tell you.

Margo got into bed.

No more affairs going nowhere, she promised herself. From now on she was only interested in men who wanted to settle down. Men who were divorced or widowed or had never been married, although she preferred divorced. That way she wouldn't be fighting ghosts and he'd have had some experience with whatever marriage was and was not. He'd have kids at least as old as hers, maybe even older. She was not interested in merging families. She had only one more year, after this one, with kids living at home. Then it was to be her turn. She wasn't about to give up that kind of freedom for some guy with kids. And he would have had plenty of experience with women, her steady man, and with life, so that settling down with her would be a pleasant relief. Not boring, of course, and not routine. But he wouldn't need to prove anything either. They would see eye to eye on important subjects. He would be politically liberal, but no longer an activist. He'd have gotten that out of his system in the sixties. He'd welcome a nice place to live, a real home, but he wouldn't get crazy over it. He wouldn't be a collector, like Leonard, who couldn't get a divorce because he was afraid of losing his de Koonings, his oriental rugs, his Ming vases. They would share a simple life, with plenty of laughter, plenty of passion, but without crazy expectations.

That's how it would be with her steady man.

Andrew was probably in bed now, thinking about tonight. Thinking about her. If they had kissed, if she had gone next door with him, they would be in bed together now, their bodies, naked, wrapped around each other. She would like to have kissed him. His lower lip was fleshy and inviting. She would have nibbled on it. It would have been nice to run her hands through his soft-looking hair, to kiss the back of his neck.

That's enough, Margo! Go to sleep.

Sleep . . . how can I possibly sleep?

Close your eyes, for a start. Then count sheep. Count lovers. Count anything. But get off the subject of Romeo next door before you start thinking you're Juliet, at forty.

12

MICHELLE HAD A RASH ON HER LEGS. THE DOCTOR SAID she had probably gotten flea bites over the summer and they had caused this allergic reaction. He prescribed a white cream, which she was supposed to apply twice a day. But most mornings she forgot because she was always in a hurry to get to school. So all during the day her legs itched and she scratched until they were bloody and sore.

School wasn't bad this year. She liked her English teacher. She liked her Chemistry teacher. She liked Gemini, a new girl in her class. She thought they might get to be friends. Real friends. She was even getting along with her mother, who had changed for the better over the summer. This year Margo wasn't on her case all the time and they hadn't had one major battle since Michelle got back from New York.

Puffin was coming to dinner tonight. Puffin was in her class too, but they had never been friends. Puffin was so spoiled, flitting around town in her Porsche. A princess from Texas. Michelle didn't see how her mother could be friends with Clare, Puffin's mother, but they were. "I don't judge my friends by their children," Margo had said one time, "any more than you judge your friends by their parents."

"But Mother," Michelle had argued, "she's a product of her environment. Clare must have made her the way she is."

"Clare has gone through many changes, Michelle," Margo had said. "And Puffin will too. It's not her fault that her parents have so much money she doesn't know what to do. Shopping to her means going out and buying a Georgia O'Keeffe. Try to remember that."

"I still don't like her," Michelle had said. "I don't like her attitude toward life."

"You're entitled," Margo had said.

And so Puffin was invited to dinner. And then Margo decided to ask Andrew Broder too, the Brat's father, because he was new in town and seemed lonely. When Michelle heard that, she asked Margo if she could invite Gemini, who was also new in town. Gemini was a Pueblo Indian from New Mexico. She was living with the family of an anthropologist from C.U. who had met Gemini a year ago while he was doing research at her pueblo. He had convinced Gemini's family to let her come to Boulder because she was a gifted student and deserved the best educational opportunities. Gemini's mother and four older sisters were well-known potters—the Gutierrezes. Their pots sold for a fortune. Margo was always admiring them in the Indian gallery on the Mall.

Gemini was definitely headed for Harvard, Yale, or M.I.T. and she knew she'd get in any place she wanted, and with a full scholarship too, because she was a Native American and all the best schools were knocking themselves out trying to recruit Native Americans. A few years ago it had been blacks, but now nobody was that interested in them.

Gemini wasn't her real name. She chose it because it suited her new life in Boulder. Michelle and Gemini had a lot in common. They were both good students, they were both virgins, and they agreed that Stuart and his preppie friends were fools who, as Gemini put it, did not know the way of the world. Michelle wasn't sure what that meant, but she thought it had to do with having your priorities in order. Having your values straight. And Michelle certainly did, which was probably why Gemini had decided to hang out with her.

So there would be six for dinner. Michelle baked whole wheat bread and, for dessert, brownies. Margo made chicken marengo, her old standby, and Andrew Broder brought the salad and the wine. Michelle did not like the way he and Margo kept looking at each other.

Puffin did not talk, she exclaimed. "Oh, Margo . . . this chicken is simply fabulous!"

"Oh, Stuart, I think you look so nice with your short haircut!"

"Oh, Mr. Broder, I hope you like Boulder as much as we do!"

And Michelle did not like the way Stuart kept looking at Puffin. Puffin was such a flirt. It was disgusting. Gemini didn't say anything. She ate quietly, taking it all in. She got rice stuck to her hair.

Margo drank too much wine and got silly. God, Michelle hated it when her mother got silly. It was intensely embarrassing. Why couldn't Margo see that? Once, Andrew Broder reached out and covered Margo's hand with his own. Oh, it was coming all right. Her mother was getting *ga ga* over this guy. Michelle thought back to that night last spring, that night she had given Margo hell for renting the Hathaway apartment for B.B.'s ex-husband. If only Margo had understood that Michelle had just been trying to protect her. She had felt what was coming, even then. She had felt that her mother was going to get involved in somebody else's life again. God, she hated that word, *involved*. If only she had been able to make Margo understand that she had been thinking of her own good. Margo should have learned her lesson the last time, with Leonard. That was all Michelle had meant. But no, Margo courted disaster. That was a line from one of the books Michelle was reading for English class. She couldn't remember which one, but it was certainly fitting.

Puffin and Stuart drank wine too. Puffin was practically in Stuart's lap by the time Michelle carried in the brownies and ice cream. Of course her mother didn't notice. She was practically in Andrew Broder's lap. Gemini watched it all without a word. She got ice cream in her hair.

They all helped clear the dishes, but then Margo shooed the kids out of the kitchen. Too small for all of them, she said, so just she and Andrew Broder would clean up. Oh, Mother, Michelle thought, who are you fooling?

Puffin and Gemini stayed until eleven, then Puffin drove Gemini home. After about fifteen minutes the phone rang and Michelle and Stuart picked up at the same time. It was Puffin, calling Stuart. They stayed on the phone for about an hour, Michelle thought. She wasn't sure because she fell asleep reading *Billy Budd*. She wasn't sure what time Andrew Broder left either. And she had meant to check up on that.

13

SARA WAS FINALLY GOING TO SPEND THE NIGHT AT HER FA-
ther's. She couldn't wait to tell Jennifer her good news. But
when she did, Jennifer said, "That's weird, Sara . . . because last weekend, when you begged to stay over at your
father's, your mother exploded, right?"

"Right," Sara said. "But this weekend she's had a
change of heart, I guess."

"Well . . . take whatever you can get . . . that's my
motto. And remember, Omar says *You have the courage of
your convictions now and know how to express them to
bring people around to your outlook.*"

Sara and Jennifer read "Omar Reads the Stars" every
day. It was a column in the *Daily Camera* and as far as
they were concerned, the only reason to look at the newspaper, except for "Dear Abby," who was sometimes interesting.

"You think that's why she's letting me go then . . . because of the courage of my convictions?"

"Could be," Jennifer said.

Sara was not about to ask her mother. She would just take what she could get.

Last weekend her mother's friend, Lewis, had come to town to see the aspen. They turned color every year at the same time, the first week in October, making the whole mountainside look like a forest of gold. Lewis brought Sara a sweatshirt that said *Minnesota is for Lovers*. Sara didn't tell him they had the same sweatshirt for sale at the C.U. bookstore, only that one said *Colorado is for Lovers*. She pictured Minnesota on top of the map of the United States that she'd had to memorize the first week of school. Her history teacher had let them color it. Sara had colored Minnesota turquoise.

Sara did not know if her mother and Lewis were just friends, if it was some kind of business deal, or if Lewis was a new lover. She worried that Lewis would be like Mitch because her mother had met him in California too. But he wasn't. He was kind of old and friendly and he showed her pictures of his grandchildren. She didn't think Lewis was her mother's new lover. For one thing, he didn't stay at the house. He stayed at the Boulderado Hotel. And for another, they didn't hold hands or anything like that.

Still, it was her mother who had suggested she stay overnight at Jennifer's last Saturday. Sara had begged to stay at her father's instead and that's when her mother had exploded.

"Why are you doing this to me?" she had screamed.

"Doing what?" Sara had asked.

"Do you want to hurt me, Sara . . . because that's what it feels like when you talk that way."

"What way?"

"I won't have this behavior, Sara. I mean it."

"All right . . . I'll go to Jennifer's."

So naturally, after all the noise her mother had made, Sara was surprised to find out that this Saturday she was allowed to go to her father's for an overnight. She got up early and tiptoed around the house, careful not to annoy her mother, afraid that if she did her mother would ground her and not let her spend the night at her father's after all. Her mother threatened to ground her all the time now. Sara didn't even know what she was doing wrong. She tried to figure it out, but she couldn't. Her mother didn't get up in time to say goodbye and that was pretty weird because Mom was always up early to go running. So Sara left her a little note, saying she had gone to Daddy's, that she'd already fed Lucy, and that she hoped Mom would have a very nice weekend.

On Saturday afternoon Sara and her father went bicycle riding. When Sara asked where he'd gotten the bicycles he said he'd borrowed them from Margo. On Saturday night they went to the movies to see *10*, which was partly funny and partly gross.

On Sunday they were wrapping cheese and bread and planning their hike into the mountains, when someone knocked at the door. It was Margo.

"I brought back the book," she said, handing it to Sara's father. It was *his* book, the one he'd written. Sara recognized the cover, without even seeing the title or Daddy's name. "I can't begin to tell you how moved I was . . ." Margo said.

"I'm glad," Daddy said. "But you weren't supposed to return it. It's for you." He walked over to his desk and pulled a felt tip pen out of a mug. "Here . . . let me sign it . . ."

Sara couldn't see what her father wrote inside Margo's book, but whatever it was, when Margo read it, she got all mushy and she looked at the floor, as if she were about to cry.

"I wrote you a note too," Margo said, shaking the book. A small blue envelope fell out and Daddy and Margo both bent down to pick it up off the floor. As they did they bumped heads. Then they both laughed.

"Sara and I are going on a hike this afternoon," Daddy said. "Would you like to join us?"

Margo stood up, smoothed out her skirt, and looked over at Sara for what seemed like a long time. Sara just stared right back at her. Finally Margo said, "Thanks . . . maybe some other time. I've got a lot of catching up to do today."

Sara felt relieved. She didn't understand why her father would have invited Margo to join them anyway. Sunday was *their* special day. She was glad that Margo couldn't go with them.

That night, when Daddy drove Sara home, he told her he'd had the best weekend and that he hoped she would come to stay for a week sometime soon.

Sara said she would like that a lot.

When she went into the house, Mom was really angry. She was almost always angry on Sunday nights now, but this night she was angrier than before. And Sara had to answer a million questions.

"What did you do today?"

"We went on a hike. We had a picnic."

"What did you eat?"

"Cheese . . . I think it was Cheddar . . . and french bread and a grapefruit."

"Did you go alone . . . just the two of you?"

"Yes."

"Did you see Margo?"

"Just for a minute. She brought a book back to Daddy's house. But I didn't see what book," Sara added quickly.

"And what else?" Mom said. "What did you do on Saturday night?"

"We went to the movies."

"What did you see?"

"*10.*"

"*10!* That's not a movie for children."

"I liked it. It was funny."

"He has no sense, no sense at all."

"It's okay, Mom . . . really. I understood everything in it."

"That's not the point."

Sara nibbled at her fingernails.

"Please, Sara," Mom said, "stop biting."

Mom looked out the window for a minute and Sara held her breath, hoping that that was the last of the questions. But when Mom turned around again she said, "Did he have clean sheets for you?"

"Yes. They had stripes."

"What do you do when you're not at the movies or hiking?"

"We talk," Sara said.

"About what?"

"I don't know. We just talk . . . like everybody does."

"About me?"

"No. We never talk about you." Sara wasn't sure she should have added that, but she thought it would please her mother. Also, it was mostly true.

"Why not?" Mom asked. "Why don't you talk about me?"

"I don't know. We just don't."

"Are you afraid to talk about me in front of him? To tell him how much we love each other?"

"No," Sara said, "I'm not afraid."

"Good."

"I just wish you wouldn't ask me so many questions every time I come home from Daddy's."

"Why?"

"I just wish you wouldn't . . . that's all."

"I don't understand that, Sara. I really don't," Mom said. "When two people are as close as we are it's only natural for one to ask the other about what's going on. Aren't you curious about how I spent my weekend?"

Actually, Sara wasn't.

"You should be curious and interested," Mom continued, "because you love me and you care about me. Don't you . . . don't you love me Sara . . . and care about me?" Now Mom had tears in her eyes and her voice had turned to a whisper.

So Sara said, "Yes, Mom. Did you have a nice weekend?"

"No," Mom said. "I was very lonely. I missed you very much."

"What did you do?" Sara asked.

"Nothing."

"Didn't you go out with your friends?"

"No."

"How come . . . last weekend when you went out with Lewis you had fun, didn't you?"

"That was different. Besides, Lewis lives in Minneapolis."

"I know, but you have lots of friends here. You used to go out with them all the time. So how come you don't now?"

"I guess it's because I miss you too much, Sara. I just can't get myself together when you're gone."

"You should try, Mom. Jennifer says that when she goes to stay with her father her mother has a really good time. That's how it's supposed to be when you're divorced." Sara didn't get it. Her mother never complained about being lonely when Sara slept over at Jennifer's.

"Well," Mom said, blowing her nose, "that's not how it is with me. But I did go out for a few hours. I went to a party at Clare's house. She's back from her trip."

"Was it a nice party?" Sara asked.

"Yes. Clare's parties are always very nice. I met Clare's ex-husband there. They're thinking about getting back together."

"Do you think you and Daddy will ever get back together?"

"Would you like us to?" Mom asked.

"Well, if you did, then you wouldn't be lonely."

"That's right. And I wouldn't have to share you, would I?" Mom smiled, a funny lopsided smile, and Sara couldn't tell if she was serious or not.

Sara felt very tired. She yawned. "I'm going to get ready for bed now."

When her mother tucked her into bed she smoothed the hair away from Sara's face, kissed her forehead, and said, "I love you, Sara."

"And I love you."

"For how long?" Mom asked.

"For always and forever," Sara said, closing her eyes.

"That's how long I'll love you too," Mom said, turning out the light.

When her mother was gone, Sara rolled over in her bed. She felt frightened. One minute her mother was full of anger, the next she was telling her how much she loved her. Sara didn't know what to expect anymore. She felt like a top, spinning and spinning, waiting to fall, but not knowing where or when she would.

14

B.B. HAD WORN A NEW DRESS TO CLARE'S PARTY, PURPLE
with a red sash. From across the room she looked sensa-
tional, she thought, catching a glimpse of herself in the mir-
rored wall of Clare's bedroom. But up close, her face looked
drawn and thin and she had had to use makeup to hide the
black circles under her eyes.

She was glad that Clare was back in town. Surprised at the
news about her ex, or whatever he was, since they weren't
formally divorced, but curious too. Clare had always said
that she and Robin had had an almost perfect marriage, until
he'd gone crazy and run off with the Doughnut. An almost
perfect marriage. She and Andrew could have had that too.
Clare had asked her once what had gone wrong with her
marriage and she had thought about telling Clare about the
accident, about Bobby, but she found she couldn't. She
couldn't risk opening the wound again, couldn't expose her-

self to the pain, so she'd said, *Oh, the usual . . . we married too young . . .* and Clare had nodded.

Robin Carleton-Robbins looked like the photos she'd seen of him at Clare's house. Tall, angular, with dark eyes, a slight stutter, and a soft accent. He seemed shy and unsure of himself at the party. Clare had told everyone that he had come to town for a visit with Puffin, but B.B. knew the truth. That Clare and Robin were thinking about getting back together.

Maybe that's what she should do too. Try to make a go of it with Andrew. It wouldn't be easy, she knew, and she had mixed feelings about taking Andrew back. On the plus side, she would no longer have to worry about sharing, or even losing, Sara. And Andrew was still attractive. She was sure she could get him to trim his hair and shave his beard. And she would buy him some decent clothes at Lawrence Covell's. Andrew was a successful author now, about to write his second book. He should look like one. Not that she had read his book, or ever would, but she knew that it had been well-reviewed. On the minus side, Andrew was still Andrew. She was never going to be able to change him or trust him. And he would never adore her, never want her the way that Lewis did. And between her and Lewis there was no destructive history. No pain. So she just didn't know.

Her mother had phoned several days ago, hinting that she was the reason that Andrew had come to town.

"Are you giving him a chance, Francie?" her mother had asked. "That's all I want to know."

"A chance at what?"

"Getting back together."

"What makes you think he wants to get back together?"

"Why else is he in town?"

"To be with Sara."

"That's not all of it . . . believe me," her mother had said.

"Do you know something, Mother? Did he say something to you before he left?"

"I know what I know."

"What's that supposed to mean?"

"That a woman shouldn't be by herself."

"Mother . . ."

"Let me finish, Francine. You're a big-time businesswoman and I'm proud of you. I couldn't be more proud. But in the long run a woman has to have more . . . a woman has to have a man."

"Mother . . . I don't . . ."

"You don't want to hear it because you know it's true."

"I don't want to talk about it," B.B. said.

"What do you want to talk about, Francine . . . the weather?"

"Yes. How's the weather down there?"

"Gorgeous."

"And how's Uncle Morris?"

"Wonderful. Playing eighteen holes a day and watching his weight. We're both on low sodium. My pressure's been up lately. How's Sara?"

"Just fine."

"When will I see her . . . Thanksgiving? Christmas?"

"Maybe Christmas. We're going to Minneapolis for Thanksgiving."

"Minneapolis? What's in Minneapolis?"

"A friend."

"Since when do you have a friend in Minneapolis?"

"Since summer."

"I see."

If Andrew was interested in getting back together he was going to have to make the first move and he was going to have to make it before Christmas, because Lewis had already asked her to join him in Hawaii for the holidays and she was seriously considering his offer.

B.B. stood in front of the massive stone fireplace in Clare's living room. It was a dramatic two-storey glass house, on top of Flagstaff mountain, with an overall view of Boulder, especially dazzling at night when the city was lit. It had been put on the market three years ago by the family of a wealthy alcoholic Buddhist who had driven off the mountainside one night and Clare had bought it, through B.B., a week later.

She looked around at the party guests. Oh God, there was Clint, the politician who called her Red. He spotted her and waved. She looked away. He got the message. If he ever said a word to anyone about her, she'd deny it.

She had met him at a party at the mayor's house several years ago. She'd had too much to drink and had flirted with him. He was going to run for Congress in the next election, he'd told her proudly, letting his hand rest on her ass. He was young and very good looking and when he offered to drive her home, she accepted. He took her to his place and fucked her quickly on the living room floor. She couldn't remember much about it except that while he was pumping her he'd whispered in her ear in Spanish.

She'd seen him a few times after that. Once she'd had a

flat and had taken·it into Big-O to be repaired and he had
been there, buying a new set of tires for his Jeep. He had
greeted her warmly. "Hey Red . . . how're you doing?"

"Excuse me?" B.B. had said.

"It's me, Clint . . . don't you remember?"

"No," she'd told him.

"The mayor's party . . ." he'd said, reminding her.

"Oh, yes. The mayor's party. Nice to see you again."

She had read about him in the *Daily Camera* recently. He
wasn't running for Congress, but he was a candidate for the
state legislature and had a good chance of making it.

And there was Margo, across the room, talking to Caprice, who owned an antique shop in town. Margo was
wearing the suede suit that B.B. had helped her select.
Margo looked up, saw B.B., said something to Caprice,
then headed toward her.

"Hello . . ." Margo said. "How are you?"

"I'm all right," B.B. answered.

"How do you like the suit?" Margo asked, turning
around for B.B.'s inspection.

"Maybe you should have gotten the next size," B.B.
said. "It looks a bit tight across the chest."

"Really?" Margo said. "It's very comfortable . . . I'm
sure it will give as I wear it."

"I suppose so."

"Have you met Robin yet?" Margo asked.

"Yes. Now the only ex-husband who's missing is yours."

Margo laughed. "It's not likely that Freddy will come to
Boulder. He thinks it's the end of the universe."

"Speaking of ex-husbands," B.B. said, "I hear you're
pretty chummy with mine."

Margo looked into her wine glass. "We run into each other . . . we live next door . . ."

"He can be quite charming, can't he?"

"I suppose so."

"But thoroughly unreliable."

"I wouldn't know."

"Have you, by any chance, seen Sara this weekend?"

"I saw her for a minute," Margo said. "She seemed to be having a good time."

"I don't like her spending too much time over there."

"I know how hard it is," Margo said. "Every time my kids fly east to visit Freddy I'm convinced I'm never going to see them again."

"How would you feel if Freddy moved into town and expected to have the kids every weekend?"

"I wouldn't mind the every weekend part as much as I would having him in town. But I'd adjust. I'd have no choice."

No choice. That's what Clare had told B.B. at lunch earlier in the week. "Face up to it," Clare had said. "He's here . . . Sara wants to see him . . . there's no point in setting up an impossible situation. Let her go . . . let her spend the night . . ."

"Why should I give in to his demands?" B.B. had asked.

"Because they're reasonable. Because if you don't it's going to tear you apart. I can see it already. I can see it in your eyes. What do you have to lose by letting her spend the night?"

"Everything," B.B. said.

"I know you love her," Clare had said, "but you can't control her whole life."

B.B. had nodded, biting her lower lip. "All right. I'll let her spend Saturday night."

"Good," Clare had said. "That makes sense. And you'll come to my party. I want you to meet Robin."

"Do you really think getting back together can work?"

"I don't know. But in four years I haven't met anyone I'd rather be with . . . and God knows, I've tried." Clare had laughed then. Her laugh echoed through the restaurant. "Let's have some outrageous dessert. How about sharing a piece of coconut cake."

"I'll have one bite," B.B. had said.

15

"So how was Clare's party?" Michelle asked Margo on Sunday night. They were having cheese omelets with parsley and sautéed potatoes.

"Very nice," Margo said. "I met Clare's ex-husband."

"He's not ex," Stuart said. "They were never officially divorced."

"Well, whatever . . ." Margo said.

"And?" Michelle asked.

"And what?" Margo said.

"What was he like?"

"Shy, but pleasant," Margo said.

"Pleasant is such a blotto word, Mother. It has no meaning . . . none whatsoever."

"I didn't get to know him," Margo said. "I barely said hello."

"Puffin hates his guts," Stuart said. "He ran off and left

them, you know . . . with some bimbo who worked in his bank.''

"At least Clare had plenty of money," Michelle said. "Some women and children are left without a penny."

"That's why you have to prepare yourself for whatever life dishes out," Margo said to Michelle, "so that you're never economically dependent on anyone else."

"Let's face it," Stuart said. "It doesn't matter if you're a man or a woman. What's important is money. You can knock it if you want to, but you can't change the hard facts. Money is power and money is living well and living well is the best revenge."

Margo lay down her fork. "Where did you hear that?" she asked quietly.

"From Aliza!" Michelle said.

"Aliza?" Margo asked. "Aliza's an Israeli . . . Aliza's a Sabra, for God's sake. I can't believe . . ."

"You just don't know, Mother," Michelle said. "Aliza is such a princess! Everything is *designer* in her house. She even has designer dishes. She's into spending Daddy's money as fast as he makes it."

"Come off it, bitch!" Stuart said. "He likes it too. They have their heads together. They're not trying to prove anything like some people. Why shouldn't they live well? They've earned it, you know . . . he's worked hard all his life and her parents were both in a concentration camp . . ." He turned to Margo. "Did you know that, Mother . . . that Aliza's parents were both in Treblinka during the war?"

"Yes, I've heard that story."

"And that's supposed to make it okay?" Michelle fumed.

"That she spends money like it's going out of style . . . and all because her parents were in a concentration camp?"

"She doesn't buy anything more than Mother!" Stuart shouted.

"Mother . . . Mother . . . oh, I just can't believe this," Michelle said dramatically, hitting her head with the back of her hand. "Mother doesn't buy anything. Well, hardly anything. When's the last time you bought a new dress, Mother?"

"I think it was . . ." Margo began, her head swimming.

"And it wasn't a designer dress, was it?" Michelle asked.

"Well . . . I might have had . . ."

"You see!" Michelle said, "Mother doesn't waste hundreds and hundreds of dollars on every dress. Mother is aware . . . Mother has values."

"You want to wear hospital rags for the rest of your life, that's up to you," Stuart said.

"What's wrong with my scrubs?" Michelle asked, smoothing out her green shirt.

Margo listened intently, trying to figure out where all of this was going. Was Michelle suddenly her champion? Had Stuart really turned into Freddy or was this just another phase like spewing facts from the *Guinness Book of World Records,* like being unwashed, like experimenting with marijuana? A phase that would pass. But if it didn't. She just didn't know.

If only she hadn't had her children with the wrong partner. She had suspected that Freddy was the wrong partner for her even before she married him. But she'd married him anyway.

* * *

The first time Margo had gone sailing with Freddy, they'd capsized in Sag Harbor Bay. She'd lost her Dr. Scholl's, her favorite sweater, and her prescription sunglasses.

At the time, her older sister, Bethany, who was visiting along with her children, said, "Maybe he can't do anything right."

"He forgot to lower the centerboard," Margo explained. "That's all."

"Yes, but if he's the kind who forgets the centerboard . . ."

"There was a squall," Margo said. "He was trying to bring us in."

"Worse yet," Bethany said, "to panic during a squall."

"He *didn't* panic. He forgot. There's a difference."

Margo's younger sister, Joell, who was then twelve, said, "At sailing camp the first thing we learned was control. C-o-n-t-r-o-l."

"Thank you," Margo said, "but I already know how to spell it."

"*And* to remain calm," Joell said. "You're hardly ever calm, Margo."

"It's not easy to be calm around here," Margo said, "with everyone telling you what you should do and what you shouldn't do and judging you every single minute of every single day!"

"Margo, darling," her mother said, "who's judging? We all think Freddy is a lovely boy . . . lovely . . . and he's going to be such a fine dentist . . . I'd trust him with my teeth completely. Don't get so huffy, sweetheart

. . . you're just upset because you're about to be married.''

"Upset because you're marrying the wrong boy," Bethany whispered in her ear.

That night Margo met Bethany coming out of the bathroom. "Suppose that were true," Margo said, "about marrying the wrong boy."

"Then get out of it now . . . while you still can. Don't make the same mistake as me. I'm telling you, it's not all it's cracked up to be."

"Are you saying you don't love Harvey?" Margo asked.

"I love Harvey, in a way . . . it's hard to explain. I wish I'd waited, that's all. And I'd hate to see you flushing yourself down the same drain. Before you know it you'll be stuck with babies and a house and responsibilities and you'll grow to hate it just like me."

"Bethany, I'm shocked. I always thought you and Harvey had a perfect life."

"Nobody has a perfect life, Margo."

"But I couldn't get out of it now, even if I wanted to . . . the invitations are out . . . there's a roomful of gifts . . . we have a lease on the apartment . . ."

"Those aren't good enough reasons to get married."

"It will be all right," Margo said.

The next morning, at the breakfast table, her mother, sensing Margo's anxiety and convinced that it had to do with the sailing mishap, said, "Darling . . . you and Freddy will laugh about this for the rest of your lives. Now eat some toast, at least. At a time like this you need your strength."

Her father, trying to turn it into a joke, said, "So who pays for the new sunglasses . . . him or me?" Then he laughed and everyone else at the table joined in, even Bethany.

And so Margo had married Freddy and they'd flown off to the Virgin Islands, to Bluebeard's Castle, for their honeymoon. While they were there they'd met another honeymooning couple, Nelson and Lainie Berkovitz, from Harrisburg, and one day on the beach Lainie had cried to Margo, had cried and confessed that she and Nelson just weren't able to do it, that it wouldn't go in and she didn't know what they were going to do or how they were going to go home and face their families with her still a virgin.

Margo suggested some of the jelly that she smeared inside her diaphragm and Lainie agreed to give it a try. Late that afternoon Lainie knocked on Margo's door and Margo squeezed some jelly into a paper cup for her. Lainie thanked her very much, then went back to her room where she hoped to convince Nelson to give it another try because by then Nelson was feeling very depressed.

Margo and Freddy laughed about poor Lainie and Nelson and felt smug because they were able to do it with no trouble at all. Of course Freddy did not know that Margo was experienced, that she had slept with James, who had died.

They came back from their honeymoon and settled into an apartment in Forest Hills and sixteen months later Stuart was born and a year after that, Michelle. When Michelle was two they moved into Manhattan, to a spacious apartment on Central Park West where they lived for the rest of their marriage.

Margo did not know exactly why she and Freddy were divorced, except that she couldn't stand it any more, couldn't stand Freddy or her life or any of the endless shit, and felt that she was headed down a long road going nowhere and that she had to get out in order to save herself.

By then Freddy was an oral surgeon with an outstanding practice and a fine reputation and Margo's parents were confused and concerned about her plan to divorce. They urged her to see a marriage counselor, but Margo's mind was made up. She wanted out. Besides, Freddy had already found an apartment on the East Side and was invited to one dinner party after another, where he was seated next to attractive divorcées who thought he was some good catch.

Stuart had been twelve and Michelle eleven when Margo and Freddy separated. Stuart had withdrawn, saying it was their problem, not his, and that he was not going to get caught in the middle. Michelle had screamed at Margo, "I hate you, you fucker . . . I hate you for ruining my life. Daddy says it's all your fault. That you're just an immature baby who doesn't know when she has it good."

"If you hate me, then go and live with Daddy!" Margo screamed back. Oh, it wasn't working out the way it was supposed to. None of it. Margo felt lonely and frightened and disoriented and was on the verge of tears from morning until night, although she still made it to work every day. "Just go and live with Daddy if you think he's so great!"

But Michelle had cried, "I won't live with Daddy. And you can't make me. I hate him as much as I hate you. I hate you both and I hope you die tomorrow because I don't give a shit about either one of you. You hear me? I don't give a shit about you or about him! You're both fucking assholes!"

Michelle carried on for more than a month. Then one day she approached Margo. "I've decided to get on with my life,'' she said. Margo had breathed a sigh of relief and had tried to get on with her own.

Seven months later she had met Leonard. It had been the middle of winter in New York and freezing. She had worn fleece-lined boots and wool socks to the party and had carried a pair of sandals to change into once she was there. The party had been given by Lainie Berkovitz, who had been divorced from Nelson for six years. Lainie was earning thirty-five thousand dollars on Wall Street. Lainie, who couldn't do it on her honeymoon, was doing it regularly now with her live-in mate, Neil, an investment banker. Margo imagined that Lainie and Neil got into bed at night and had long, involved discussions about money.

Leonard was Neil's friend and a tax lawyer. At the time Margo had had no idea that he was married. He had approached her, offering a cracker spread with caviar.

''Thanks, but I don't like caviar,'' she'd said.

''Everybody likes caviar,'' he'd told her.

''Not me.''

He had sat down next to her, had eaten the cracker himself, and had made small talk for more than an hour, letting his arm brush against hers, letting his hand rest on her knee. She'd felt warm and excited and very desirable and when she'd excused herself for a minute to use the bathroom, he'd followed her down the hall, to Lainie's bedroom, and had locked the door behind them. They had kissed without speaking, then had fallen onto Lainie's bed, on top of the coats that were piled there. He'd unbuttoned her silk shirt and kissed her breasts. She'd raised her skirt and kicked off her panties and had felt something soft and furry under her ass. Mink, she'd thought, as she came.

She and Leonard had met every day for a week and at the end of that time he'd told her about his wife and children. About how he kept a small apartment in Gramercy Park that he used weeknights, but that on weekends he went home, to Pound Ridge, to his family. He wanted a divorce, he'd explained, but Gabrielle wouldn't give him one, although he was sure she would eventually. Margo believed him.

Their affair had lasted more than a year and had ended, finally, because Margo realized that it wasn't the family he couldn't leave, but his collections. And then, of course, there was the incident with Gabrielle and the gun.

Leonard had flown out to Boulder once, to try to convince Margo to return to New York, but by then she had begun her new life, her children were set in school, and she was involved with her boss, Michael Benson. Even though she was wise enough this time to know that she and Michael weren't going anywhere, he did help her understand there were other fish in the sea and for once she was able to look at Leonard objectively and she didn't like what she saw, an infantile man who wanted it all, on his own terms, without giving an ounce to anyone.

Margo took a sip of coffee and was surprised to find that it was already cold. She heard music coming from her children's rooms and hoped that they had started their homework. She stood up, cleared away the dinner dishes, and picked up the phone. Margo was concerned about Clare. She had been in a frenzy at the party last night, the sleeves of her long silk kimono flapping like the wings of a bird trapped in a glass house. Last weekend, before Clare had flown to Dallas for a reunion with Robin, Margo had tried to warn her. "People don't change," she had said. "They may try, they may pretend for a while, but then they revert."

"Look," Clare had said, "if Robin hadn't run off with the Doughnut we'd still be together."

"But he did run away with the Doughnut," Margo had reminded her. "That's the whole point."

Margo dialed Clare's number and Clare answered the phone on the third ring.

"It was a wonderful party," Margo said.

"Really . . . I couldn't tell . . . I was a wreck."

"I know."

"Tell me it's going to be okay . . . that I'm not making a terrible mistake," Clare said.

"I can't tell you that."

"Suppose you're right . . . suppose he runs off again . . . with or without a Doughnut . . ."

"We all make mistakes," Margo said. "You can always get out of it."

"You're only allowed so many mistakes," Clare said.

"No . . . you're allowed as many as you need," Margo told her. "There's no limit."

"You're sure?"

"Yes . . . look at me!"

Clare laughed. "I want it to work. God knows, I really want it to work. Maybe I shouldn't have had a party . . . maybe it was too soon. He used to love parties, but last night he was like a frightened child."

"Give it some time," Margo said.

After they'd hung up, Margo made herself another cup of coffee. She took it into the living room and settled on the sofa with the Sunday *Camera*. But she found herself thinking about Clare's party again. It had been strange seeing Clint there. She had once had a fling with him. He had whispered to her in Spanish while they were making love. She hadn't understood a word he was saying, but she had thought of whispering back to him in Yiddish, if only she could remember some of her grandmother's favorite expressions. The idea of speaking Yiddish to him had made her laugh. He had been offended, thinking she was laughing at him. Last night Clint had been putting the make on Margo's friend Caprice, who owned the antique shop where she had bought her rolltop desk. She wondered if she should have warned Caprice about Clint. But what would she have said?

Margo was tired of Boulder parties. She longed to stay at home on Saturday nights, working on her quilt, sharing a quiet evening with someone special. She thought about Andrew Broder and how, when she had returned the book to his house that morning, he had invited her to go hiking with him and Sara. Margo had been tempted, but when she'd seen the look of surprise and hurt on Sara's face she'd decided against it. She wasn't about to come between a man and his daughter.

She didn't see him again until Wednesday night, when he called, asking if she'd like to take a drive. It was clear and brisk outside and she zipped up her vest as she walked to his truck. They drove up to the Red Lion Inn, found a table in the back, and ordered brandies. She thought about telling him that she couldn't see him again. That she felt she had to stop before it was too late. That Boulder was a small town and since she and B.B. lived here, worked here, and were raising children here, she simply could not risk getting involved with him.

But as soon as they sat down he took her hand, looked directly into her eyes, and said, "I've missed you. Where've you been?"

"I've been working on a fund-raiser for the Democratic Professional Women's Organization."

"I didn't know you were active politically."

"I'm not. I mean, I might be, but I can't work up any enthusiasm for Carter. This is just a luncheon I was asked to co-chair. And Michael was out of the office for a few days . . ."

"Michael?"

"Michael Benson . . . one of the partners in the firm."

"Oh, I thought maybe there was competition."

She didn't laugh. She swished the brandy around in her glass. "And I've been thinking too . . . about us."

"So have I. Your note was beautiful. Thank you."

She had written a note about his book, telling him that it was tender, funny, sad. She shouldn't have written anything.

"The book is based loosely on the accident," he said, "but I guess you knew that."

"The accident . . . what accident?"

"When Bobby was killed."

"Bobby?"

"My son. He was ten."

"Oh God." Her throat closed up. She looked away from him. Tears came to her eyes. She'd had no idea.

"You've known Francine since you came to Boulder and you didn't know about Bobby?"

She shook her head.

"Jesus!" He ran his hands through his hair. A vein in the center of his forehead stood out. "Does anybody here know?"

"I doubt it," Margo said softly. "I would have heard." She wished she'd known sooner, wished she'd known all along.

"I was driving," Andrew said. "She blames me. And for a long time I blamed myself. Writing the book was a cathartic experience. My way of dealing with it . . . of facing up to it."

Margo thought of B.B.'s cool exterior, the vacant eyes.

"It tore us apart," Andrew said. "She's never forgiven me."

Suppose Freddy had been driving, had had an accident, and Stuart or Michelle had been badly injured, had been killed. Would she have been able to forgive him? God, what an impossible situation.

"I don't know what to say," she told him, covering his hand with hers. Suddenly she understood so much.

"I was sure you knew," he said. "I was sure everyone knew."

"No wonder B.B. didn't want you to come here."

"I came because of Sara."

"Stop, please . . ." Margo said. "I don't want to hear anymore. Not now. Not tonight."

"Sorry. I usually don't go on about it."

"I'm glad you told me. I just need a little time to digest it."

"One thing," Andrew said. "I don't feel sorry for myself anymore and I don't want anyone else feeling sorry either. Got it?"

"Got it," Margo said.

They sat quietly for a long time, nursing their brandies.

And then Margo began to talk. She told him about her marriage to Freddy, about the divorce guilt and how it affected her relationship with her children, about her fears of not being a good enough mother, of screwing things up with

Michelle, of blaming herself for a million little things that she knew, at some other level, were not really her fault.

She told him about James and how James reminded her of him. She told him about Ruby, who had been her neighbor in Forest Hills, and how their first babies had been born just two days apart. About how, one summer day, while they were pushing their infants in their carriages, Ruby had asked, "If you had to choose between your husband and your baby who would you choose?"

"I can't answer that," Margo had said. "It's a crazy question."

"I'd choose my husband," Ruby had said. "We could always make another baby."

Margo had looked down at Stuart's sweet sleeping face. I'd choose my baby, she'd thought, and find another husband.

She babbled on and on, anxious to share the intimate details of her life.

By the time they got back to her house it was after midnight and Stuart and Michelle were asleep. She invited Andrew in for a soak and he accepted.

"You're not going to pass out, are you?" she asked as he stepped into the tub.

"Not tonight," he said.

"Fifteen minutes . . . that's all you get," Margo told him, setting the timer.

"I'll try to make the most of it," he said.

They sat on opposite sides of the tub, facing each other, not speaking, not touching.

When the buzzer went off Margo stepped out of the tub, wrapped herself in a robe, handed Andrew another, and told him that he could go home through the gate in her fence.

He grabbed her by the shoulders then, spun her around, and kissed her. She didn't resist. It was a long, warm, wet kiss and from it she knew how it would be to make love with him. But before it could go any further she broke away, saying, "Not yet . . . not yet . . ."

"Why?"

"I don't know . . . I'm not ready."

"When . . . tomorrow, the next day?"

"I don't know."

"Don't you ever act on impulse?" he asked.

"I'm one of the most impulsive people you'll ever meet," she told him. "And right now I'm fighting it harder than I've ever fought anything."

"Why fight?"

"I need to think about it."

"Goddamn it, Margo. You're acting like some fifteen-year-old tease."

"I don't know if I can handle this, Andrew."

"Does anyone ever know?"

"Some people . . ."

"That's bullshit and you know it. What is there to handle?"

"You . . . us . . . the complications . . . the consequences . . . please, Andrew . . . go home and let me think."

"I hope you know what you're doing," he said.

"I hope so too."

He kissed her one more time, then gathered his clothes and left. She watched him walk away. Then she went into the house and climbed into bed.

Well, Margo . . . the voice began, *I'm proud of you!*

I figured you would be.

You really thought things through tonight.

I've just postponed it, that's all . . . because I really like this man . . . hell, I'm crazy about him.

Think, Margo!

I am thinking. I've been thinking.

She tossed back her covers and sat up.

Margo . . . the voice warned.

I'm a fool. There may never be another night like this one. He could be dead in the morning. I could be. The bomb could fall. The world could end . . .

She got into her robe, slipped her vest on over it, stepped into her sandals, tiptoed out of the house, and went next door, pausing for a minute at the foot of the staircase leading to his apartment. Then she ran up the stairs and knocked on his door, timidly at first, then stronger.

He opened the door. He was wearing his jeans but no shirt and no shoes.

"I was wondering if I could borrow a box of raisins," she said.

He closed the door behind them, took her in his arms, and kissed her. She threw her vest on the floor. Her robe fell open and she felt the warmth of his skin next to hers. He took her hand and led her into the bedroom. They made love for hours and finally, worn out and exhausted, fell asleep in each other's arms, their bodies covered with sweat, the sheets damp and sticky. When they awoke it was close to five and she put on her robe and crept back to her house. She got into her cold bed and thought, I am in love.

And then she fell asleep.

PART
TWO

16

MICHELLE WAS SO PISSED AT MARGO! HOW COULD SHE LET him move into their house, into their *home*, without discussing it, without bothering to find out how she and Stuart would feel about it, without a second thought?

One morning in November, while they were in the kitchen, Margo had announced it. "Andrew is going to move in next week." Just like that.

Michelle had been gulping orange juice at the time and had choked on it. Margo had had to whack her on the back. "His lease is up and since we're together all the time anyway . . ." Margo went right on talking, never mind that Michelle's throat was closing up, that she couldn't breathe, that she might die right on the spot.

"Does this mean congratulations are in order?" Stuart asked, stirring two sugars into his coffee.

"If you want to congratulate us on being happy, sure . . ." Margo said.

"That's not what I had in mind," Stuart told her.

"Well, we're not talking marriage at this point," Margo said. "We're talking living together."

Michelle got her breath back. Living together! *Him*, living here. As if he belonged. It was one thing for Margo to have a boyfriend, one who slept over sometimes, one who was around a lot. It was another thing completely to have her boyfriend move in, to take his showers there, open their refrigerator whenever he wanted, put strange foods into it, shit in their toilets, to be around *all* the time. "Is he going to pay," Michelle asked, "or just live here free . . . just live off us?"

"I don't see that it's any of your business, Michelle," Margo said.

"It's *all* my business, Mother. This is *my* house too . . . remember? And as I recall my father pays child support that goes toward our house payments and our grocery bills and so I have every right to know what kind of arrangement you've made with your boyfriend."

"He's going to contribute the same amount of money that he was paying next door."

"Which is?"

Margo sighed. "Three hundred and fifty dollars a month."

"And what about food?"

"He'll pay for his share of the groceries. We'll divide our bill by four. Anything else?"

Margo was really tense now. Michelle could tell by the tightening of her mouth, the crease in her forehead. Her mother looked old when she got tense. Michelle had no trouble visualizing her as an old old woman, her face all lined, her mouth puckered and sunken, her flesh loose and hanging from her bones, her fingers arthritic, like Grandma Sampson's. And how many boyfriends would she have then?

"Yes," Michelle finally said, answering Margo's question. "There is one more thing. What about the Brat? Because if you think she's going to stay in my room when she comes over, you can guess again. And I mean it, Mother!"

"Well, she certainly can't stay in my room," Stuart said. "I need my privacy."

"We all need our privacy," Margo said.

"So what about it, Mother?" Michelle said.

"We're working on it," Margo said.

"Working on it? What does that mean?" Michelle asked.

"It means we're thinking about it," Margo said. "Sara has to feel welcome here. Andrew is her father."

"But it's not *his* home," Michelle said. "It's ours! The Brat has her own home in Boulder . . . with her mother."

"You are acting selfish and unreasonable, Michelle," Margo shouted, "and I'm getting sick of it!"

"You should have thought about all of this before you decided to let him move in, Mother. You could have waited. Stuart will be gone next fall and I'll be gone a year later. You could have waited until then to let him move in."

"No, I couldn't have waited," Margo yelled, "because this is also *my* home, and *my* life, and I'm tired of waiting."

Margo's voice choked up and she started to cry. Michelle knew she would. She was such a baby.

"We're going to be late for school," Stuart said.

"I'm ready," Michelle told him.

"Then let's go."

They left Margo with her head on the breakfast bar, sobbing. Serves her right, Michelle thought.

17

MARGO WAS IN LOVE AND NO ONE WAS GOING TO SPOIL IT for her. Not Michelle and her hostility, not Stuart and his blasé attitude, not B.B., not Sara, not anyone.

It wasn't as if they'd made the decision to live together on the spur of the moment. They had been inseparable from the first night they had made love, running back and forth from her place to his, having dinner together, laughing and talking into the night, feeling exhausted but exhilarated the next morning.

Andrew had brought up the subject of living together on the night that Steve McQueen had died. They had lain in bed talking about how fragile, how unpredictable life was and Andrew had asked, "Would you go to Mexico for laetrile treatments?"

"No," she answered. "Would you?"

"Yes, I'd try anything."

"If it comes down to that, I'll take you."

"Even though you're not a believer?"

She wrapped her arms around him. "Even though . . ."

They had made love tenderly.

Later, Margo was curled beside Andrew, her head on his chest, her finger tracing an imaginary line from his belly to his neck and back again. She loved the smoothness of his skin and the soft hair that ran from his chest to his belly, then spread out so that his lower half was covered with a downy fur. It was hard to be near him and keep her hands to herself. Like Puffin and Stuart, she thought. But Puffin and Stuart were new at the game and Margo and Andrew weren't.

He had stroked her face. He loved her cheekbones, he'd told her. He loved to kiss them and touch them and nibble at them. She'd never been aware of her cheekbones, but now, when she looked in the mirror she noticed them first and tried to see herself as he saw her.

"My lease is up in a few weeks," Andrew had said. "I can't renew it. Hathaway has rented the place for the whole winter. I could look for another place . . ." He hesitated.

Or you could move in with me, Margo thought.

"Or I could move in with you," Andrew said. "That is, if you'd have me."

If she'd have him! She tried to think reasonably, but she couldn't. She wanted to jump up and shout, *Yes, move in with me*, but a mature adult did not react solely on an emotional level. A mature adult thought things through, considered both sides of the issue. Finally she said, "There would be a million complications."

"I can only think of nine hundred thousand," he said.

She reached down and pulled up the quilt, then snuggled close to him again. "It would be nice to have you here every night, to wake up next to you every morning, but moving in together . . . I don't know . . . are you saying that you're going to stay in Boulder? Are we talking serious commitment?''

"We're talking about being together as long as it works . . . as long as we both want to be together."

"But suppose one does and the other doesn't?"

"Then we'd have to figure out what happened and why and make adjustments."

"Adjustments," she said, more to herself than to him. "You wouldn't just walk out . . . without discussing it?"

"No," he said. "And you wouldn't just kick me out, would you?"

"No . . . not unless you did something to make me hate you."

"Such as?"

"Being dishonest with me . . . or making love with someone else."

"Ah . . . so you're the jealous type."

"Monogamous. I couldn't live with you unless I knew it was a monogamous relationship, unless I could trust you."

"There's more to trust than sexual faithfulness."

"Oh sure, I know, but it's a good place to start. How would you feel if I made love with another man?"

"I probably wouldn't like it," Andrew said.

"You're supposed to say you'd hate it, that you'd kill him, or me, or both of us."

"But then I'd go to jail."

"I'd visit every Sunday."

"Assuming I spared your life."

"Right."

"Would you bring me raisins?"

"By the carton."

"Then it's a deal," he said.

"What is?"

"Living together in a monogamous, trusting relationship."

"For how long?" Margo asked. "I need to have some idea so that if we ever have a difference of opinion, which I realize is unlikely but still possible, I won't worry that it's all over between us."

"How does six months sound for a start?" he asked.

"Six months . . ." she said, mentally counting. "No . . . six months is no good because that would put us right in the middle of May and I can't take the chance that my life is going to fall apart this spring, because Stuart will be graduating and Freddy and Aliza will be coming to town. It would have to be until the end of the school year, at least."

"Okay . . . fine," Andrew said. "At least until the end of the school year and much, much longer, I hope."

"I hope so too."

They were quiet for a while, then Andrew said, "Margo . . ."

"Hmmm . . ."

"I love you . . . at least I think I do . . . and if I think I do that must mean something."

"I'm sure it means something," she said, "because I've been thinking that I love you, too, but I've been afraid to say it, afraid that you wouldn't respond, that you'd be embarrassed or say, *Well, I like you a lot, Margo, but love, that's a different story, that's . . .*"

"Come here," he said, taking her in his arms, kissing her. "Right now there's not a doubt in my mind that I love you, that I'm going to keep on loving you."

"Sounds good to me," she said, climbing on top of him, kissing his face, his neck, his mouth. In a minute she knew it was going to be another night of very little sleep.

Afterwards, she said, "If you live here we'll be able to make love like regular people and still get some sleep."

"We'll never make love like regular people, Margarita," he said, "because regular people don't have this much fun."

Margo and Clare were at the Overland Sheepskin Company, looking at gloves. Although the temperature was in the low seventies, snow was forecast, with a thirty degree drop expected overnight. Tomorrow morning it would be winter if the weatherman was right.

"Andrew is moving in at the end of the month," Margo said as she tried on a fleece-lined glove.

"Are you sure you know what you're doing?" Clare asked.

"We feel that it's right for us. We seem to be . . ." She hesitated, looking at her hands in the gloves, then went on, ". . . in love." She could feel her cheeks redden and she smiled.

"After two months?" Clare asked.

"It's closer to three and anyway, don't you think we're old enough and wise enough to know quickly?"

"I'm not sure we're ever old enough to know," Clare said, "and wise enough is out of the question."

"Still . . . it feels right to us."

"It could be such a mess, Margo."

"I know, but it's not fair to us, to Andrew and me, to say we can't be together because . . . look, I wish I didn't know his ex-wife, but I do. I can't change that. Anyway, I hear she has a new man in her life."

"Yes. A doctor from Minneapolis. Robin and I had dinner with them a few weeks ago. He's a nice man and obviously adores her."

"Well, that's great. Is it serious?"

"I think it could be, on his part anyway. But it's a long way from Minneapolis to Boulder."

"I'm going to take these gloves," Margo said to the saleswoman.

"You're sure it's not just sex?" Clare asked as they left the store and headed back to work.

Margo laughed.

There had been moments, at the beginning, when Margo thought it might be just the sex, because neither of them ever tired of it and because it worked so well between them. Margo had read all the books. She knew about the limits of limerance and the three-to-six-month life of the typical affair. But she also knew that if you never tried, you would never find out what it might grow into.

Okay, so they'd only known each other a couple of months, but still, there was so much promise. This was what she'd had in mind when she'd left Freddy. And certainly, one of the reasons she had left was that they had brought their resentments to bed with them. How could you feel loving toward someone who was constantly putting you down? How could you respond in bed to someone you wanted to smash with a baseball bat? For a long time after Margo left Freddy she thought it might not be possible to find the kind of love she had imagined.

Okay, so it was too soon to be able to trust completely, to feel secure all the time. There were still moments of panic, of doubting, but she got through those moments, often with Andrew's help.

Ten days after Andrew moved in, Margo invited Clare and Robin to dinner. Puffin came too, of course, since she and Stuart had also become inseparable. Clare had met Andrew a few times in town, but they hadn't had the chance to get to know each other. And Robin was meeting him for the first time. Robin seemed more relaxed than at Clare's party and Margo was pleased at how well dinner was going when Michelle turned to Andrew and said, "Did you know when we first moved to town my mother joined Man-of-the-Month Club?" Michelle paused for a second, making sure everyone had heard what she'd said and that she had their attention. Then she went on. "First there was her boss, Michael Benson . . . then there was that asshole physiologist from the University, who always had to have the last word . . . then there was Bronco Billy . . . remember Bronco Billy, Stuart?" But Michelle didn't wait for Stuart to answer. She kept going. "Bronco Billy used to clean his fingernails with his pocket knife . . ."

"Eeeww . . . gross . . ." Puffin said, listening intently.

"Then there was . . . oh, what's his name . . ." Michelle said, "the one with the bad arm . . ."

Margo swallowed hard and fought back tears. Why did Michelle want to hurt her this way? Clare and Robin had stopped eating. Clare gave Michelle a look of such contempt that it should have shut her up, but it didn't.

"Oh, I remember now," Michelle said. "His name was Calvin and he was a lawyer . . . and after him there was Epstein, Mom's token Buddhist . . ."

149

"That's enough, Michelle," Margo said quietly. She wanted to take Michelle and shake her by the shoulders, wanted to slap her face, scream, *Why . . . why are you doing this?*

"But, Mother . . ." Michelle said, wide-eyed, "I'm just getting started."

Before Margo had a chance to respond, to really blow it, Andrew placed his hand over hers and said, "Oh, those were just alternate selections, Michelle. They don't count. I'm a main selection. There's a big difference. Besides, I thought you knew, Margo's quit the club." He smiled at Michelle and then at Margo, letting her know that it was okay, that he could take it. And Margo, relieved and deeply grateful for his understanding, for his sense of humor, smiled back. The awkward moment passed.

"Well, Andrew," Michelle said, "at least you're a useful one . . . *you* can cook."

"Thanks, Michelle," Andrew said.

Everyone laughed self-consciously, then went back to eating the lemon chicken with snow peas.

"A Buddhist named Epstein?" Andrew asked later, when they were in bed.

Margo laughed. "He wasn't born a Buddhist."

"I never knew Buddhists fucked."

"Oh yes . . . quite a bit."

"How was it . . . was it different . . . did he chant while you were making love?"

"Not that I noticed," Margo said.

Then they both laughed and when they stopped they made love.

18

MICHELLE HAD SET OUT TO TEST ANDREW AS SOON AS HE'D moved in, because it was better to find out now if he could take it, and if he couldn't, to get rid of him quickly, before she got to know and even like him. So she'd given it to them good at the dinner party, figuring if they couldn't handle a little scene like that then they didn't have a prayer of staying together. And really, if she could scare him away so easily then it was better for Margo to know, even though she might be angry for a little while. Eventually she'd get over it and thank Michelle for making her see the light.

Also, Margo had been a bitch about the dinner party. She wouldn't let Michelle invite Gemini.

"Look," Margo had said, "this dinner is for Clare and Robin to get to know Andrew."

"What about Puffin? She's invited too."

"Puffin is Clare's daughter."

"God, Mother, you're always telling me who's related to who around here, as if I've got an acute mental disorder."

"If Stuart had another girlfriend, someone who was not my best friend's daughter, she would not be invited to dinner tonight. Now try and get that through your head, Michelle, and if you feel that you can't behave in a civilized way, then don't come to the dinner table . . . all right?"

Michelle might not have come to the dinner table except that during English class, while Ms. Franzoni was telling them they could become members of a book club for only one dollar and get four books free, she had dreamed up her Man-of-the-Month-Club number.

And it had worked beautifully. She'd waited until just the right moment to face Andrew and tell him about Margo's lovers. Michelle had expected to ruin the dinner, had expected Clare, Robin, and Puffin to get up and leave the house, had expected her mother to dissolve into tears, and then, just maybe, to be slapped around a little by Andrew so that Michelle could call her father and tell him that Margo had a live-in boyfriend who was into child abuse. Upon hearing this news her father would order Andrew out of the house . . . *or else.* Michelle wasn't sure what the *or else* would be, but her father would think of something, she was sure.

Michelle had been surprised that Andrew had taken it so well. You just never knew.

That night, after the dinner party, after Clare and Robin and Puffin had gone home, Andrew and Margo had put on their vests and had gone for a walk. Michelle was in bed reading *Franny and Zooey* when Stuart burst into her room. "What the fuck were you trying to pull tonight?"

Michelle did not answer. She kept her book in front of her face and pretended to go on reading. Pretended that she didn't even notice that Stuart was standing over her, his face red, his breath coming hard.

But then he swatted the book out of her hands and sent it flying across the room. "I said, what the fuck were you trying to pull tonight?"

She could feel Stuart's anger and it frightened her. But the best way to handle it was to stay calm. So she said, "Oh ho . . . aren't we getting violent?" She scrambled across her bed and reached down to the floor to retrieve the book.

Stuart yanked her back by the arm. "It's about time someone got violent with you, you little bitch!"

She was sure he was about to smash her. She tried not to cower, she tried to stare him down, and after a minute he punched her panda bear instead.

"I just don't want Mom to be hurt again," she explained. "I don't want to go through another Leonard."

"Leonard was years ago," Stuart said. "Why don't you just leave her alone for once. She's happy. Or is it that you can't stand to see her happy?"

"I'm the one who has to suffer through it every time one of her love affairs fizzles. Me . . . not you!"

"It's her life, Michelle, so just butt out of it."

"It's my life too. And when she's miserable, I'm miserable."

"You better cut the cord, Michelle, before it's too late. Besides which, she's not miserable, she's in love."

"Oh, sure. Now. Today. But what about next week, next month, next year? You'll be gone, so what do you care? But I'll still be around."

"You worry too much," Stuart said. "You're getting to be just like Grandma Sampson."

"I am not! But somebody around here has to think ahead. And since when do you care about her anyway?"

"I've always cared."

"Yeah . . . well, you'd never know it."

"I keep my feelings to myself."

"I'm glad to know you have feelings, Stuart. That's a real revelation."

"Hey, bitch . . . I'm the one who defends you every time somebody makes a rude remark about you and your Indian maiden."

"What do you mean?"

"Wake up, Michelle . . . everybody's saying you've got a thing going with Gemini."

"That is the most intensely stupid remark I've ever heard."

"Hey, look . . . it's nothing to me if you're gay."

"I am not gay!"

"Or bi . . ."

"I am not bi!"

"Then don't get so defensive. I just thought you should know what everybody's saying."

"Some people don't recognize friendship because they've never experienced it. All *you* know is sticking it up Puffin."

He grabbed her by the arm again, roughly, his fingers digging into her flesh. "I swear, Michelle, I'll kill you if you ever say anything like that again!"

She pulled away. "Get out of my room, you fucking asshole!" He turned and left. As he did she threw her copy of *Franny and Zooey* at him, but it missed, hitting the wall instead. She looked at her arm. His fingers had left red marks on it. She began to cry into her pillow. Life was not turning out the way she had planned. Everything was screwed up. How could they say those things about her and Gemini? Gemini was the best friend she'd ever had. Gemini even understood her poems, calling them outstanding examples of contemporary thought.

A couple of times Michelle had thought about showing her poems to Margo. But at the last minute she'd always changed her mind. Margo was too busy. Margo wasn't interested in Michelle, especially now that she had a live-in boyfriend.

One day Margo would be sorry. Sorry that she'd had a daughter and hadn't bothered to get to know her. Sometimes Michelle thought about slitting her wrists, the hot blood flowing out of her body. She pictured her family finding her on the floor, dead. They would blame themselves, each of them feeling guilty forever. Plenty of poets killed themselves. Even modern poets like Sylvia Plath and Anne Sexton. The only trouble with killing yourself, or with dying in general, was that you wouldn't be around to find out how everyone took it. It would be different if you could come back and say, *Well, all right, now you have another chance and this time you better treat me right.*

Anyway, Michelle wasn't about to kill herself. There were other ways to get even with people. Like when her poems were published and Michelle was interviewed on the *Today Show* and Jane Pauley said, *Tell us, Michelle . . . did your mother encourage you to write?* Michelle would say, *My mother? My mother was too busy with her boyfriend to even notice.*

Michelle got out of bed and walked across the room to her desk. She picked up a pencil, opened her special notebook, and jotted down a few lines. She yawned then, feeling incredibly tired. She closed her notebook. She would finish her poem in the morning. She got back into bed and fell asleep.

19

SARA COULD NOT BELIEVE IT. HER FATHER, WHO HAD COME to Boulder to be with her, had moved in with Margo Sampson. And Sara was never going to forgive him. Never! Now all of her plans, her secret plans, were spoiled. Because she had been thinking that maybe she would tell her father about her mother's screaming fits and that Daddy would say, *Well, Sara, in that case, why don't you come and live with me?* And she would.

Jennifer said that Sara was more than disappointed. Jennifer said that Sara was depressed. And Jennifer should know. One time Jennifer had been so depressed she'd had to see a shrink three times a week. That had been a long time ago, when they were in fifth grade. Jennifer said that she would help Sara through her depression. Jennifer was the one who had clued her in on what was going on between Margo and her father in the first place.

It was on the Saturday night before Halloween and Jennifer had come to Daddy's house with her. The three of them had played a marathon game of Monopoly and then Daddy had cooked them baked ziti, which Jennifer refused to eat until Daddy explained that it was just spaghetti in a different shape. After dinner Margo had come by and she and Daddy had gone for a walk while Sara and Jennifer had watched a movie on TV.

That's when Jennifer had asked, "Are Margo and your father lovers?"

"I don't think so," Sara said. "Do you?"

"Yes," Jennifer told her, "without a doubt."

"How can you tell?"

"I've had experience with my own parents."

"I don't think you're right," Sara said. "They're just friends is all."

"You're so naive, Sara," Jennifer said. "If you don't believe me you can smell the sheets."

"Smell the sheets?"

"Yes."

So she and Jennifer went into her father's bedroom and pulled back the blanket and Jennifer bent down and sniffed the sheet. "What'd I tell you?" she said. "They're doing it all right."

Sara sniffed the sheets too, but she didn't smell anything strange. Still, it gave her a funny feeling to think about her father doing it with Margo. She had noticed that one time Daddy and Margo were holding hands, but still . . .

There was just one way to find out for sure. On Sunday night, when her father drove her home, she asked him. "Are you doing it with Margo?"

"Doing what?"

"You know . . . sex."

Her father took a deep breath and tightened his grip on the steering wheel. "What makes you ask?"

"I'm curious."

"Well, it's true that Margo and I are very good friends."

"But are you doing it?"

"Sometimes, yes."

Sara squeezed her eyes shut for a minute.

"Does that bother you?" her father asked.

"I guess not," Sara said, biting her nails. "I just like to know what's going on." Damn her mother! If only her mother had been nicer to Daddy then he wouldn't be doing it with Margo. He'd be back home, where he belonged. "Margo's not as pretty as Mom, is she?"

"They're very different," her father said.

"But Mom is prettier, don't you think?"

"This isn't a contest, Sara."

Even if her father wouldn't admit it, Sara knew it was true. Her mother was the prettiest woman in Boulder. Everybody said so. It would be nice to look like her mother, Sara thought. But she didn't. She looked more like her father's family, like a Broder. Sometimes she couldn't remember what her father looked like underneath his beard, so she'd take out her photos, the ones she kept hidden away, and she'd study them. In the photos Sara could see that she and her father had the same eyes. Bobby had had them too. Sleepy-looking eyes that changed from gray to green, depending on the light. And she had her father's thick hair which Jennifer called *dirty blonde,* but which her mother called *honey,* and she had her father's teeth, which was why

159

she had braces and couldn't eat raw carrots anymore. She wondered what Bobby would look like if he hadn't died. He'd be about the same age as Stuart Sampson. Maybe they'd be friends.

"Do you like Margo better than Mom?" Sara asked.

"Sara, honey . . ." Daddy said, "your mother and I are divorced and have been for a long time."

"I know that! Don't you think I know that? What I mean is do you like Margo more than you liked Mom when you first met her?"

"I can't answer that."

"Why not?"

"Because it's not fair to compare how I felt at twenty-two and how I feel at forty-two. It's very different."

"But suppose you were just meeting Mom now, for the first time. Wouldn't you think she was beautiful?"

"Yes, I suppose I would."

"I thought so," Sara said.

When her father pulled up in front of Sara's house he turned off the engine and faced her. "You're beautiful too, Sara. Your beauty comes from inside, like Margo's."

"I'd rather look like Mom than like Margo," Sara said.

Daddy took her in his arms and talked into her hair, so softly that she could hardly hear what he was saying. "Just because Margo and I are close friends . . . are lovers . . . doesn't have anything to do with the way I feel about you. You know that, don't you?"

"I guess," Sara whispered back.

"Because I love you very, very much and nothing will ever change that."

Sara let him hold her that way for a long time. She liked

being close to him. She liked the way his hair smelled from that shampoo he bought at the health food store. She liked the feel of his denim jacket, which was so old it was soft against her cheek. She liked being absolutely alone with him. She wished they were the only two people in the whole world. She wished that Margo and her mother were both dead.

It was that night, after she'd said goodbye to her father, that she'd gone inside and had made the terrible mistake. She never should have told her mother that Daddy and Margo were sleeping together. And maybe she wouldn't have if her mother hadn't started in on her right away.

"God, you stink when you come back from his place, Sara. Doesn't he ever make you take a bath or brush your teeth? And look at your hair. I'll bet you didn't brush it once all weekend, did you? Now get into the shower and scrub everywhere, or else I'll come in and do it for you!"

"I'll do it later," Sara said. "First I want to call Jennifer."

"You'll do it now!" her mother shouted, grabbing her by the arm and dragging her toward the bathroom.

"Get off my case!" Sara shouted.

"Don't you talk to me that way."

"Daddy and Margo are lovers. Did you know that?"

There, she'd surprised her mother all right. She could see the change in her face. Well, it served her mother right.

"What did you say?" her mother asked.

"I said that Daddy and Margo are lovers," Sara repeated, more quietly this time.

"Where did you ever get such an idea?"

"I asked Daddy and he told me."

"Do you know what that means, when two people are lovers?"

"Yes. It means they're fucking."

Her mother slapped her across the face, stunning her. Her mother had never hit her before, not even on her bottom when she'd been little. Sara could feel the sting long after the slap. Tears came to her eyes. But she wasn't going to cry. Instead she thought about how good it would feel to slap her mother back. But a wild look came into her mother's eyes and Mom began to make these strange sounds, like a puppy yelping. Then her mother took off, running down the hall. Sara heard a door slam shut and the yelping turned to screams. The screaming grew louder and louder until there was just one horrible, continuous sound.

Sara covered her ears with her hands and prayed, *Please God, let her stop . . .*

20

B.B. DID NOT KNOW WHAT TO DO. AND SHE FELT AFRAID. Sometimes the screaming just started in the back of her throat and came out, surprising her. She had to work harder at controlling it. Control was the key to success. If she could not control the screaming, if she ever let go completely, she would never stop, she was sure. And then she would lose everything. Everything she had worked so hard for. Everything that mattered.

She almost lost it in Jazzercise, the day after Sara told her that Andrew and Margo were lovers. That morning, after her run, while she and Sara were in the kitchen having breakfast, B.B. had said, "I hope you didn't think I was angry at you last night. It's just that I have so much on my mind. We're so busy at the office. I didn't mean to slap you. You understand, don't you, Sweetie?"

"Sure," Sara had said.

"And Sara, about Margo and your father . . ."

Sara looked up from her bowl of cereal. "What about them?"

"Well . . . I just want you to know it's nothing but a convenience."

"How do you mean, a convenience?"

"You see, a man needs a woman for sex and since he's living right next door to Margo and since he's new in town and doesn't know anyone else, it's convenient for him to be having sex with her."

"Doesn't a woman need a man for sex too?"

"Yes, of course . . . that's what I'm saying. Margo and your father are both lonely people, and somewhat neurotic, and so they . . ."

"What do you mean, neurotic?"

"Oh, nothing . . . nothing . . . just forget it."

"No," Sara said, laying down her spoon. "I want to know."

"It's hard to explain," B.B. said. "Margo and your father are two people who aren't especially steady or reliable . . . they flit around a lot, like bees . . . the first convenient flower is the one the bee sits on . . ."

"Bees don't sit," Sara said. "They cross-pollinate."

"Right. So you see what I mean."

"Are you saying they don't really like each other?" Sara asked.

"Oh, I'm sure they like each other, but it's just a diversion. It's not an important relationship or one that's going to last."

"Is it like you and Lewis?" Sara asked.

"No. Lewis and I have an important relationship."

"Are you going to get married?"

"It's much too soon to talk about marriage. We've only known each other since last summer and he's only been to Boulder twice."

"But you're lovers, right?"

"Well, yes. But we're good friends first."

"That's just what Daddy said about Margo and him."

"Really . . ."

"Daddy thinks you're very pretty," Sara said. "Did you know that?"

"Did he say so?"

"Yes. It would be nice to have him come home, wouldn't it?"

"Home? Do you mean back here with us?"

"Don't you think that would be nice?" Sara asked.

"Is that what he wants? Is that what he told you?"

Sara shrugged. "Not exactly."

B.B. felt tense, confused. After breakfast she offered to braid Sara's hair, but Sara said, "No thanks. I'm going to wear it loose today." B.B. walked Sara to the front door. "Bye, Sweetie. I love you."

"And I love you," Sara mumbled.

"For how long?"

"For always and forever." Sara did not look at B.B. as she said it.

"That's how long I'll love you too," B.B. said, hugging Sara, feeling her warmth, not wanting to let her go. Sara stood there stiffly, allowing B.B. to embrace her, but not responding.

God, B.B. thought, suppose Sara decided to go and live with Andrew? Suppose they went to court and Sara told the judge that her mother screamed all the time, that she had even slapped her face once, that she was afraid of her? Surely any judge would allow a child to live with the other parent in that case. And Andrew would be there, ready and willing to take Sara away.

B.B. watched Sara run down the front steps, jump on her bicycle, and head off to school. Then a sadness washed over her, a sadness so unbearable she had nothing to compare it to, except for the day that Bobby died.

They had reached her at the Millar house that afternoon, which she had been showing to a family from Pennsylvania, assuring them they could get it for under three hundred thousand dollars, if they didn't waste any time, and that all they would have to do was paint inside and clean up the landscaping. They had told her over the phone and she had politely excused herself, had driven to the hospital, and hadn't felt anything, hadn't reacted at all until she had asked to see Bobby's body. They had tried to dissuade her. But she had insisted and when they took her to him, when she held him in her arms for the last time, when she refused to let go so that they'd had to pry her loose, she had finally screamed and cried and cursed Andrew.

It had been his fault. She knew it. Never mind that the witnesses, the police reports, later Andrew himself, told her that the other car had crossed the dividing line, had crashed into their wagon. She knew that he had been talking over his right shoulder, the way he always did, to the boys in the back, probably telling them a joke, probably laughing, oblivious to the road. The boys in the back had been banged up, a bruise here, a cut there, nothing serious. Only one had required stitches. And Andrew had cut his head, had been in shock, had been hospitalized overnight.

But Bobby was dead.

Dead on Arrival.

Ten years old and still wearing his Little League uniform and his new cleats.

Now, at the idea of losing Sara, B.B. felt as if she were surrounded by grayness, a thick cloud, separating her from the rest of the world.

Later, when she was in her office dictating a letter to Miranda, the tears came unexpectedly and once she began to cry she could not stop. She put her head on her desk and sobbed uncontrollably. Miranda left the room quietly and returned a few minutes later with a glass of water and two small yellow pills.

"Here, B.B. . . . take these . . . you'll feel better."

"What are they?"

"Valium. I keep them in my desk for emergencies."

"No," B.B. said, waving them away. "I don't take tran-quilizers."

"I know you usually don't, but in this case . . ."

"No," B.B. said again. "I don't need them."

"All right," Miranda said, tucking them into her pocket. "Is there anything I can do?"

"No. It was just a touch of the blues. It's over now."

Miranda nodded. "You're supposed to meet a client at ten-thirty, at the Russo house. Would you like me to cancel, or ask someone else to show them around?"

"No, I'm all right. And I'll go directly to Jazzercise from there, so I'll be back here around one-fifteen."

"Shall I get you something for lunch?"

"A container of strawberry yogurt would be nice."

"Sure," Miranda said, "no trouble."

B.B. was late getting to Jazzercise because the clients, two women from Detroit, insisted on inspecting every square inch of the Russo house even though they weren't serious buyers. B.B. could tell from the moment she met them. They were just tourists, looking for a cheap way to spend the morning, trying to see the *real* Boulder. And she'd told them so. Had even called them bitches.

They'd been surprised by her outburst and threatened to report her to the Board of Realtors. But she'd just laughed, telling them to go ahead, telling them that she was the chairperson of that Board. She'd laughed so hard she'd had to run back inside the house to use the toilet. She'd laughed until tears were rolling down her cheeks, but when she looked at herself in the mirror her face looked contorted, as if she were crying. *Control . . . control* she reminded herself as she drove to Jazzercise. She had never been rude to a client before. Never. Well, she could always explain it as a bad day. It happened to the best agents. That it had never happened to her until now proved that she was more patient than most and that's why she was on top. Still, she could not stop her hands from shaking.

She came into Jazzercise in the middle of the second number. She stood in the back instead of at her usual place down front, between Margo and Clare. Jazzercise always relaxed her, relieved her tensions in a way that was different from running or yoga. The beat of the music, the burning sensations in her muscles, the stretching and toning. Yes, she felt better already. Just being here was therapeutic.

After class there was the usual scramble for the showers. Clare waved at her from across the crowded locker room, then disappeared into a shower stall. Margo's locker was next to B.B.'s. Margo was humming the tune of the final number as she pulled off her leotard and tights. Humming and smiling to herself.

B.B. watched as Margo undressed. Margo's breasts were big and round with full pink nipples. In a few years, if she wasn't careful, she'd look like a cow, B.B. thought, enjoying the idea. She'd seen Margo naked a million times, but today was different. Today B.B. saw Margo as Andrew's lover, Andrew kissed this woman's lips, Andrew caressed this woman's breasts, Andrew lay on top of her or under her or alongside her and thrust his penis into her.

"What is it?" Margo asked.

"What do you mean?" B.B. said.

"You've been staring at me for the longest time."

"I hear you're sleeping with Andrew," B.B. said. Oh, she shouldn't have said anything, shouldn't have gotten started, but she couldn't help herself. Maybe Sara had made it all up, maybe Margo would deny it.

Margo's face turned red. "How did you . . ."

"Sara told me," B.B. said.

"Sara," Margo said. "How did she . . ."

"Andrew told her."

"Andrew."

So, it was true. B.B. grabbed her towel and headed for the showers.

Margo caught up with her. "Look, I . . ."

"He's just using you," B.B. said. "Can't you see that? You're nothing to him but a convenient hole."

"I don't think we should discuss it," Margo said.

"Why not?" B.B. asked, her voice rising. "Everyone else is." She turned around. "Well . . ." she said to the women in the locker room, "aren't you all discussing it? Aren't you all talking about Margo and Andrew fucking their heads off?"

"Please," Margo said.

"You're such a fool," B.B. told her. "I never thought you'd turn out to be such a fool!"

Margo pushed ahead of B.B. and stepped into the shower. B.B. pulled aside the shower curtain and shouted into the steamy stall, "Does he still cry out when he comes? Does he call you his beautiful darling?"

Margo jerked the shower curtain out of B.B.'s hand. It had grown very quiet in the locker room, the only sounds were the water running in the showers and B.B.'s own voice. "What are you looking at?" she shouted at the silent women watching her. "Haven't you ever seen a naked body before?"

They turned away and busied themselves dressing.

"B.B.," Clare said softly. "Come on . . . let's get dressed and go have a cup of coffee."

Clare drove to the Mall. They went to the New York Deli, chose a table in the back, and B.B. sat facing the wall. "Well," she said, biting into a piece of toast, "I certainly made a scene, didn't I?"

"Yes," Clare said, "you certainly did."

"I didn't mean to, you know . . . it just happened."

"I know." Clare squeezed B.B.'s shoulder. "It's all right."

B.B. shook her head. "I can't believe the things I said."

170

"Look," Clare told her, "we all blow it sometimes. You should have seen me when Robin ran off with the Dough-nut."

"He's sleeping with Margo. Did you know that?"

Clare nodded.

"I guess everyone knows."

"I don't think so. Not until you announced it in the locker room. Anyway, what difference does it make?"

"It's the idea of them together. It's just so tacky."

"Do you still love him, is that it?"

"No, but I don't want anyone else to either, especially not Margo, especially not right under my nose." She paused. "I guess that's selfish, isn't it?"

"Margo doesn't want to hurt you," Clare said.

"Then she shouldn't be sleeping with my husband."

"He's your ex-husband."

"So he's really not cheating on me . . . is that what you're saying?"

"That's right," Clare said.

"Well, he'll be gone soon," B.B. said, swirling the tea bag around in her cup. "His lease is up at the end of November. I'll just have to hang on until then."

B.B. wrote a note to her Jazzercise instructor, apologizing for her outburst in the locker room and explaining that she was transferring to the Monday-Wednesday class for personal reasons.

She toyed with the idea of making an appointment to see Thorny Abrams. Clare thought she should. But B.B. felt she could handle the situation herself, that the worst was over. It had been the shock of hearing the news about Margo and

Andrew from Sara that had set her off. So instead of calling Thorny Abrams, B.B. called Cassidy, her masseuse, and set up an appointment for the following afternoon. During the massage, when B.B. told Cassidy she was going through a difficult time, Cassidy suggested that B.B. consult with Sensei Nokomoto, the acupuncturist. Acupuncture could do wonders for the mind as well as the body, Cassidy explained, by regulating the pulses. B.B. agreed to give it a try.

She spoke with Lewis almost every night. Talking with her was the highlight of his day, Lewis said. He had seen a beautiful ring, gold with three diamonds. Could he interest her in becoming engaged? And had she decided about Christmas in Hawaii yet?

"So many questions all at once," B.B. said, laughing, not answering any of them.

"You're my fantasy woman," he told her.

"What happens when you find out I'm real?" she asked.

"I'll love you even more."

"Promise?"

"Promise."

For a few moments each day her spirits lifted. But as soon as she hung up the phone she plunged deeper into grayness. It was so hard to go on pretending to be all that Lewis and the rest of the world expected her to be. Sometimes she wanted to tell him to forget it, to forget her, that it was just a game. But she couldn't let go that easily. It was comforting to have him there, on the back burner. It wasn't fair to go on using Lewis, she knew, but wasn't he using her too, inventing her to serve his own needs? In the long run don't we all use each other, she wondered, isn't that the way we make it through the day?

When Andrew phoned a few weeks later, asking to see her, B.B. was not entirely surprised. Although she hadn't mentioned it to anyone it was possible that Andrew was simply using Margo to make her jealous, to make her beg him to come back. This was a possibility she could not ignore since both Sara and her mother had hinted at the idea of a reconciliation.

She hoped that Margo hadn't told him about her outburst in Jazzercise and that Sara hadn't told him about her screaming fits because she'd been doing so much better lately. She had seen the acupuncturist three times and it was true that her pulses had been out of sync. She was following the diet he had prescribed and could feel the poisons leaving her body. She rarely felt out of control now, but when she did she was careful not to show it. She would lock herself into her bathroom and shred Kleenex, or she would go for a long run.

She agreed to meet Andrew on Thursday afternoon, at four, while Sara was taking her piano lesson at Mrs. Vronsky's. She hadn't seen Andrew in more than a month, since the evening he'd dropped Sara off while she had been outside walking Lucy.

She came home from the office early to shower and change her clothes. She dressed in white. He had always liked her in white. She wondered if he liked Margo in white too. God, she didn't see how he was fucking Margo. She knew there had been other women in his life. After all, it had been six years. But the others were just faceless creatures who satisfied his physical needs.

173

When he rang the bell she was in the kitchen arranging crackers in a basket. She'd already put out the cheese, a sharp Vermont Cheddar she'd picked up at Essential Ingredients on her way home, along with a bottle of Blanc de Blanc.

"Hello, Andrew," she said, opening the front door. "Come on in." She felt calm, in control.

He stepped inside and followed her into the living room. "Nice," he said, looking around.

"Would you like a quick tour?"

"I'd like to see Sara's room."

"Of course." She led him upstairs and down the hall to Sara's bedroom with its white wicker furniture, its canopied bed, its blue and white ruffles and pillows and curtains.

"Pretty," Andrew said, "and so neat."

"I expect Sara to keep her room in order and she does."

She showed him the guest room and the hall bath, but not her own room, then led him back downstairs to the sun porch and the kitchen. He kept nodding and muttering, *nice*. The pots of geraniums on the kitchen window sill flourished in the late fall sun. Her copper pots and pans, gleaming, hung on a rack from the ceiling. The spices were arranged in alphabetical order.

He followed her back to the living room and sat on the sofa. B.B. sat on the love seat, opposite him. "Wine?" she asked.

"Please."

She poured a glass for him and then one for herself. She cut a slice of Cheddar, laid it on a water biscuit, and passed it across the glass table separating them.

"Thanks."

"Didn't my mother knit that sweater for you?" she asked. It was dark green with cables.

"I think mine did," he said. "Your mother made me a blue one that's similar."

"I remember this one," she told him. "It always looked nice on you . . . made your eyes very green . . . still does."

He took a bite of the cheese and cracker, followed by a long drink of wine. He seemed uncomfortable. Probably because they were on her turf. She tucked her bare feet under her and sat back seductively. She wanted him to want her. She wanted him to compare her to Margo and see that there was no comparison. If he would take the first step, she would take the second. She would prove to him that Margo was second best.

"Well," he said, clearing his throat, "the reason I asked to see you . . ."

She tossed her hair away from her face, sipped her wine, and waited.

". . . is that the lease on the Hathaway place is up at the end of this month."

"Oh, right," she said. "It was just a three month lease, wasn't it?"

"Yes, although I'd hoped it was renewable."

"You can't always get a renewable lease around here. Hathaway probably rents to the same people every winter." She paused and sipped her wine. "So, you'll be heading back to Miami at the end of the month?"

"No, I'm going to stay here, at least until the end of the school year . . . maybe longer. And that's what I wanted to talk to you about."

He was either going to ask her to find him another place or he was going to ask if he could move in with her, B.B. thought. And she was not going to give him a definite answer now. There was too much at stake.

"I'm moving in with Margo," he said.

"What?" she asked.

"I'm moving in with Margo at the end of the month. I wanted to tell you now since that's where Sara will be staying when she's with me and I hope we can make arrangements for her to spend at least one week each month."

"No. Never." She stood up. "Why are you doing this to me?"

"It has nothing to do with you," he said.

A pounding began in her left temple. "Haven't you already hurt me enough?"

"I'm not trying to hurt you."

"I'll never let Sara stay there. Those children are horrors." Her voice sounded as if it was coming from very far away. "I don't understand why you're doing this."

"Because I want to be with Margo."

She picked up her wine glass and threw it at him. He ducked. The glass hit the piano and shattered. She reached across the table for his glass, but knocked over the bottle of wine instead. The wine dripped down onto her Navajo rug. "Look at that . . . look at what you've made me do."

"Where's a sponge?" he asked.

"Never mind a sponge. Don't you think I know what you're after? You're out to destroy me. You killed Bobby and now you're trying to take Sara so that I'll have nothing left, nothing to live for. You won't be satisfied until then, will you?"

His mouth opened as if to speak, but she couldn't hear what he was saying.

"What?" she screamed. "What did you say?"

He shouted at her. "You're making this more difficult than it has to be."

"Who sent you . . . my mother? The two of you planned it together, didn't you? She wants me out of the way because I know the truth. That's it, isn't it?"

"You're inventing things, Francine."

"Don't call me that."

He came toward her and tried to put his hand on her shoulder, but she pulled away. "You better calm down before Sara gets home," he said.

"Don't tell me what to do! You and my mother both think you can run my life, but you're wrong. You can't. So get out . . . out of my house and out of my life." She picked up a stone carving as if to throw it, but before she could, he was gone. He had turned and said something as he'd slammed the door, but she had missed it. The cloud was forming, making her head feel fuzzy.

She ran into the kitchen and turned on the cold water tap. She stuck her head under the faucet, letting the icy water wash away the grayness. When her scalp felt numb she turned off the water and shook out her hair. Then she went back into the living room. She washed the rug with club soda, swept up the broken glass, Windexed the glass tabletop, and plumped up the pillows on the sofa. She carried the cheese and crackers to the kitchen, where she dumped them into the trash can. She brushed off her hands. There. She had removed every trace of him. It was as if he had never been there, as if this afternoon had never happened.

21

FROM THANKSGIVING UNTIL CHRISTMAS MARGO WORKED late into each night stitching the commemorative quilt she had designed and appliqued for her parents' fiftieth wedding anniversary. She had constructed a series of connecting circles in primary colors. The center circle represented her mother and father, the next three, Margo and her sisters, the small circles, the five grandchildren. The idea for the quilt had come to her more than two years ago when she had been afraid that her mother would not live to see her next birthday, let alone her fiftieth wedding anniversary. In some childlike way Margo believed that by working on the quilt she could keep her mother alive. Now, she was determined to finish it before they left for the west coast and the anniversary bash that Bethany was throwing at her home in Beverly Hills.

Long after Stuart and Michelle had gone to sleep Margo

and Andrew would sit in the living room, in front of the fire-place, Andrew reading, Margo stitching, the stereo turned to KBOD. During this time Margo felt a peacefulness she had never known. She would sometimes look up at Andrew, just to be sure that he was still there, and he would smile at her or reach out and touch her hair or squeeze her hand. As it grew later and her eyes became tired she would lie in his arms as the fire died and think, this is the way it's supposed to be. Sometimes they would make love on the rug and Margo would bite Andrew's shoulder as she came, to keep from crying out. Then they would creep downstairs, climb into bed, and fall asleep, his arms wrapped around her.

For five years Margo had slept in a bed by herself. And even during her marriage to Freddy she had really slept alone, although he had been there, in his half of the bed, with a can of Mace on the bedside table, ready to protect her. But he had not slept with his arms around her, had not made her feel warm and safe and well-loved. There had been no tender kisses in the middle of the night as she'd rolled over in her sleep. No wonder she was sleeping so well these nights.

Margo hadn't told her family about Andrew until he had moved in and then only because she felt she had to since the kids might mention something. She knew, once she told them, there would be questions.

"What a surprise!" her sister Bethany said. "How long have you known each other?"

"Since August."

"Since August . . . I see."

Margo could tell that Bethany did not approve of living together after only three months.

"And what does he do?" Bethany asked.

"He's a writer," Margo said.

"One of those Boulder types?"

Bethany did not like Boulder types. Every time she came to visit she walked along the Mall and disgustedly pointed out aging hippies to Margo. *They must all come here to retire,* she once said. *Not all,* Margo assured her. *Some go to Santa Fe.*

"He's new in town," Margo said. "He's from Florida."

"Oh, Florida," Bethany said. "I wonder if he knows Harvey's older brother. They moved to Florida a few years ago. You remember Ike and Lana, don't you?"

"I think so, but it's been a long time."

"Well, you'll see them at the party. You'll see everyone at the party." She paused and Margo pictured her sitting on her bed, the phone tucked between her ear and shoulder as she picked last week's polish off her nails. "You're bringing him, aren't you?"

"He doesn't have a tux," Margo said.

"Can't he rent one?"

"He'd rather not."

"Is he one of those avant-garde types?"

"Not really."

"Well . . . if he won't feel out of place, it's okay with me."

"I thought everything's so casual out there anyway. How come the party's formal?"

"It's an affair, Margo. And even if we are living out here, I'm still a New Yorker at heart and to me affairs are always black tie."

"Oh."

"I hope you can convince Stuart to bathe in honor of his grandparents. The last time I saw him you could smell him a mile away."

"Oh, that's all changed," Margo said. "You can't get him *out* of the shower now. He's got a girlfriend."

"Really?"

"Yes."

"Well, you just never know, do you?" Bethany said, laughing. "You sound happy, Margo."

"I am."

"I'm glad. I was thinking the other day about how I warned you not to marry Freddy . . . remember?"

"Yes."

"But it wasn't so much Freddy I was talking about. It was marrying and having babies too soon. Before you were ready. I had a lot of my own problems in those days. But now, after so many years, Harvey and I have worked it out. It's not passionate, but it's nice. Is it passionate with you and Andrew . . . is the sex really good?"

"Yes," Margo said.

"I guess the second time around you make sure of that," Bethany said wistfully. "I know I would."

Within the hour, before Margo had had a chance to call her parents, her mother called her.

"Margo, darling . . . Bethany just told us the good news . . . that you have a *significant other*."

"Significant other?" Margo said.

"Yes. Isn't that what you call it out there? That's what Joell calls it. She has one too, you know. And to tell you the truth, it sounds so much better than saying she has a boyfriend. So much more grown up. Don't you think so?"

"Yes," Margo said. "I guess it does."

"So darling, tell me . . . he's a real mensh?"

"He's a very nice man. I'm sure you'll like him."

"So it's serious?"

"Well, yes. We're trying it out for six months."

"For six months?" her mother said. "What does that mean . . . for six months? I never heard of such a thing."

"Not necessarily *just* for six months," Margo said, trying to explain. "It could be for much longer. We hope it will be. We'll stay together as long as it works."

"Works?" her mother said. "What does *works* mean?"

"You know," Margo said, wishing she could get out of this conversation. "If we continue to get along and continue to care about each other . . ."

"Where's love?" her mother asked. "Don't people fall in love anymore?"

"Yes, of course," Margo said. "We're in love."

"Then it's settled. After six months you'll get married."

"We haven't discussed marriage yet."

"You should discuss it, darling."

Later, when she and Andrew were in bed, Margo said, "My mother refers to you as my *significant other.*"

Andrew laughed. "Come over here and I'll show you *how* significant your other is."

Margo moved toward him.

"Feel that . . ."

"Wow . . . that's exceptionally significant."

Margo had been living in Boulder for just three months when her father had phoned. She had known right away it was going to be bad news. She had heard it in her father's voice.

"Dad," Margo had said, "what is it . . . what's wrong?"

"It's Mother," he'd said. "She's in the hospital . . . just tests . . . she didn't want me to tell you."

"What kind of tests?"

"Well, it looks like it could be . . . she found some little lumps . . . under her arm . . . it's probably nothing . . . but just to be sure, the doctor put her in."

"I'll be there as soon as I can," Margo had said.

She had flown east the next morning, after making some hasty arrangements with Michelle's English teacher, a young woman she had met and liked who had told her that she often stayed with her students while their parents traveled.

She had taken a cab directly from LaGuardia to New York Hospital. As she'd rounded the corridor, looking for Room 412, she could hear her sisters' voices. Her father was there too, all three of them standing at her mother's bedside. Her mother had been sitting up, wearing a pink lace bed jacket. Her hair, which was usually teased around her face, was brushed back, making her eyes look bigger and her face very small and white. But she had been trying to make the best of it, of whatever was about to happen, by laughing and joking. She had always told Margo that humor was the only way to get through life.

"Margo, darling . . ." her mother said, holding out her arms. "You didn't have to fly in for this. It's just a few tests. Abe . . . why did you have to go and tell her?"

"I'm glad he did," Margo said, kissing her mother's soft

cheek. She smelled from Shalimar, her favorite perfume. "I want to be here with you."

The nurse came in then, to take her mother's blood pressure. She was a big black woman, with steel-gray hair and oversized glasses. "This is my daughter, Margo," her mother said.

"The one who's from Colorado?" the nurse asked.

"That's right." Her mother began to sing, doing her John Denver imitation. "Rocky Mountain high . . . aye aye aye aye . . . Rocky Mountain low . . . ooh ooh ooh ooh . . ."

The nurse laughed. "You're such a card, Mrs. Kaye."

"You should only know," Margo's father said.

Later, when Bethany, Joell and their father went down to the cafeteria, Margo's mother lay back against the pillows and said, "So tell me darling . . . how are you, how are the children?"

"We're all fine."

"You like it out there?"

"I think I will. It's still too soon to say for sure."

"I'll never understand why you had to move so far away."

"You know it's not that far. Did you study the map I sent? Did you see that Colorado and Arizona, where Aunt Luba lives, come together? And that Colorado's not nearly as far as California?" Her mother shared Steinberg's view of the world.

"You couldn't have just gone to New Jersey?" her mother asked.

Margo laughed. "No. I had to make a clean break, had to start a new life . . . you know that. But never mind me . . . tell me about you."

"What's to tell?" her mother asked. "If it's malignant they'll operate. I told them, *Go ahead, take it off. Abe will love me with one breast as much as with two.* And if they have to take them both off, that's all right too."

And they had. A double mastectomy. And even then they hadn't been sure they'd gotten it all. But they'd hoped that with radiation followed by chemotherapy . . .

It was Margo's father who needed the comforting. "Without Belle, I don't want to live."

"She's going to be all right," Margo said, trying to reassure him.

"But suppose she's not? Suppose they didn't get it all?"

"We can't plan ahead, Dad," Margo said. "We're just going to have to wait and see."

"She's my life," he whispered, tears in his eyes. "I love you girls, I love my grandchildren, but she's my life."

Oh, to be loved that way, Margo had thought. To be loved so completely. Would she ever know such love, such devotion? She doubted it. Maybe people just didn't love as intensely anymore. Maybe they were afraid.

"Look at this," her mother said, two days after surgery. "Flat as a pancake . . . just like a boy . . ."

And a few days after that, "This morning I had a visit from a beautiful young woman, Margo. She reminded me of you. She had a double herself, not that you'd ever know it, and she told me all about the possibilities. So what do you think . . . falsies at my age and maybe reconstructive surgery?"

"Why not?" Margo said.

"You know something, darling . . . even when they tell you it's cancer, you don't give up . . . you keep making plans. I keep telling myself I'm going to beat it. I suppose it's because I'm an optimist.''

"You are going to beat it," Margo said. "And at a time like this an optimist isn't such a bad thing to be.''

"Of all my children, Margo, you're the one who's most like me. I don't know if that's good or bad.''

"I think it's good.''

Her mother smiled. "Deep down I think so too.''

Margo had called Freddy. "I'm in New York," she'd told him. "My mother's in the hospital.''

"Nothing serious, I hope," Freddy said.

"A double mastectomy.''

"I'm sorry to hear that. I'll send flowers.''

"You don't have to send anything . . . I just thought you'd want to know.''

"I said I'll send flowers." There was a long pause. Then Freddy said, "So how are you doing out there, in the middle of nowhere?''

"I think it's going to work out very well.''

"I could go to court, Margo. I could go to court and get an injunction against you for taking the kids so far away. You're going to ruin my relationship with them. Some day they'll blame you.''

"I thought you agreed that if it was necessary for my work . . .''

"I made a mistake. I never should have agreed to let you take them.''

"I couldn't concentrate on solar design in New York, Freddy . . .''

"Don't feed me any of your crap, Margo.''

"Let's not get started," Margo said. "This is a hard time for me."

"When isn't it a hard time for you? You thrive on hard times."

"Okay. If you say so. How's Aliza?"

"Aliza's fine."

"Good."

"Who's with the children?" he had asked.

"Michelle's English teacher."

"Is she a responsible person?"

"Would I have left her with the kids if she wasn't?"

"Probably."

"Goodbye, Freddy."

"Goodbye, Margo. And I am sorry about your mother."

She had hung up the phone feeling all the old anger, all the old resentments. She had not been the wife that Freddy had expected. He still blamed her for having had her own needs and he was still able to make her feel guilty. Freddy had wanted a Stepford Wife. Margo had once told him so in the heat of a bitter argument over the menu for a dinner party. She had hurled a copy of the novel across the room, catching him on his left shoulder. "A plastic princess who doesn't think!" Margo had yelled. "That's what you want, isn't it? A plastic princess who'll give elegant little dinner parties and fuck whenever you feel like it!"

"Right," Freddy had said, rubbing his shoulder. "That's exactly what I want."

At home Stuart and Michelle were full of questions about Grandma Belle. Margo tried to be honest, but at the same time, not to worry them, assuring them that the doctors would do everything possible and telling them that Grandma Belle was in very good spirits.

"Is she tap dancing, yet?" Michelle asked.

"No, not yet. But I'm sure she will be soon."

Margo's mother had taken up tap dancing at the age of sixty-two. She took three lessons a week, inspired by Ruby Keeler's performance in a revival of *No, No, Nanette*. And she was good. She used to love to dance for the grandchildren, before Bethany moved to the west coast and Margo moved to Boulder. Margo did not tell Michelle that she was afraid Grandma Belle would never put her tap shoes on again.

Margo was not sure that she should bring Andrew to the anniversary party. Too much too soon, she feared. But when Bethany offered them the use of her condominium on the peninsula at Marina del Rey, how could she refuse? A week alone with Andrew. A week of making love with no one else around.

It had been Andrew's idea to drive to L.A. They would drop Stuart and Michelle at the airport in Denver and hit the road by themselves. It had sounded romantic at the time. No kids, no responsibilities, no phone calls from B.B., accusing Andrew of ruining her life and of filling Sara's head with his fucked-up values. Margo urged Andrew to hang up when B.B. became hysterical, but he would not. He believed it was better to let her vent her feelings. Sometimes when Margo answered the phone, B.B. would lay it on her. "He has no sense. Can't you see that? All he's after is a quick fuck and a place to live. He doesn't give a shit about you or anyone else."

* * *

The evening Andrew had returned from B.B.'s house in mid-November, after telling her that he was moving in with Margo, Margo had asked, "How did it go? How did she take it?"

And Andrew had answered. "I don't know. She seemed hyper at first, almost flirtatious, and then she became hysterical."

"She'll get used to the idea. Don't worry."

"You're such an optimist," he said. "You always think everything will work out."

"It will."

"That's not realistic, Margo. Some things don't work out. Some things get screwed up and stay screwed up."

"I know," she said. "I've had my share of disappointments."

"I'm not talking about disappointments." He lay down on the bed, covering his eyes with his hand. "I don't know if this is going to work."

"What?"

"Me, living here. I might be making it harder on Sara instead of easier. Maybe I should leave, go back to Miami."

"I thought we made a deal," Margo said, her throat tightening.

"You'd come with me."

"I can't come with you . . . not now . . . you know that. I have responsibilities here."

"Fuck responsibilities."

"I can't and neither can you. What would Sara think if you walked out on her?" *Don't do this. Don't leave now when it's just beginning. I don't know if I'll ever allow my-*

self to try again if you do. But she could not say her thoughts out loud.

"Maybe I shouldn't have come here in the first place."

"Maybe not, but you did . . . and I'd like to think . . ." Her voice trailed off. *I would like to think you love me,* she thought, turning away.

He got off the bed and put his arms around her. "I'm sorry," he said. "It's not you. I'm glad I found you. You know that."

"It'll be okay," she said into his shoulder. "There's a lot to get used to, that's all."

Margo found herself avoiding B.B. She stayed away from The James at lunch, meeting Andrew at the library instead or eating alone at her desk. She no longer browsed in the Boulder Bookstore at noon or met friends at the Boulderado for a drink after work. Anyway, she was too busy for friends. But surely after the holidays, after the mad rush to get everything in order, both at work and at home, so that she and Andrew could enjoy their trip, she would have more time. Unless what Clare had said about having a steady man was true. That it was hard to keep that kind of intimacy going with more than one person at a time. And in the past two months Andrew had become everything—friend, lover, confidant.

Margo had been disappointed to hear that B.B. had put the land for the cluster housing project back on the market. Clare had told her.

"She feels that she can't work with you," Clare had said. "Not anymore. And she doesn't want to start in with another architect."

"But to put the land back on the market . . ."

"This is very hard on her," Clare said. "It's not just knowing that Andrew has moved in with you . . . it's the way you flaunt your happiness."

"I don't mean to flaunt it," Margo said.

"I know that, but it's there. You shine . . . you sparkle . . ."

"I try to think of her feelings . . . to put myself in her place . . . really. But she's making it so hard. She's so hateful, so off the wall. Does she want him back, is that it?"

"I think it's more that she doesn't want anyone else to have him. Look, Margo . . . you're both my friends. I can't take sides. I can't choose between you."

"I don't want you to," Margo said.

Margo kept reminding herself that B.B. had lost a child. She almost said something to Clare one day, but caught herself in time. If B.B. wanted Clare to know she would tell her herself. She tried to imagine how she would feel if she had lost a child, but the idea was so horrible she could not. Once, when Stuart was small, he had been very sick, running a fever of 105, and the doctors could not find out what was wrong with him. He lay in his bed for days while they awaited test results and Margo had slept on the floor next to him, rubbing his small body with alcohol every hour. She had known she might lose him and had felt utterly helpless. Well, B.B. had lost a healthy ten-year-old son. Margo tried to remember that, tried to sympathize, not allowing herself to hate.

But when they ran into B.B. and Lewis at the airport at the start of the holidays and B.B., cool as could be, introduced Andrew to Lewis, ignoring Margo and her children, Margo was pissed. And she was still feeling hostile when she and Andrew got back into the car to begin their drive to L.A.

If only B.B. hadn't been at the airport, Margo thought, there wouldn't be this tension in the car now. Andrew tried, singing along with country-western music on the car radio, but it was forced gaiety and they both knew it. After "Mamas, Don't Let Your Babies Grow Up to Be Cowboys," Andrew said, "Back in Hackensack, New Jersey, when I was about nine, I wanted to be a cowboy more than anything."

"Did you ride a horse?" Margo asked.

"Nope . . . a bicycle."

"It's hard to be a cowboy without a horse," Margo said, forcing a laugh, "although you certainly drive like one."

Andrew turned pale and slowed down. "I didn't mean to go over sixty."

"I didn't . . ." Margo began, "that is, I wasn't . . . oh, shit . . . I'm sorry . . ."

"It's okay," Andrew said.

But it wasn't okay. None of it was okay. She had reminded him of Bobby and the way he'd died. Bobby's death was always there, always with Andrew, and she was going to have to learn to accept it, along with his occasional bouts of melancholy. At first she had assumed his moodiness had to do with something she'd done or said, but now she knew that wasn't the case. Any reminder of Bobby brought on a sadness, a withdrawal. She had tried to talk to him about it, but he hadn't responded. The few times she had pressed he had become even more withdrawn. She remembered the night he had told her about Bobby. *I don't feel sorry for myself anymore and I don't want anyone else feeling sorry for me either.* Okay, she would not feel sorry for him.

During the rest of the trip to L.A. they were quiet, taking turns driving and dozing, twenty-four hours, straight through. Not exactly the romantic interlude they had planned.

22

At first Michelle had not wanted to go to the anniversary party. She'd wanted to fly straight to New York instead of spending five days in Beverly Hills at Aunt Bethany's house. If it hadn't been for hurting Grandma's and Grandpa's feelings that's exactly what she would have done. She always got headaches when she was around Aunt Bethany. Aunt Bethany never shut up. Michelle tried to follow her endless stories, but the harder she tried the more her head hurt. Little Lauren, who was Aunt Bethany's *mistake*, said that her mother was lonely living in Beverly Hills and that's why she talked so much. Maybe Little Lauren was right.

Margo and Andrew dropped Michelle and Stuart at the airport in Denver. It had been Andrew's idea to drive to L.A. and, of course, Margo did whatever Andrew wanted. Well, that was their business. As long as she and Stuart didn't have to spend twenty-four hours in the back seat of Margo's Subaru listening to the lovebirds, who cared? Every time he called Margo *Margarita,* Michelle gagged.

God, it was so strange bumping into B.B. at the airport. Michelle thought that B.B. was going to pass out when she saw them. She hung onto this guy, Lewis something or other, as if he were her lifeline. He was older, but not bad. He had a nice smile. B.B. looked really sophisticated. She had her hair pulled back, showing off gold earrings, and she was carrying one of those expensive bags you see in *New Yorker* ads.

Michelle could not understand what Andrew saw in her mother after having been married to someone like B.B. Although, Michelle had to admit, B.B. was not the friendliest person around. When she introduced Lewis she said, "Lewis, this is Andrew, my former husband." And that was it. She acted as if the rest of them didn't exist.

But Margo offered her hand, saying, "I'm Margo Sampson and these are my children, Stuart and Michelle." Michelle was really proud of her mother then. If only Margo hadn't been wearing her faded jeans and that baggy sweater.

There was this awkward moment when no one said anything, and then everyone spoke at once. Finally they parted and walked off in opposite directions.

"God," she said to Stuart when they were on the plane, "I'll bet that really shook up Andrew."

"What?"

"Meeting his ex-wife and her new boyfriend."

"He's tough," Stuart said, yawning.

"Don't you wish we were going to Hawaii instead of Aunt Bethany's? Hawaii sounds so exotic." When she looked over at Stuart for some reaction she saw that he had fallen asleep. She didn't see how anyone could sleep on a plane, but Stuart was out cold and they had barely taken off.

She clutched her canvas purse. Gemini had loaned her gobs of jewelry to wear to the anniversary party and she was worried that if she lost it she would never be able to repay her. Michelle was going to do herself up for the party. Maybe she would meet someone exciting there. Not a poet or a true intellectual, because Aunt Bethany wouldn't know anyone like that, but possibly a movie star. Since Uncle Harvey was some big deal at one of the studios she was sure there would be some movie star types at the party. Not that she was interested in movie stars, because they wouldn't know the way of the world, but just for the night it might be interesting.

She took out her copy of *The Book of Daniel* and began to read. She wished her parents had done something dramatic with their lives, like Daniel's had.

23

GOING TO FLORIDA FOR TWO WEEKS WAS SUPPOSED TO BE A privilege. That's what Sara's mother told her. Sara didn't think it was such a privilege. Her mother had gone to Hawaii for the holidays to a place called Maui. Now that sounded like a privilege. Her mother should have invited her to go too. Not that she'd have gone, but she should have been invited. And her father! She'd spent every Christmas vacation with him since the divorce. But this year he was in Los Angeles with Margo. And he hadn't invited her either. It was just like Jennifer said. You couldn't trust parents. They were only interested in you when they didn't have anyone else. As soon as they had lovers, forget it.

"They'd probably get rid of us completely, if they could," Jennifer had said.

"What do you mean, completely?" Sara asked. "Do you mean they wish we were dead?"

Jennifer laughed her head off. "No, stupid. They'd never go that far. Then they'd feel guilty for the rest of their lives. They're really subtle about it. What they do is, they send us away to school, except they act like it's for our own good instead of theirs. They say stuff like, *Wouldn't you like to go away to school next year . . . someplace where you could get a really fine education. You'd get to meet lots of interesting new people . . . people from all over the world . . .*

"And you say *No.*

"So they say, *But think of it in terms of expanding your horizons . . .*

"And you still say *No.*

"So then they say, *Well, we think you should give it a try, at least for one year . . .*

"And you say, *I won't go and you can't make me.*

"And they say, *It's already settled. We've paid the tuition and you leave on August fifteenth.*"

"Nobody is trying to send me away to school," Sara said.

"Yet," Jennifer said. "They wait until you're going into ninth grade or even tenth. That's how they did it with my sisters. And I know they're going to do it with me too. I'll bet you anything I'm going to be sent to the same school my mother went to when she was a girl."

"Where is it?" Sara asked.

"In Virginia. I'll be able to have my own horse."

"That doesn't sound so bad."

"The horse is the only good part of it."

So Sara went to Florida and spent the first week of her vacation with Grandma and Grandpa Broder. They wanted to hear all about Daddy and Margo.

"What does Margo look like?" Grandma Broder asked.

"She's all right. Not as pretty as Mom."

"A nice figure?" Grandpa Broder asked.

"Okay," Sara said. "Not as skinny as Mom."

"You like her . . . she's nice to you?"

"She's okay."

"You didn't bring a picture of her?" Grandma asked.

"No." Why should she have brought a picture of Margo? Who cared what Margo looked like anyway? It was just a passing fancy. That's what her mother told her. Sara really liked that expression—a passing fancy. It was just a convenient place for Daddy to live while he wrote his book. So why were her grandparents making such a big thing out of it? Unless they knew something she didn't. Oh, she hated grownups and all their secrets!

It was the same at Grandma Goldy's and Uncle Morris's the next week. They wanted to hear all about her Thanksgiving trip to Minneapolis. She didn't tell them anything except that Minneapolis had been so cold her lips had been blue the whole time. And she told them that Lewis was seventeen years older than her mother. But they already knew.

Sara did not want to spend her vacation answering questions about her parents. She wanted to swim and play with the other kids who were down visiting their grandparents. If they were going to talk at all then Sara wanted to talk about *her* life. And she wanted them to tell her what a wonderful kid she was and how they hoped her parents appreciated her and that if ever her parents weren't paying enough attention to her she could fly right back to Florida.

"You're getting little bosoms," Grandma Goldy said,

the first time Sara put on her one-piece Speedo. "Pretty soon you'll have all the boys after you, just like your mother."

Sara wanted to shout that she was nothing like her mother. And that the boys weren't even interested in her. They all liked Ellen Anders, who was always in trouble in school and who took Quaaludes every weekend.

24

B.B. FELT WONDERFULLY REMOVED IN MAUI, WITH JUST THE sun and the sea and Lewis, adoring her, making her feel young and beautiful, making her feel that her whole life was ahead of her. She remembered Andrew once saying, *Fuck responsibilities!* Well, maybe that's exactly what she would do.

She'd been proud of herself at the airport. She had really been in control. The night before she had phoned Andrew, had shouted at him.

"What do you want?" he'd asked.

She'd thought about saying, *I want you back,* but that was too demeaning and she wasn't even sure it was true, so she'd said, "I want you out of my life. I want you off my turf. Sara is mine."

"She's ours," he'd answered.

"No, not here. Here she belongs to me." Then she had slammed down the receiver.

She phoned their house at odd hours, when she thought they might be talking about her or making love. She hated the idea of them in bed together, snuggled close, Margo's head on his chest. She hated the idea of him telling Margo stories about their marriage, sharing the most intimate details of their lives. Sometimes she would phone in the middle of the night, then hang up. She didn't want to phone. She didn't want to show them that she cared, that knowing they were together hurt, but she couldn't stop herself. If only he would go away. If Margo loved him so much let her go with him. Love . . . the idea of it made her laugh.

She and Lewis made love every afternoon. Sometimes she would keep her eyes open and stare at the lovely designs on the ceiling of their villa. Sometimes she would become confused and think that Lewis was her father. There was something about his hands, something so familiar. She came close to calling him Daddy several times, but caught herself in time. Lewis was older than her father had been when he had died. She couldn't remember exactly how old her father had been then. She could remember only that her mother had told her he had died in some girl's bed. Some girl with red hair. Poor and Irish. But maybe her mother had made that up because her mother had been having an affair with Uncle Morris, hadn't she? She remembered her father accusing her mother of doing it with her own sister's husband. But none of it mattered. Because Daddy had loved *her* best. She had been his darling, his Francie. And now Lewis loved her the same way.

One afternoon, after making love, B.B. said, "I never tell

anybody anything . . . you know that? I'm a very secretive person."

"You're the most together person I've ever known," Lewis said.

"You think so?" B.B. asked.

"I know so," Lewis said.

"I have a cloud that sometimes forms around my head, making everything fuzzy."

"You should see an ophthalmologist when you get back. Sounds like you need glasses." He kissed her fingers then, one by one.

B.B. laughed, could not stop laughing. She laughed until her body ached. Lewis didn't know. Lewis had no idea. And she was not going to spoil it by telling him about herself, by taking the chance that if he knew what she was really like he would stop loving her.

"I may never leave here," she said one day, as she oiled her legs.

"B.B., darling, if that's what you want I can make arrangements. Let's look for a place, a glass house on the ocean. What do you say?"

"Oh, Lewis, would you honestly do anything to please me?"

"Yes," he said seriously, sitting on the edge of her lounge chair. "Yes, I would."

"There's so much about me you don't know."

"If you want me to know, you'll tell me. Otherwise, it doesn't matter."

She had not yet told him about Bobby.

She wondered if she could spend the rest of her life pretending. Pretending to be happy. Pretending to be the most together person he had ever known. It was so hard to pretend. It took up almost all of her energy. Sometimes she felt so tired from pretending that she just wanted to let go, to slip away quietly, to let the warm ocean water cover her and carry her away.

"Marry me," Lewis said. "Marry me right now."

25

ANDREW SAT ON THE DECK OF BETHANY'S CONDOMINIUM peering through a pair of binoculars that he had found in the kitchen cupboard. Margo assumed he was watching the parade of long, graceful sailboats leaving the marina. She lay back on a chaise, letting the sun warm her. No more serious sunbathing for her, though. She had more than enough lines around her eyes and mouth from years of careless sunning, when the most important goal of the summer was to have a good tan. She tried to warn Michelle to use a sun block routinely, especially in Colorado, where the high altitude made you even more vulnerable, but Michelle wouldn't listen. Michelle didn't believe she'd ever be forty.

"Have a look," Andrew said, passing Margo the binoculars. "It's tits and ass from here to Venice Beach."

Margo held the binoculars to her eyes. God, he was right. The beach was filling up with bodies—long, lean, gorgeous bodies—tanned, oiled, and wearing the skimpiest bikinis she had ever seen. She handed the binoculars back to Andrew without commenting.

"Put on your suit, Margarita," he said, "and let's hit the beach."

She went upstairs to the bedroom and got into her bathing suit, a black strapless one-piece with a diagonal pink stripe. As she appraised herself in the full-length mirror waves of insecurity washed over her. How could she possibly compete with all those leggy young things on the beach, their long hair flying in the breeze? Andrew was such an attractive man and his slim athletic body was very appealing. He would attract all those young girls on the beach, all those girls who wanted older men, so they could pretend they were fucking their daddies.

It's not how you look, dummy, she said to her reflection. *It's what's inside that counts.*

Bullshit. It's how you look, nothing more, nothing less.

But looks don't last.

Exactly. And you're a good example of that, aren't you? Look at the flab on the inside of your thighs.

Come on, I'm not flabby. For forty I'm in great shape.

Oh, sure. But if you really worked at it, if you ran, say, four or five miles a day, if you followed a strict macrobiotic diet, if you plunged your face into a basin of ice water three times a day like Paul Newman . . .

It's best not to think about aging. It's best to just accept it. Besides, it's not as if he's never seen my body . . .

But he's never seen it in a bathing suit, never compared it to a beachful of gorgeous California girls.

"Margo," Andrew called. "What are you doing?"

"Coming . . ."

Look, Margo said, trying to convince herself, *European women wear the tiniest bikinis no matter how old they are, no matter what their bodies look like, and they exude a kind of sexiness that women here aren't expected to have after a certain age. It's all in how you see yourself, in how you move.*

"Margarita . . ." Andrew called again.

"Here I am," she said, running down the stairs. She had pulled a t-shirt on over her bathing suit. She was furious at herself for feeling insecure.

They walked along the ocean's edge, holding hands. When they got down to the Venice Pier, they sat on the beach, watching a family with three children. The young mother, pregnant again, the father, building sand castles with the smallest. Suddenly it occurred to Margo that she and Andrew had never discussed the possibility of having children together.

"Have you ever thought about having more kids?" Margo asked tentatively. She picked up a handful of sand and let it trickle through her fingers.

"I used to think I'd marry again and have more kids, but not anymore. You can't replace a child you've lost. And anyway, I don't want to go through it all over again. I'm glad your kids are older. That makes it easier." He paused. "You don't want more, do you?"

"No." She leaned over and kissed him. "It would have been nice to have a baby with you though."

"How do you know?"

"I just do." Margo choked up and turned away.

"What is it?" Andrew asked.

"I don't know," she managed to say. "Just the idea that we always have our kids with the wrong person."

"Not always."

"A lot of the time."

"It works out okay in the long run."

"Now you sound like me," Margo said. She bit on her lip to keep from crying.

"Too many people have the mistaken idea that when they love someone they'll make a baby that will be just like that person . . . and it's not true."

Margo looked away.

"Do you want another baby, Margo . . . is that it?"

She shook her head. "No, I don't want to start all over again either, especially now, especially knowing what I know about raising kids. I'm just being sentimental, that's all, wishing we had met in college, married young, had our kids together."

"We still would have had a lot to get through, and who's to say we would have come through it together?"

"I suppose you're right," Margo said. "But look at my parents . . . fifty years and they still love each other. Not just a comfortable kind of love, but *in* love. I just wish we had met sooner so we could have had a chance at that."

"You want fifty years together?" he asked.

She nodded.

"You've got them."

Margo felt nervous and upset dressing for the anniversary party. She popped two Rolaids into her mouth, hoping they would ease her queasiness.

"What's wrong?" Andrew asked. He had already finished dressing and was relaxing on the bed, watching her. He liked to watch her get dressed, he said. He liked the way she used her lipstick, then blotted almost all of it off, sliding a layer of clear gloss over it, making her mouth slick and inviting.

Margo crossed the room and sat beside Andrew. She touched his cheek, then his hair. "Look," she said, "this might be too much for you. It's not just a question of meeting my parents and my sisters. It's everyone all at once . . . aunts, uncles, cousins, old family friends . . . people I haven't seen in years, people I haven't seen since my own wedding. Are you sure you want to expose yourself to that?"

"It's probably easier to do it all at once," he said.

"You're brave," she told him. "I'm not sure I wouldn't opt to stay here and read a book."

"What's the worst that can happen?" Andrew asked.

She stood up, smoothed out her long skirt, and looked out the bedroom window. The sun was beginning to set over the ocean, turning the sky pink and the water golden. "They can ask you when we're getting married," she said, turning to face him.

"I'll tell them we haven't picked the date," he said easily. He got off the bed, came over to her, put his arms around her, and kissed her ear. "Would you?" he asked. "Would you get married again?"

"Maybe," she said. "Would you?"

"Maybe . . . if the right person came along."

"I'll remember that," she said. And then he kissed her mouth and she kissed him back and they both looked at the bed, rumpled and inviting, but knew that there was not time now. That they would have to wait.

26

AT THE ANNIVERSARY PARTY MICHELLE SAT AT A LITTLE
table by the side of the pool, watching Grandma and
Grandpa dance. Grandma was wearing white chiffon and
she looked like she was floating. You'd never know she'd
had cancer, Michelle thought, sipping some kind of fruit
punch with rum. You'd never know that she'd had both
her breasts removed. God, what an idea. Michelle was
still waiting for hers to grow. She was almost seventeen
and her breasts were still the same size as when she was
thirteen.

There weren't any movie stars at the party. Just a lot of
family and friends who had flown in from all over the place
and who did a *My, haven't you grown since the last time I
saw you* number on Michelle and Stuart and the cousins.

Margo and Andrew were slow dancing, their bodies
pressed very close. Every now and then Andrew kissed

Margo near her ear and she looked up at him and smiled. Michelle finished the rum punch.

Aunt Joell, who had just turned thirty, was dancing with her boyfriend, Stan, who was divorced and had three kids. Aunt Joell ran this big travel agency in New York and said she was never going to have kids because they ruined your life. Imagine talking that way about having kids! How would she know? Did Michelle and Stuart look like they were ruining Margo's life? Not at all. On the contrary, Margo was very glad she had them. Otherwise she would be lonely and depressed. It was going to be very hard on Margo when both she and Stuart went off to college. Michelle wanted to have a child some day. But she wasn't sure she'd get married, unless there was some guarantee that her marriage would turn out like Grandma Belle's and Grandpa Abe's. That would be different.

The music stopped, then started again. Andrew walked across the dance floor and stopped at Michelle's table.

"How's it going . . . are you having a good time?"

"Yeah . . . sure."

"Want to dance?"

"Me?"

"Yes."

"I don't know how to do these dances."

"I saw you dancing with your grandfather. You looked like you were doing fine."

"That was different."

"Come on, Michelle, live a little."

"Well . . ."

He took her hands and practically pulled her to her feet, then out to the dance floor, which was a patio covered by a striped tent. He didn't try to hold her close or anything, but he looked directly into her eyes and smiled. "You look very pretty tonight," he said.

"I do?"

"Yes."

"Well, I tried, for Grandma and Grandpa. Gemini let me borrow all this jewelry." Michelle did think she looked kind of exotic. She had outlined her eyes with a silver green pencil and she was wearing a gauzy blouse with a Navajo sash tied around her waist.

"You look exotic," Andrew said. "You have good cheekbones, like your mother."

Michelle felt funny dancing with her mother's boyfriend. She had read an article about stepfathers putting the make on young girls at home. So as soon as the music stopped she ran for the house.

"Wait a minute . . ." Andrew called, coming after her.

She stopped outside the French doors.

"Look, Michelle . . . there's something I want to say to you . . ." he began.

She hoped he was not going to embarrass her. She fiddled with her Navajo sash, pretending that it was not tied properly.

"Michelle . . ." he said, "I know you weren't happy when I moved in . . . and I don't blame you . . . but I hope in time you'll accept me . . ."

He paused, as if he expected her to say something, but she didn't.

"I'm not going to try to be your father," he continued. "You already have a father. I know that. I guess what I'm trying to say is that I'd like to be friends."

212

"I've got to go in now," she said and she opened the French doors and stepped inside.

Later, Grandma put on the gold tap shoes that Grandpa had given to her for their golden wedding anniversary and she did a number to "You Are My Lucky Star," with double pullbacks and everything. Then they opened their gifts. The best one was the quilt that Margo had made. Grandma cried when she read the card, especially the part about the quilt being called *Circles of Love.* So did Margo. Even Andrew had tears in his eyes. And Michelle felt this gigantic lump in her throat and wanted everyone to love each other as much as they did then . . . forever.

27

It was the end of January and freezing. Sara wore her fisherman's sweater over her yellow turtleneck and sat close to the fire in the living room. She had a Spanish test coming up. Her mother was quizzing her, asking her all the words that began with the letter *N*. Last week they'd had *M* words and the week before that *L* words. So far Sara had an average of 100 on her quizzes. She wasn't sure if her good grades were the reason her mother had finally let her sleep over at Margo's house or not.

Her mother hadn't even told her she was going until last Thursday night, while they'd been sitting at the table, finishing their Jell-O. Sara liked to let the Jell-O melt on her tongue. When her mother told her about going to Margo's overnight she had been so surprised some of it had drooled out of her mouth and had landed on her white sweater. "How come?" Sara had asked. "How come you're letting

me stay there? I thought you said you'd go to court first."
Sara knew she shouldn't ask her mother questions, that she
should just accept it, but she couldn't help herself.

"If you don't want to go you don't have to," her mother
said.

"It's not that."

"Then what?"

"The way you keep changing your mind," Sara said. "I
never know what's going on."

"Lewis convinced me that since your father didn't have
you for Christmas he should have you one weekend a
month."

"One weekend a month!" Sara said. "That's nothing."

"Why aren't you ever satisfied?" her mother shouted.
"Don't you know what it means to me to let you stay there
overnight? Have you any idea? Do you ever think of my
feelings . . . because I have feelings too."

"Yes, Mom. I do try to think of your feelings."

Her mother stood up and paced the kitchen. Back and
forth, back and forth, making a fist with one of her hands
and smacking it into the other.

Sara started to feel all tangled up inside. She pushed her
dish of Jell-O away and fooled with the crumbs from her
Carr's biscuit.

Her mother whirled around, pointing a finger at her.
"Ever since you've come back from Florida you've been
acting like a selfish little bitch. What happened . . . didn't
you have a good time there?"

"It was all right," Sara said. "I told you when I came
back it was all right. There were just other things that I

would rather have done over vacation.'' Like go to Hawaii, Sara thought. But she didn't say it.

"Your grandparents would have been very disappointed.''

"All right!'' Sara shouted. "So I went, didn't I? I stayed with them, didn't I?''

"Go to your room, Sara. And don't come out until you can control yourself.''

"No! I don't feel like going to my room.''

"Goddamn it, Sara! Do as I say.''

"You're the bitch,'' Sara muttered, not caring if her mother heard her or not. "Come on, Lucy . . .'' she said. Lucy followed her to her room. Sara slammed her bedroom door and flopped on her bed. "I hate her, I hate her, I hate her,'' she cried into Lucy's soft fur.

She knew she shouldn't argue with her mother. It only made things worse. But sometimes she got so sick of Mom she just felt like letting her have it. Mom was crying and carrying on in the living room, yelling about how she was a good person, how she had always been a good person, had always tried her best, and this is what she got for it. And why had God punished her . . . her of all people . . . why . . . ?

Sara did not want to hear anymore so she turned on her clock radio. It was small and white. Her father had given it to her for Christmas. Let her mother act like a nut, she thought. Who cares?

Suddenly Sara heard her mother running down the hall, but before she could figure out what was happening her mother threw open Sara's bedroom door, grabbed her clock radio, and hurled it across the room.

"Didn't I tell you to turn it down?'' Mom yelled.

"What's the matter with you, Sara . . . are you deaf? I told you at least four times."

"I didn't hear you," Sara said, jumping off her bed.

"Of course you didn't! How could you possibly hear me with that thing blasting? Blasting and making my head feel as if it's splitting in two?"

Sara ran across the room and picked up her clock radio. Its case had cracked. "You broke it!" she cried. "You broke my new clock radio. I hate you! You shouldn't be a mother!"

Her mother turned and left the room and in a minute Sara heard the front door slam, then the car start, and the tires screech. She ran to the living room window in time to see her mother's car racing down the street.

She felt dizzy then and sat on the piano bench, lowering her head between her legs. That's what you were supposed to do when you felt dizzy, to keep from fainting. Grandma Broder was always doing it. Her mother shouldn't be driving, she thought. You weren't supposed to drive when you were upset. You were much more likely to have an accident.

Sara waited half an hour. She pictured her mother's car smashing into a tree. Mom's head would have gone through the windshield of the car and would be covered with blood. Her eyes would be open, staring straight ahead, which meant that she was dead. Sara started to shiver. She went to the phone in the kitchen and dialed Clare's number, which was posted there for emergencies.

Clare answered.

"Hello . . . this is Sara. My mother's not home and I wondered if maybe she's at your house, or else, if you know where she is."

"I haven't seen her," Clare said. "Didn't she tell you where she was going?"

"No . . . see, we had a little disagreement and then she left and . . ."

"How long has she been gone?" Clare asked.

"About half an hour."

"Are you all right, Sara? Should I come over?"

"That's okay," Sara said. "You don't have to."

"I think I will," Clare said. "I'll be right there."

"Well, if you really want to."

On Friday afternoon her father had picked her up after school and brought her over to Margo's house. Sara had found out from Clare that Mom was meeting Lewis in Colorado Springs for the weekend. So that was why she had decided to let Sara go to stay with her father. Why hadn't Mom just told her the truth? Sara wondered if Lewis knew about her mother, about how she sometimes acted crazy.

Sara felt funny going to Margo's house, even though her father lived there now. Stuart and Michelle were out of town for the weekend, at a ski race, and Sara was glad. She knew Michelle didn't like her, would never like her, and that there was nothing she could do about it. Well, she didn't like Michelle either, so they were even. She didn't want to sleep in Michelle's room, but she had no choice.

Margo said, "This will be your room for the weekend. If you need anything just ask . . . okay?"

Sara would rather have stayed in Stuart's room. Stuart reminded her of Bobby, of what it might be like if she still had an older brother. She wished she had brought Lucy with her. Lucy would have helped her feel more at home, but Mom had said absolutely not and she'd hired a dog sitter for the weekend.

Michelle's room was filled with plants and posters. Sara was not allowed to tape posters to her wall. Her mother thought posters were tacky. Michelle's bed was covered with a brightly striped quilt. Sara lay down on it. The mattress was very hard. She looked up at the ceiling and counted the beams. There were seven of them. After a few minutes she got off the bed and opened her knapsack. There was no point in unpacking since she was just staying two nights, although Margo said she'd emptied a dresser drawer for her. Sara pulled a book out of her knapsack and lay down on the bed again. She tried to read, but she couldn't concentrate. She put the book down and crossed the room to Michelle's dresser. She opened one drawer at a time, poking around. Everything in Michelle's drawers was folded and stacked. Sara was surprised. She'd figured Michelle would be a slob. Only her socks were tossed into one drawer and weren't in pairs.

Sara found Michelle's diary under a pile of sweaters. She wanted to read it, but she was too scared. Probably Michelle was the kind who kept strands of hair in her diary so that she'd know if anyone ever tried to open it. Sara could not take that kind of chance. She put it back exactly where she'd found it. Then she tried on a couple of Michelle's sweaters. There was one she especially liked, a fuzzy blue one with a V neck.

She went through the bathroom cabinet too. You could find out a lot about a person by doing that. She'd done the same thing at her grandparents' apartments. But they'd had zillions of bottles of pills and Michelle had only one. *Mi-*

chelle Sampson: one tablet twice a day for stomach cramps.
So, Michelle got stomach cramps too, Sara thought. Now
that was interesting. Sara pictured Michelle sitting on the
toilet, doubled over, with tears in her eyes from the pain,
feeling as if her insides were about to come out.

Sara put the pills back into the cabinet and continued to
look around. Michelle used Secret deodorant, washed her
hair with Sassoon Salon Formula shampoo, and had a box of
Tampax Regular. Sara hadn't started her period yet, but
when she did she was going to use Tampax brand tampons
too.

Sara had a weird feeling the whole time she was at Margo's house. She knew that Margo was trying to be nice, trying to make her feel welcome, but still, there was something
about being there that made her uneasy. Maybe it was knowing that her father slept in Margo's room. In Margo's bed.
Knowing that they did it. That they fucked. She didn't like
to think about them doing that, but sometimes she couldn't
help herself and then she'd get this funny feeling down
there, between her legs, like an itch, and she'd have to rub
and rub until the itch went away.

On Saturday afternoon she and Daddy took a drive to the
National Center for Atmospheric Research. Everyone who
came to Boulder wanted to see it. It was on Table Mesa and
the view was spectacular—that's how the guidebooks put it.
But Sara wasn't as interested in the view as she was in the
deer who browsed beside the road.

On the way back to town Daddy said, "Is everything all
right at home, Sara?"

"What do you mean?" Sara asked.

"Are you getting along okay . . . no problems?"

"What kind of problems?" Sara asked.

"I don't know . . . any kind."

Sara knew that her father expected an answer. But she could not tell him the truth. She could not tell him about her clock radio, although she wanted to ask him if he thought the store would give her a new one. She could not tell him without going into the details of how and why it had cracked. And so she said, "Everything's okay."

"You're sure?" he asked.

She nodded.

When she got home on Sunday night she was glad she hadn't said anything, because there, on her bedside table, was a brand new clock radio, exactly the same, but without a cracked case. It was tied up with a red ribbon and there was a note propped in front of it.

Dear Sara,
I'm so sorry I broke your clock radio. You know it's not like me to lose my temper that way. It's just that I had a terrible headache. I hope you will forgive me. I love you, always and forever.

Mom

Sara didn't know what to say. Her mother was standing in the doorway. "Sweetie . . . will you forgive me?"

"Yes," Sara said. "But I wish you would just talk it out when you feel that way, instead of screaming and running off in the car and scaring me. You were gone for almost two hours."

"I didn't mean to scare you. It's just that sometimes I

need to be by myself, to let it all out. You can understand that, can't you?''

"Yes," Sara said quietly. But she really meant, *No. No, I can't take any more of this.* She pictured her mother's cleaver, the one she was never supposed to touch, and the way it could split a chicken breast in half just like that—thwack—with one solid movement. That's what her parents were doing to her.

28

MICHELLE RETURNED HOME FROM THE FIRST SKI RACE OF the season with two blue toes. She had been skiing for years, but she had never raced. Stuart convinced her to go out for the team this year, but she had known from the moment it began to snow that she was going to regret it.

She'd been sitting up front in the school van, a wad of Doublemint in her mouth, praying she would not get car sick. The coach was driving and Michelle was sure that he could not see more than six inches in front of him.

She heard Stuart's voice from the back of the van. She heard Puffin giggling. The van skidded. If they crashed and Stuart got out before the gas tank exploded, engulfing the rest of them in flames, which one would he try to save, Puffin or her? Probably Puffin. He loved her. He had shouted about his love for her over the holidays. He had shouted it across Freddy and Aliza's pale gray living room. "Goddamn it, Dad, I love Puffin!" He had shouted it in the midst of a monumental blowup because Freddy would not let Puffin, who was flying to New York, stay at his apartment over New Year's weekend.

"You'll have a million more girlfriends before you finally settle down," Freddy had told Stuart.

"You don't understand, do you?" Stuart had yelled. "You don't understand that Puffin and I have a serious relationship and I will not . . . repeat, will not . . . have you acting as if it's some kind of puppy love."

"I don't know what's gotten into you, Stu," Freddy had said, "but I don't like it."

If the coach didn't slow down none of them were going to have to worry about love, puppy or otherwise. Kristen, the girl squeezed between Michelle and the coach, was dozing and her head wobbled, finally landing on Michelle's shoulder. Michelle inched away. She wished she were home on her bed, reading a Stephen King novel.

Suppose the van careened off the highway and plunged into the canyon? Suppose she and Stuart were both killed? Margo would fall apart. Andrew had had a kid who was killed in a car crash. Michelle had just found out about that. She had asked Margo if she could read Andrew's book. She was curious. She'd read some of his magazine pieces, but they were just bullshit articles about prison reform and politics. The book was different. After she'd read it she couldn't stop thinking about the characters. And when Margo had told her about Andrew's kid, Bobby, Michelle had locked herself in her room, bawling her eyes out for hours.

Michelle closed her eyes and tried to think pleasant

thoughts, tried to erase the picture in her mind of the van turned upside down, their bodies splattered across the highway, their blood turning to red ice.

She tried instead to remember the good, warm feeling she'd had at Grandma's and Grandpa's anniversary party. The feeling that if only everything could stay this way forever, life would be perfect.

On Monday morning Margo took Michelle to the doctor. "Frostbite," he said, examining her toes, "but I don't think you're going to lose them. You're lucky it's not your big toe. Big toes are the most useful, you know."

"Do I have to quit the ski team?" Michelle asked. She was hoping he'd say yes. She had never been so scared as when she'd been whizzing down the mountain full speed, totally out of control, and then, near the end of the run, catching her ski on the tip of a rock and falling. Falling and falling, head over heels, sure she would never stop, or that when she did both her legs would be broken, or even worse, her neck, paralyzing her for the rest of her life.

"I know you don't want to quit," the doctor was saying, "especially in January, when the season is just beginning, but if I were you I'd stay off the slopes and give those toes a chance to heal. They'll never be the same. You'll probably always experience pain in cold weather, but . . ." He paused for a minute and looked at Margo, then back at Michelle. "How did this happen anyway? Weren't you wearing thermal socks?"

"I forgot to loosen my boots after the race," Michelle said. "I rode all the way from Wolf Creek to Boulder without loosening them."

"That was not good thinking," the doctor said. "I'm surprised at you, Michelle . . . you've always struck me as a good thinker."

"These things happen," Michelle said seriously.

So, she had frostbite on two toes. Well, that was certainly more interesting than a sore throat, which was what Stuart had.

"I've got to get to the office now," Margo said, dropping Michelle off at school. "You think you'll be okay?"

Michelle did not answer her mother. She got out of the car and slammed the door shut. She was so pissed at Margo! While she had been at Wolf Creek, close to killing herself, Margo had let the Brat sleep in *her* room, in *her* bed, and Margo had not even asked *her* permission. Had not even told her, probably would never have told her. But Michelle had known instantly. Those little flowered cotton underpants at the side of her bed. The kind Michelle had worn in junior high. And her room had smelled differently too. The Brat never took baths and even when she did you could still smell her feet a mile away because she never bothered to wash them.

"You let Sara sleep in here, didn't you!" Michelle had yelled at her mother, the minute she'd surveyed her room. "How could you? How could you have done such a thing?"

"I changed the sheets for you," Margo said, sounding guilty as hell.

"Changed the sheets! You think changing the sheets makes it all right?" Michelle ripped the quilt off her bed and sprayed her sheets with Lysol. Then she checked every one of her drawers and her closet to make sure that nothing was

missing, that nothing was out of place. She would never forgive her mother for this. Never! Suppose the Brat had read
her diary? Suppose she'd seen some of the books Michelle
kept buried under her sweaters or the letters she had written
but never mailed?

Margo was always yapping about respecting privacy.
Well, this showed how much she respected Michelle's privacy. But Michelle had made it very clear that the Brat was
never to go near her room again.

29

B.B. HAD NOT BEEN TO MIAMI IN ALMOST SEVEN YEARS, but in the midst of a late February snowstorm she was on her way. The drive from Boulder to Denver had taken more than two hours and the plane had been an hour and a half late taking off from Stapleton.

She did not know why her mother had had to have a stroke in the middle of winter.

Clare had driven her to the airport. At least she was able to get an aisle seat on the plane. Dinner was served an hour after takeoff. Chicken Kiev. The flight attendant smiled sweetly as she served it. The man squeezed into the seat next to B.B., a jowly, heavyset man in a three-piece polyester suit, ate everything on his tray. He sopped up the Kiev juices with his roll, smacking his lips together as he did. Afterwards he picked his teeth with his fingers.

B.B. nibbled on a cracker.

The phone call from Uncle Morris had come at five in the morning. Her mother couldn't move, couldn't speak.

"Not hungry today?" the flight attendant asked, eyeing B.B.'s untouched dinner tray.

"Not especially," B.B. said. "But I would like some coffee."

The flight attendant, who wore too much green eye-shadow, poured the coffee sloppily, spilling some on B.B.'s lap. "Oh, no . . . I'm terribly sorry," she said. "Here, let me help you." She tried to wipe up the coffee that was seeping into B.B.'s beige pants, burning her thighs. "If you'd stand up," she said, "I think it would be easier."

"Here . . ." the man next to B.B. said, passing his napkin.

"Club soda," the woman in the window seat said. "It works every time."

"If you'd just stand up . . ." the flight attendant said again, sounding annoyed, as if this had been B.B.'s fault instead of hers.

"I don't *want* to stand up," B.B. said.

"Well, I can't help you unless you do."

"Club soda," the woman in the window seat repeated. "Believe me, I know."

B.B. was trying very hard to hang on, to keep from crying out or screaming.

Her mother had gotten up to use the toilet at one A.M. and had passed out on the bathroom floor. Uncle Morris had been awakened by the thud. Thank God the bathroom floor was carpeted, he'd said on the phone.

The man next to B.B. leaned over and said, "You pay three, four hundred bucks and this is what you get. That's why they're all going out of business . . . know what I mean?''

B.B. nodded.

She had begged Andrew to stay at her house with Sara and not to take her to Margo's.

Now two flight attendants approached her, the one who had spilled the coffee and another. ''When you reach your final destination and have your trousers cleaned, please send the bill to the airline,'' the older one told her.

''Yes . . . all right,'' B.B. said.

She had phoned Andrew at six that morning. Margo had answered the phone sounding sleepy. ''Honey . . . it's for you,'' she had heard her say. ''It's B.B.''

Tears came to B.B.'s eyes and spilled over, running down her cheeks.

''Please accept our apologies,'' the senior flight attendant was saying.

''Yes, all right . . .'' B.B. answered. ''Just leave me alone, please.''

''Of course.'' One looked at the other, then both flight attendants walked down the aisle, away from her.

''My mother is just sixty-one,'' B.B. said quietly.

''Mine's eighty-four,'' the man next to her said, as if she'd been talking to him, ''and senile . . . don't know a thing . . . don't recognize us . . . it's no good . . . who wants to live that long? When my turn comes I hope it's quick.''

She did not answer him. She closed her eyes and kept them closed until they landed in Miami.

At the airport B.B. rented a car, a Dodge Dart, green, smelling of newness. She had not been to Miami since the accident.

Bobby had been ten. He'd be seventeen now, tall and handsome, with a deep voice. Almost a man. Her mother should have died instead of having a stroke. Death was clear. The ones who were left knew what to do. Arrange for the funeral. Go through the motions of mourning. The other feelings, the ones that lived deep inside, the gnawing empty feelings of loss, of unbearable sadness, you kept to yourself.

B.B. had been packed and ready to go by the time Sara was up that morning. They'd had a quick breakfast together and B.B. had told Sara what had happened.

"Is Grandma Goldy going to die?" Sara had asked.

"I don't know. She's very sick."

"What's it like to have a stroke?"

"I don't know that either. I imagine it's like being inside a tunnel but you can't get out, no matter how hard you try."

Sara began to cry.

"Don't, Sweetie . . . it will be all right . . . come on now . . ."

Sara had come to her then, had let her hug her for the first time in a long time. "I don't want her to die."

"Neither do I, but it's not up to us to decide. You better get ready for school now."

Sara had looked out the window. "Do you think school will be open with all this snow?"

"I don't know. Why don't you put on your radio and find out."

"If it's closed I'll go over to Jennifer's . . . okay?"

"Okay."

"How long will you be gone, Mom?"

"I'm not sure . . . probably four or five days."

"And Daddy's coming here to stay with me?"

"Yes."

"Will you send Grandma Goldy my love?"

"Yes."

B.B. drove directly to the hospital. Uncle Morris was slumped in a chair outside the intensive care unit. He looked exhausted. He was seventy-eight, an old man, seventeen years older than her mother. She had a vision of Lewis at seventy-eight—seventeen years older than her. This is how he would look. Uncle Morris should have been the one to have had the stroke, not her mother. Then his children, her cousins, could have come running, eager to get their hands on his money at last. All but her mother's share, two hundred and fifty thousand dollars or half the estate, whichever amount was greater at the time of his death. Her cousins had hated the prenuptial agreement, had believed that their father's entire estate belonged to them.

"Francie . . ." Uncle Morris stood up when he saw her and they embraced.

"How is she?" B.B. asked.

"No change . . . still nothing . . . we don't know what's going to be. I only wish it had been me instead. She's still so young."

"Can I see her?"

Uncle Morris checked his watch. "Every hour, for ten minutes. That's the rule. But it's been more than an hour so go ahead."

B.B. entered the intensive care unit, whispered her mother's name to the nurse in charge, and was escorted to her mother's bedside.

"Hello, Mother . . . I'm here . . ."

Her mother did not respond. Her eyes were closed, as if she were asleep. B.B. stayed for a few minutes, then went back outside. She told Uncle Morris that he should go home, should get some rest, that she would stay and if there was any change she would call him.

"You're sure, Francine . . . you're not tired yourself, after your trip?"

"No, I'm fine. I want to stay here."

"All right then. I'll go have a nap, take a shower, maybe heat up some soup."

"Yes."

Uncle Morris kissed her cheek and walked slowly down the hallway. His bald head was tanned. B.B. had always liked the way bald men tanned on their heads.

In an hour she went back inside to see her mother. Her mother seemed so small, and although her skin was suntanned, a grayish color had seeped through. Her bleached hair, stiff with spray, stuck out like porcupine quills. B.B. took her hairbrush from her purse and gently brushed it back, away from her mother's face.

Her mother opened her eyes and looked at her.

"Mother . . . it's me . . . Francine . . ."

Her mother made a small noise, like a cat mewing, then her eyes closed again. Had she recognized her? B.B. couldn't be sure. She sat at her mother's side holding her hand until a nurse asked her to leave. It was eleven o'clock.

She walked down the hall to a pay phone and dialed her home phone number. It would be just nine o'clock there. The phone rang twice and then her answering machine clicked on with Andrew's voice saying, *You have reached*

555-4240. If this is an emergency please phone 555-6263. Otherwise, please leave a message and someone will get back to you. Thank you.

Damn him! She hung up and dialed the other number, Margo's number. Michelle picked up on the third ring. "Hello . . ."

"Is Sara there?"

"Who's calling?"

"Her mother."

"Just a minute . . ." B.B. heard Michelle calling, "Hey, Sara . . . it's for you . . . it's your mother."

"Hello, Mom . . ." Sara said, coming on the line. "Where are you? How's Grandma?"

"I'm at the hospital. She's asleep. What are you doing at Margo's?"

"Oh, it was really snowing and Daddy decided it would be better for all of us to be together since he's the only one with a four-wheel drive, in case of an emergency . . . you know . . ."

"Where's Lucy?"

"Lucy's here, with me."

"Don't let her drink out of their toilets."

"Why not?"

"Because I said so. Where are you going to sleep?"

"I'm not sure. Upstairs on the sofabed, I think."

"Watch out for those children, Sara. They're drug addicts."

"Not really, Mom."

"Listen to me, Sara. I know. Don't take anything they give you. Promise me that . . . promise me that you won't take anything."

234

"Okay . . . I promise."

"Let me talk to your father now."

"Hang on . . . I'll get him."

Andrew came on the line a minute later. "Hello, Francine . . . how's your mother?"

"Why did you take Sara there? I asked you not to, didn't I?"

"Because of the storm, but that's not important . . . how's your mother doing?"

"I'll decide what's important!"

"Look, don't worry, everything is fine here. Lewis is trying to reach you. He asked me to have you call him as soon as you can."

"I want to talk to Sara again."

"Yeah, Mom?" Sara sounded annoyed this time.

"Sara, I want you to make your father take you home tomorrow. It's not safe for you there. Do you understand?"

"Okay, Mom. I'll try."

"I love you, Sara."

"And me you."

"For how long?"

"You know . . ."

"For always and forever?" B.B. asked.

"Yes."

"Then say it, Sara."

"I can't right now."

"Why not?"

"You know."

"Because they're listening?"

"Something like that."

"Are you embarrassed to have them know you love me?"

235

"No, Mom."

"Then say it."

"For always and forever," Sara said, softly.

"For always and forever what?"

Sara didn't respond.

"For always and forever what?" B.B. said again.

"I love you for always and forever," Sara said quickly.

B.B. began to cry. "The flight attendant spilled hot coffee on my lap. My pants are all stained."

"I guess you'll have to wash them," Sara said.

"Yes," B.B. said, hanging up the phone. She had lost Sara too. She could feel it. Sara would be happier if she never came back.

B.B. awoke at dawn with a cramp in her foot and a kink in her neck. She had fallen asleep in the chair in the hallway outside the intensive care unit. It had been hours since she had seen her mother. But surely if there had been any change they'd have called her.

She went inside. Her mother was still asleep, or whatever it was that looked like sleep. B.B. sat beside her, looking down at her, feeling an intense anger building up. "Damn it, Mother! I was such a good girl. I always tried so hard to please you. I never did anything wrong, did I? Never got into trouble like other kids. Never let the boys touch me. I did everything right and now look! Look at what a mess I'm in. How come? I mean what's the point in being a good girl if this is what you get for it? My son is dead. My daughter doesn't care about me any more. My husband's living with another woman, right under my nose. My whole life is such a disappointment. Why didn't you tell me what to expect?

Why did you lie to me, saying I had everything? I expected to be happy and now I can't remember what being happy feels like. I haven't felt happy since Daddy died.''

She turned the gold bracelet she was wearing around and around on her wrist. "Did he really die in that girl's bed, Mother, or was that just some story you invented because you were playing around with Uncle Morris? I remember that time I walked in on the two of you and your blouse was unbuttoned, but you just laughed and said that Uncle Morris was tickling you. I believed you, Mother . . . I believed you because Uncle Morris liked to tickle me too. Did you know that? Did you know that he felt me up on my wedding day? That he said he'd like to shtup me himself . . .

"You told me when things get unpleasant I should just put them out of my mind and then I wouldn't feel unhappy or angry. Why did you tell me that?" She grabbed her mother by the shoulders, "Why are you just lying there like that? Why won't you answer me? Why am I being punished this way?" She shook her mother and shouted, "Why did you have to go and have a stroke? Haven't I had enough . . . haven't I?"

"Now, now . . ." a nurse said, restraining her. She led B.B. out of the intensive care unit. "We must pull ourselves together, dear. At a time like this it's important to . . ."

"Fuck off!" B.B. yelled, wriggling free.

"We're going to have to be quiet," the nurse said, "or we're going to have to leave."

"Don't talk to me as if I'm a three-year-old." B.B. turned and ran down the corridor to the emergency exit, then through the parking lot until she came to her rental car. She had to think, had to clear her head. She drove off, as the sky turned from black to gray. She drove for ten minutes, for

twenty, for forty, until she came to the cemetery. She
parked the car, leaving the door on the driver's side open,
and ran past row after row of grave sites. *Turn right . . .
turn left . . . across the hill, beyond the trees . . .* until she
came to a small grave, covered with ivy. In the early morning light she looked down at the simple gray headstone with
block letters carved into it.

ROBERT ALLAN BRODER
1964–1974
BELOVED SON OF ANDREW AND FRANCINE
BELOVED BROTHER OF SARA
REST IN PEACE

She lay down on the ivy and wept.

She did not know how much time had passed when a
caretaker, young and black, kneeled beside her, tapping her
shoulder. "You all right, lady?"

"Yes," she said, standing up.

"You all wet."

"Yes," she said, surprised. She had not been aware of
the rain until then.

"You gonna catch cold, you not careful."

She walked away, her feet squishing in the soft ground.
She walked back to the rental car. The seat was wet. She
turned on the ignition, but she did not know how to turn on
the windshield wipers. It didn't matter. She drove away.
She drove across the Causeway. Just a flick of the wheel,
she thought, just a flick would send the car jumping off the
bridge, into the black water below.

PART
THREE

30

MARGO HAD PALE, PUTTY-COLORED PAINT IN HER HAIR.
When school had been cancelled that morning because of
the heavy snowfall, she had decided to stay at home and finish up the trim in the new room. It was a beautiful room,
light and spacious, with two skylights, a window wall facing
south, rough wood walls, and brick floors. Even she was
surprised that they had been able to turn the garage into this
handsome space in just four weeks. They had done the work
themselves, with some help from a carpenter who owed
Margo a favor. Andrew had worked full time, Margo had
worked weekends and evenings, and Stuart and two of his
friends, after lengthy negotiations over hourly wages, had
worked after school each day. Even Michelle had partici-
pated, helping to set the brick floor in sand, and then applying eight coats of glossy sealer to it.

It had become clear to Margo when Sara stayed overnight

for the first time, in January, that they did not have enough space in the house for a visiting third child. She had been thinking of converting the garage for a long time anyway, at first as a studio for herself, then, after Andrew moved in, as a hideaway for the two of them. But after Michelle's indignation over Sara having spent the night in *her* room, without *her* permission, Margo knew that what they needed most was a room that could serve as a kid's bedroom now and someday double as a workspace for her and Andrew.

"You're not going to give this room to the Brat, are you?" Michelle asked, as she and Margo were painting the trim around the windows.

Margo had anticipated that question and was surprised it had taken so long to come. "No, I think it should be Stuart's for the rest of this year and then, when he goes off to college, it should be yours. We'll give Stuart's old room to Sara so that when she comes over she'll have a place to sleep."

"All this trouble for one weekend a month?" Michelle asked.

"Andrew is hoping she'll come more often once she has her own space. And this will give all of us more privacy."

"So you're saying that next year this room will be all mine?"

"Yes . . . if you want it."

"What about when Stuart comes home from college?"

"I guess he can have your old room."

"I think he'd rather have *his* old room."

"Well, we could certainly arrange that."

"But that would mean the Brat would wind up with *my* old room."

"I think we shouldn't worry about this now."

"Don't you ever think things through, Mother?"

"Some things."

"I like to think things through totally," Michelle said. "I like to know what's going to happen next."

"No one can know exactly what's going to happen."

"I like to try."

"You have to bend a little, Michelle. Otherwise life gets to be unbearably hard."

Michelle turned away. "Who paid for this room anyway?"

Margo felt herself stiffen. She was not comfortable discussing the financial arrangements between her and Andrew and she did not know why. "Andrew and I split the cost fifty-fifty."

"Does that mean that part of the house is his now?"

"No, but if I decided to sell I'd pay back his share."

"Suppose you get married . . . what happens then?"

"We haven't discussed it."

"Do you think you will . . . get married?"

"I don't know. Does it matter to you?"

"I wouldn't mind . . . then I wouldn't have to worry so much."

"Honey, it's my life . . . you don't have to worry about it."

"I do have to worry, Mother. Suppose next year you come home with someone else and I don't like him at all?"

"It's unlikely that I'll be coming home with someone else next year."

"But you can't guarantee that, can you?"

"No, but things are working very well between Andrew and me. You can see that, can't you?"

"Yes, but it's only been a couple of months."

"The first months are the hardest," Margo said.

"Not according to this book I read about *affairs*. It said that *affairs* last three to six months and then *poof*, the magic is gone."

"Well, since it's the end of February, it's already been six months and the magic is still intact."

Michelle gave her a long look, then said, "I'm going out to build a snowman."

Margo sighed and went upstairs to the kitchen. She put the kettle on and grabbed a wedge of Gouda. One minute Michelle seemed to be an old woman, taking on the worries of the world, the next, she was a child, building a snowman. Margo found the child easier to understand.

"It's fabulous!" Clare said, a few hours later, as she stood in the middle of the new room. She had stopped off at Margo's on her way back from driving B.B. to the airport to catch a plane to Miami. B.B. had called Andrew early that morning to tell him her mother had had a stroke and to ask him to look after Sara while she was away.

"I'd take it for myself if I were you," Clare said. "It's so much roomier than your bedroom."

"I know," Margo said, "but we don't want to give up the bathroom or the hot tub."

"I guess I wouldn't either. Especially the hot tub. I wouldn't mind a soak right now. It's been a long day."

Margo checked her watch. "Good idea."

Clare sprawled out on Margo's bed while Margo stepped outside to get the hot tub going. When she came back inside she closed the sliding glass doors and leaned back against them, blowing on her hands. "It's cold out there."

"You're telling me?"

"How did it go this morning?"

"Two hours to get down to the airport. We'd have missed the plane except it was delayed."

"How was B.B.?"

"Couldn't tell, really. She slept most of the way to Denver. Didn't say a word about her mother."

"She doesn't deal well with reality," Margo said.

"How can you say that?" Clare asked. "She has the best business sense of anyone I know."

"In her personal life, I mean." Margo went to her closet and pulled out two terry robes.

"I can't discuss B.B. with you, Margo. It's too hard. I feel disloyal. I know now what it must be like for kids caught in the middle of their parents' divorce, because I sure as hell feel caught in the middle. On the one hand I'm glad that you and Andrew are so happy. On the other, I hate seeing B.B. so unhappy."

"I don't want to see her unhappy either. But it's not as if I stole him away," Margo said. "They'd been divorced for years."

"I know . . . I know . . ."

"And she's got Lewis. He seems like a nice man."

"He is . . . but something's wrong . . . I can't put my finger on it, but it scares me."

"I think it will all work out. It just takes time. The tub should be ready now."

"Good, my bones are aching," Clare said. "Do you remember having had aching bones when you were younger?''

''I've only become aware of my bones recently,'' Margo said, laughing.

''See what I mean? Our bones are aging,'' Clare said, as she undressed, ''like the rest of us.''

''I refuse to believe it.''

''So did I, but every day I look into the mirror and see more signs.''

''I only look when I have to.'' Margo knew that wasn't exactly true, but she liked thinking of herself as a person with more important things on her mind than how she looked, except, of course, for that week in L.A., when she'd realized she no longer had the body of a young girl.

''If we had been ugly kids we'd be better off now,'' Clare said.

''Why . . . you think it's easier for ugly people to adjust to growing old?''

''Yes, I do. It's losing your looks that's hard. If you never had them in the first place you wouldn't miss them.''

''I've heard that about money,'' Margo said, ''but never looks.''

''About money, I wouldn't know.''

Margo knew that Clare never thought about money. It had always been there for her, like her eyes or her teeth. Clare's money made some people afraid, especially men. To Margo, money meant freedom from economic dependence, which is what kept her sister Bethany from leaving Harvey. But people with a lot of money never knew what to do with it. It complicated their lives. She did not want money, or the lack of it, to dominate her life again, the way it had right after her divorce.

They stepped outside, threw off their robes, and shrieked as they lowered themselves into the steaming tub.

"Has Andrew started the new book yet?" Clare asked after a few minutes.

"No, he's still doing research and he's been so busy with the new room, he hasn't even had time for that."

"I can't stand having Robin around and not working . . . it's driving me up the wall, although next week he's flying to Montana to look for land."

"Really?"

"Yes, he's got this idea that he wants to ranch . . . says he needs to get in touch with nature."

"You're not going to Montana, are you?" Margo asked.

"Can you see me in Montana?" Clare asked, laughing. She stopped abruptly. "He's bored," she said. "He's never satisfied. I don't know what we're going to do."

Margo reached over and touched Clare's shoulder. "I'm sorry," she said. "I didn't know you were having trouble. I know how much you want it to work."

"What I want doesn't seem to matter. God, I wish he'd grow up, face up to responsibilities, make a commitment and keep it. You know what he says . . . that women spend their lives building nests and men spend theirs flying away from them—that women are interested in loving, but men are only interested in fucking. He says he doubts he could see a nipple without wanting to suck on it. I tried to point out that that's because his development was arrested at the infantile stage. He says plenty of men follow their cocks through life. I told him fine, but if you're going to follow yours and it takes you beyond our bedroom, forget it, because I won't be here waiting next time. And I won't. I wish I'd never let him back into my life.''

''If that's the way it is, let him go, Clare. You were doing fine without him.''

''I know . . . but I went and got my hopes up thinking it would work this time . . . that we'd both learned a lot. Why do smart women keep getting themselves involved with shmucks?''

Margo laughed. ''I love it when you use words I taught you.''

''You taught me *shmuck?*''

''Didn't I?''

''Margo, shmucks are not necessarily Jewish men found exclusively on the east coast. Shmucks can be found everywhere, sometimes where you'd least expect them.''

''I feel really lucky to have found Andrew,'' Margo said. ''I feel so lucky I'm embarrassed.''

''You don't have to be embarrassed. You *are* lucky.''

''That's not to say we're without problems.''

''When you're without problems,'' Clare said, ''you're dead.''

That night after dinner Andrew and Margo and the three kids played Monopoly in front of the fire. Lucy sniffed at the board, at the Monopoly money, then settled down for a nap with her head in Michelle's lap.

''She likes you,'' Sara told Michelle.

''Animals always do,'' Michelle said.

''So how come you don't have any animals?'' Sara asked.

Michelle looked at Margo.

"We have a pig," Margo said.

"You have a pig?" Sara asked.

"A wooden pig," Michelle said. "It's Mother's little joke."

"Oh, that pig," Sara said.

"I wanted a cat," Michelle said, "but Mother wasn't able to handle any extra responsibilities."

"That was three years ago, Michelle," Margo said. "And at that time . . ."

"Cats are easy," Sara said. "They take care of themselves. All you have to do is feed them. You want me to look around for one for you?"

"We'll have to discuss that," Margo said. "We don't want to jump into something . . ."

The conversation was interrupted by the telephone. "I'll get it," Margo said, relieved.

"Maybe it's Mom," Sara said.

It was Lewis, telling Margo that her number had been left on B.B.'s answering machine. Margo explained that B.B.'s mother had had a stroke and that B.B. had flown to Miami to be with her. She promised to have B.B. call him in Minneapolis as soon as she heard from B.B. herself.

"That was Lewis," Margo said to the group. "He wondered why he couldn't reach B.B."

"I thought it would be Mom," Sara said.

"It's your turn, Mother," Michelle said to Margo. "You're on Park Place."

B.B.'s call came half an hour later and after it Sara lost interest in the Monopoly game. She yawned several times, until Andrew asked, "Tired?"

"A little."

"Want to get ready for bed?"

"Where am I going to sleep?"

"You can sleep in my room," Stuart said, "and I'll try out the new room."

"You'll be cold," Margo told him. "We don't have the heaters in yet."

"I'll use my sleeping bag. It's good for ten below."

"That's okay," Sara said. "I'd rather sleep up here, on the sofabed. And I'll keep Lucy with me for company."

"What about our game?" Michelle asked. "Aren't we going to finish our game?"

"Could we finish it tomorrow?" Sara said.

"I'm not promising I'll play again tomorrow," Stuart said. "If I don't you can divide my properties."

"It's no fun that way," Michelle said.

"Why don't we leave the board set up on the coffee table," Margo suggested, "and we'll decide what to do about it tomorrow."

"This family never finishes anything!" Michelle said.

"We finished the new room," Stuart told her.

Margo and Andrew went downstairs and listened to the news on the radio. Margo wanted to tell Andrew about Clare and Robin, about how Robin said men follow their cocks through life. But Andrew seemed preoccupied. Margo was feeling very tense herself. Maybe she was getting her period. Andrew turned off the radio and the lights. They got into bed. But they did not make love.

In the middle of the night Sara called out in her sleep and Andrew rushed upstairs to make sure she was all right. When he came back to bed he tossed and turned for hours.

Finally he took a magazine and went into the bathroom. Margo was cold without him and pulled on socks, but she still could not sleep.

The next morning, after Sara and Stuart had left for school, the phone rang. Margo was in the bathroom, dressing for work. She heard Andrew saying, "What . . . when?"

She came out of the bathroom, carrying her hairbrush, and went to his side. He was sitting on the edge of the bed, the phone to his ear. His face was drained of color, his body tense. "What?" she asked.

Andrew shushed her. "Yes," he said into the phone. "Yes, thank you for calling. I'll be back in touch later."

"What happened?" Margo asked. "Is her mother worse?"

"It's not her mother," Andrew said, hanging up the phone. "It's her."

31

MICHELLE THOUGHT SHE MIGHT BE COMING DOWN WITH something, probably the flu. Gemini had it and so did half her class. Her head hurt and her body ached. She woke up thirsty and gulped down two glasses of orange juice, then felt incredibly nauseous. "I'm sick," she announced in the kitchen, while everyone else was having breakfast. "I'm going back to bed."

She had fallen asleep when the phone rang, waking her. Maybe it was the clerk at school, calling to find out where she was. She lifted the receiver off the hook and heard Andrew saying, "Yes . . . you have the right number." Then some guy began telling Andrew this weird story—something about a cemetery and this woman lying on a grave in the rain. Something about a caretaker who had notified the police, giving them the number of her license plate because the woman had seemed dazed and he had thought she shouldn't be driving. When the police had finally caught up with her she had been sitting in her car, in the middle of the Cause-way, with her hands over her ears. She would not speak. She would not communicate in any way. She seemed to be ex-tremely disturbed. They took her to the nearest hospital, Mt. Sinai, where she was being held for observation.

When the guy on the phone had finished talking Andrew said, "I see." His voice was all trembly. Then the guy said something else, something that Michelle didn't get and An-drew answered, "Yes, I do understand, but I'd like to call my personal physician in Miami and ask him to take a look at her first. I'll get back to you as soon as I can, within the next few hours."

"You're her husband?" the guy asked.

"I was," Andrew said. "We're divorced."

Suddenly it hit Michelle. They were talking about B.B. Mi-chelle got a picture in her mind of B.B. sitting in her car on the Causeway, her hands covering her ears. And then the police, two of them, coming up to her car, knocking on the window, asking, *Are you all right, Ma'am?* But obviously she's not. One look and they can see they've got a case on their hands. They suspect drugs or booze or a combination. They search the car but don't find a thing except her purse, with her wallet and her driver's license. *Hmmm,* they say, *Colorado.* They com-pare the photo on the license to B.B. and agree that it is the same woman, even though her long red hair is sopping wet and her eyes have this wild, crazed look. She will not answer their questions. She will not speak at all. They try sign language, thinking she might be deaf. Still no response. They shake her, but that doesn't work either. She just sits there with her hands over her ears and will not respond.

Michelle had had thoughts about blocking out the world

253

that way, but she had never carried them to such extremes. When she had been in ninth grade a boy in her class had suffered from extreme mental exhaustion—that's how the teachers had put it—and he had been sent off to some private hospital in the mountains. What Michelle remembered most about him was that when he smiled only one side of his mouth turned up. But how could someone like B.B., someone who was so beautiful, someone who had everything, go crazy? It didn't make any sense.

Michelle turned her pillow onto the cool side. She was sure she had a fever. She was shivering under the weight of her quilt. She would probably miss a whole week of school.

She wondered if her father would take charge the way Andrew had if something happened to Margo, if Margo, say, was found on I-25 with her hands over her ears. Probably not, Michelle decided. She and Stuart would have to do it on their own.

Her bedroom door opened and Margo walked in, smelling of Chanel No. 19. She sat on the edge of Michelle's bed and placed a hand on her forehead. "You feel warm, honey. Have you taken aspirin?"

Michelle nodded.

"I've got to go to work now, but Andrew is here if you need anything. I'll call at noon to see how you're feeling."

"Who was that on the phone a few minutes ago?"

"Oh, that was nothing," Margo said. "Stay in bed and take more aspirin if you feel feverish. I'll try to get home early." She dropped a kiss on Michelle's forehead, then left.

Nothing, Michelle thought. B.B.'s gone bonkers and Margo calls that nothing! What about Sara?

Right before noon the phone rang again. School, Michelle thought. She picked up the phone, but Andrew was already on. This time it was Lewis, B.B.'s boyfriend. Michelle listened as Andrew told him the whole story. He finished by saying, "I've already been in touch with my doctor down there. He knows Francine. She was his patient. I'm sure that whatever he recommends . . ."

But Lewis interrupted. "I'm taking the next flight out. I'll be in Miami by tonight."

"That really isn't necessary," Andrew said.

"You don't understand," Lewis told him. "I'm taking charge of the situation. She's my wife."

"She's your what?" Andrew said.

"My wife. We were married in Hawaii on New Year's Eve. She wanted to keep it a secret for a few months, until we had a chance to make some plans."

Michelle held the phone away for a minute. She was breathing so hard she was afraid they would hear her. When she put the phone back to her ear she heard Andrew asking, "Does Sara know?" His voice was barely a whisper.

"No," Lewis said. "B.B. and I were planning to tell her the next time I came to Boulder."

God! Michelle thought. B.B. had married Lewis and they hadn't told anyone, not even Sara. How could they have done such a thing? Michelle would never forgive Margo if Margo got married secretly. Marriage was a family matter and the children had a right to know. Now somebody was going to have to tell Sara not only that her mother had gone off the deep end, but also that she was married to Lewis. What a mess, Michelle thought. What an intensely ridiculous mess!

32

SARA WAS SICK FOR TWO WEEKS, LONGER THAN ANYONE else in the house. The doctor had come twice and Clare had come over every day, bringing soup and Jell-O and dog food for Lucy, but then Clare had come down with it too. Everyone in the house was still coughing, but Sara's cough was the worst. Her cough kept her up at night and sometimes she felt like she couldn't breathe. Then she'd get scared and knock on Margo's bedroom door, asking her father to come sit with her. And he would, holding her hand until she'd fallen back asleep.

Now her father said it was time for her to go back to school. She didn't want to go. She cried and begged him to let her stay home a few more days. But he said it would do her good to get out of the house, to be with her friends again. He said it would help take her mind off her mother.

She could not stop thinking about her mother, imagining

her in a hospital that was exactly the same as the place where they took Jack Nicholson in the movie *One Flew Over the Cuckoo's Nest*, which she had seen on HBO at Grandma and Grandpa Broder's house over Christmas vacation. It was a scary place, filled with weird patients and mean nurses. Her mother would not like it there. She would cry herself to sleep every night. Sara could see her, wearing an old hospital gown, lying on her small cot, her knees pulled up to her chest, her fingers twirling several strands of hair the way Sara sometimes did when she was tired or frightened. Sara could hear her mother crying, *Help me, Sara . . . please help me . . .* And Sara wanted to help her mother, but there was nothing she could do. Sometimes, in the middle of the night, Sara would wake up crying.

She had cried too on the day that her father had told her that her mother had had a mental breakdown.

"Do you mean she's cracked up?" Sara had asked.

"Yes, I guess so," Daddy had said.

"But why?"

"Because sometimes life just gets to be so hard," Daddy explained, "that one more crisis sends you over the edge. It must have been very hard for your mother to deal with Grandma Goldy's stroke."

"But the last time Mom had a crisis it only lasted a week and she didn't have to go to the hospital."

"When was that?" her father asked.

"The day she found out you were coming here."

Daddy covered his eyes with one hand and shook his head back and forth, back and forth. Then he took her in his arms and stroked her hair as if she were a puppy and said, "Poor Sara . . . this has been very hard on you, hasn't it?"

"Sometimes." That was all Sara was going to say. She was not going to tell him how her mother had been screaming and crying and acting crazy for months. *Crazy.* That's what had happened. Her mother had gone crazy, although no one would say that word. Sara wasn't all that surprised either. She had known something was very wrong, but she had not known what to do about it. In a way it was a relief that it had finally happened and that it had happened far away. But Sara knew she should not be glad, even though she had secretly wished that her mother would go away and never come back. She had wished worse things too, but they were too terrible to think about. She began to cry again.

"It's temporary," her father said, misunderstanding her tears. "She'll get better."

"When?" Sara asked.

"No one can say for sure."

"A week? A month?"

"Longer than a week. Maybe even longer than a month."

"I want to talk to her," Sara said.

"She can't have phone calls now," Daddy said.

"Why not?"

"Her doctors think it's best that way."

"But when you're sick you want to talk to your family."

"Look, Sara . . . your mother . . ."

"Stop calling her *your mother,*" Sara shouted. "I hate it when you call her that!"

"I'm sorry," Daddy said. "I didn't know. What should I call her?"

"Francine. That's her name."

"All right," Daddy said, "from now on I'll call her Francine."

They were quiet for a few moments. Then Sara cried, "It's all my fault."

"No," Daddy said, "it has nothing to do with you."

"You don't know," Sara said.

"Don't blame yourself for Francine's problems. None of it is your fault."

"You don't know anything about it." Sara bolted from the room. Her mother would be angry if she said anything more and she would be angrier still if Sara stayed at Margo's house. She would never forgive her for that. Sara would have to get her father to take her home and stay there with her until her mother returned.

But then they had all gotten sick, one right after the other.

The day before Sara was to go back to school her father took her home to pack up some of her things. She had not been home in more than two weeks. Everything looked the same and yet it all seemed different. She ran her hand along the polished wood of the piano. Maybe she wouldn't have to take piano lessons any more. She didn't like piano lessons, but her mother said it was important to learn to play. Sara didn't see why, but Mom kept telling her she would understand when she was older. It had something to do with being popular at parties. Sara sometimes went to parties, but nobody ever played the piano. Twice this year when Sara had come home from parties her mother had stood her under a bright lamp and had looked into her eyes to see if her pupils were dilated. Mom thought all kids did drugs. She had also smelled Sara's clothes and her breath. Sara had been really angry. "You don't trust me, do you? You don't trust anyone!"

"It's hard for me to trust," her mother had said.

"You could at least try to trust the people you love."

"Try to pack up quickly, Sara," Daddy said, sitting down on the sofa in the living room with a copy of *Newsweek*. "There's a lot to do at home."

"This *is* home," Sara said, "and I don't see why we can't stay here. I don't see why you can't just move in until Mom gets better and comes back."

"Try to understand," Daddy said. "I can't live with you in this house. I don't belong here."

"Well, I don't belong there, in Margo's house," Sara argued.

"I know you feel that way now, but as soon as we fix up your room . . ."

"I already have a room. A very pretty room. Right here."

"We're going to paint your room at Margo's," Daddy said. "What color would you like?"

"I don't give a damn about that room!" Sara shouted. "It's Stuart's room, not mine. It will never feel like my room even if you paint it purple."

She ran upstairs to her bedroom and slammed the door behind her. Her room looked perfect. Mrs. Herrera had been in to clean. Sara could tell because Mrs. Herrera always tilted the pictures on the wall so Mom would know she had dusted them. She did the same thing at Margo's house. It was weird seeing Mrs. Herrera cleaning there too. Yesterday she had taken Sara aside and had asked, "You're all right here? They're treating you okay?"

"Yes," Sara had said.

"If you want my opinion it should never have happened. They shouldn't have let it happen. You get what I'm saying?"

"I guess," Sara had said. But she wasn't really sure.

Sara turned on her clock radio. It reminded her of the night her mother had thrown it across the room, screaming at Sara, and Sara had screamed back, *You don't deserve to be a mother!* That was the night she had secretly wished that her mother would go away and never come back. Well, Sara's wish had come true. She felt the beginning of tears and swallowed hard. If she had been nicer to her mother, if she had said, *For always and forever* that night Mom had phoned from Grandma Goldy's hospital . . .

Sara went to her closet and took out a canvas duffel. She packed her clothes. Then she walked down the hall to her mother's room. It still smelled from her perfume. She opened the door of Mom's closet and looked at her clothes, all lined up, all the hangers facing the same way. She grabbed her mother's blue silk blouse and tucked it into her duffel. "Why did you have to go and have a mental breakdown?" Sara whispered. "I'll bet you didn't stop to think about me, did you . . . about what would happen to me if you had to go to the hospital for a long time. Now look, now I have to go and live at Margo's."

"All set?" Daddy asked, when she came into the living room carrying her duffel.

"I guess," she told him.

In the truck on the way home, she asked, "Who's going to water the plants?"

"Miranda has arranged for a house sitter."

"Oh," Sara said.

"Have you thought about what color you'd like me to paint your room?" Daddy asked.

"Purple," Sara said, staring out the side window.

* * *

261

Two days later she came home from school to find that Stuart's room had been painted purple. Margo said the room needed a nice rug and asked if Sara would like to go shopping with her. "You need some plants and posters too."

"I can tape posters to the wall?" Sara asked.

"I think it's probably better to tack them up because tape pulls off the paint," Margo said.

Sara nodded, thinking about the posters she would choose. She liked animal posters best, but she might get a couple of rock stars too.

She had to remember that Margo was only being nice to her because of her father. She could not allow herself to like Margo, not even a little, because that wouldn't be fair to her mother. No one ever mentioned her mother, except Daddy, and he didn't bring up the subject that often. He did tell her that he had talked with Lewis and that Lewis had been to Miami to visit Mom and had arranged for her to be transferred to a very nice private hospital, one with a swimming pool and tennis courts and arts and crafts studios. It sounded more like a camp than a hospital, Sara thought.

Sara was having trouble in school. She tried to pay attention, but her mind was always someplace else. The teachers knew that her mother was sick and in the hospital so they didn't hassle her. The kids knew that she had moved into Margo's house and from the way they looked at her she was sure they knew that her mother was on a funny farm. She remembered that when David Albrecht's father hung himself from a rafter in his garage everyone talked about it behind David's back. No one knew what to say or how to act in front of David, and David didn't either. That's how it was with her now.

At least Jennifer was not afraid to talk about it. She said,

"Look, parents crack up all the time. It's no big deal. I'll bet you half the kids in our class have parents who've gone off the deep end. That's why Boulder has one hundred and nine shrinks."

Sara bit a sliver off her left thumbnail.

"Your mother had a lot on her mind," Jennifer said. "She's a very intense person. Probably a classic Type A personality."

"Type A's have heart attacks," Sara said. "I read it in my grandmother's *McCall's*."

"Yes, but they also crack up. It's like a warning that they should slow down. It's probably good that this happened. She's been acting weird all year, Sara."

"I know."

Sara was in bed, trying to read, but she couldn't make sense of anything. Jennifer had given her the book *I Never Promised You a Rose Garden*. It was about a girl who goes crazy. Jennifer thought it might help Sara understand her mother, but the girl in the book wasn't anything like her mother. The girl in the book had invented a secret world with a secret language and everything. Sara did not believe that her mother had created a secret world inside her head.

Lucy was asleep on Sara's legs. Sara liked watching Lucy sleep. She listened for sounds that would tell her what kind of dream Lucy was having. If Lucy sighed and seemed serene, then she was having a good dream. If she shuddered and whimpered and her body twitched, she was having a nightmare. Sara wondered if Lucy dreamed about dogs or people, if she dreamed in color or black and white.

Sara heard someone coming down the hall. She could recognize each of them by their footsteps. Margo's were soft and quick; Stuart's, in his Topsiders, were squeaky; Michelle clomped in her clogs or hiking boots. These were her father's footsteps and he was wearing his Nikes. "Dad . . ." Sara called.

"Yes, honey . . ."

"Could you come here for a minute?"

"Sure." He came into her room and sat on the edge of her bed. She put out her hand and he took it.

"I love you, Daddy."

"I love you too."

"For how long?"

"What do you mean, for how long?" Daddy asked.

"You're supposed to say, *For always and forever*," Sara explained, "and then I say, *That's how long I'll love you too.*"

"Who made that up?" he asked.

"Mom. We say it every day."

"Maybe we could come up with something new and original," her father said.

"No! I don't want something new and original. I want you to say this one."

"Okay, sure . . . let's start again."

"I love you, Dad," Sara said.

"I love you too."

"For how long?"

"For always and forever."

"That's how long I'll love you too." Sara thought that saying it would make her feel better, but it didn't. It sounded babyish and stupid. And probably her mother would be angry that she had taught it to Daddy. It was supposed to be their special ritual. Sara looked down at her father's hands.

She liked the way his fingernails ended in half moons. "Do you think she misses me?" Sara asked quietly.

"I'm sure she does."

"Do you think I could write to her?"

"I think that's a very good idea," her father said.

She started her letter the next day, in English class. She slipped a piece of notebook paper into her American Poetry book and wrote:

Dear Mom,

I'm sorry you're sick and I hope you feel better very, very soon. I had the flu. It lasted almost two weeks. But now I'm better. Lucy is fine. We had a lot of snow but now it's getting nice and I hope to go skiing next weekend. I wish you could . . .

"Sara . . ." Mrs. Walters called. "Sara . . . are you listening?"

"What?" Sara asked. "Me?"

"Welcome back to earth, Sara," Mrs. Walters said.

Everyone laughed. Sara could feel her face turn red.

"We were discussing what Robert Frost had in mind when he wrote the lines, *But I have promises to keep,/And miles to go before I sleep.*"

"I'm sorry," Sara said. "I wasn't paying attention."

"We know. Try to pay attention from now on," Mrs. Walters said.

"I will." Sara folded the letter and tucked it into her math book. It wasn't any good anyway. It sounded like the kind of letter you write because you have to, not because you want to.

33

"FRANCINE, YOU HAVE A LETTER FROM SARA."

She would not speak.

"Would you like to read it?"

She would not think.

"Would you like me to read it to you?"

She would not feel.

"I'll leave it here, on your table, in case you change your mind."

And no one could make her.

She closed her eyes.

34

IT WAS NO LONGER AN AFFAIR, MARGO THOUGHT. IT WAS no longer just a live-in situation. It was a merging of families, a merging of histories. She had wanted Andrew. She had wanted him to share her life, but she had not given enough thought to sharing his. She should have considered the possibilities earlier in the relationship. She should have sorted out her feelings in advance, so that they would not come spilling out now, when she needed to remain clear-headed. She had never expected Sara to move in with them. She had had no time to prepare, no time to get used to the idea, yet she wanted it to work. She had helped Andrew paint Sara's room—which until a few weeks ago had been Stuart's room—a soft violet color, hoping to make Sara feel more at home. But she was not sure that Sara would ever feel at home here.

Every time Margo approached her Sara put up a barrier. She was polite to Margo, but she did not relate to her.

"Sara, I know this is a hard time for you," Margo had said once, "but if you ever feel like talking . . ."

"That's okay," Sara had said. "Where's Dad?"

Another time Margo had begun, "Sara, if there's anything I can do to help . . ."

"That's okay," Sara had answered, and then she had quickly changed the subject. "Do you have an old shopping bag? I need to take a project to school tomorrow."

"Sure, under the kitchen sink," Margo had said.

Sara reminded Margo of the windup mouse that Stuart had loved as a baby. He would watch it travel across the room, waiting for it to bump into a piece of furniture, shrieking with delight each time it changed directions.

Margo was not at all sure that she would make a good step-parent. She thought of Aliza and what it must be like for her, trying to build some kind of relationship with Stuart and Michelle. She warned herself to go slowly, to be patient, not to expect too much.

When Margo and Andrew had first talked about B.B.'s breakdown, Andrew had cried, blaming himself. Margo had held him in her arms, comforting him, telling him over and over that it wasn't his fault, that his guilt wasn't going to help B.B., wasn't going to help Sara, wasn't going to help any of them. He began to have nightmares. All through that long week when they'd been sick, he had dreamed about Bobby. He had cried out in his sleep, reliving the accident—the sound of the glass shattering, the bodies tossed at impact, the children screaming. Margo had urged him not to confuse B.B.'s breakdown with the accident. "This is her problem," Margo had told him, "and the answer to it is somewhere inside of her."

She'd sounded so reasonable then, so perceptive, so certain, she had almost convinced herself. But the feelings of guilt did not belong exclusively to Andrew. There were moments when Margo blamed herself for B.B.'s breakdown. If only she hadn't met Andrew, hadn't allowed herself to fall in love with him, hadn't invited him to move in with her. Everyone has a breaking point, Margo thought. Everyone.

On the night Margo had told her children about B.B.'s breakdown she'd said, "This is going to be very hard on Sara. I hope you'll both be understanding."

Michelle, who had come down with the flu that morning, spoke in a whispery voice. "You don't have to tell us how to behave. We can appreciate how it would feel to have your mother go bonkers. We came pretty close ourselves."

Stuart had shot Michelle a poisonous look.

"Well, we did," Michelle said, coughing. "Mother was just hanging on by a thread when Leonard's wife came over with the gun. Isn't that right, Mother?"

"It was a difficult time in my life," Margo said.

"You can't count on anyone or anything," Stuart said, his voice breaking. "Life is shit . . . this proves it."

"Stu," Margo said, going toward him. It was not like Stuart to break down, to show emotion, although Margo wished he would more often. "Is everything all right with Puffin?"

"What do you mean?" he asked.

"I don't know. I just thought . . ."

269

"This has nothing to do with Puffin." He had spun on his heels and left the room.

Two weeks later, when they had all recovered from the flu, Andrew came into the bathroom one night while Margo was brushing her teeth. He sat down on the edge of the tub and said, "Do you think I should take Sara home and stay there until Francine comes back?"

Margo dropped her toothbrush into the sink. "Is that what you want to do?"

"Don't get defensive."

"I'm not getting defensive. I'm just asking a simple question." She looked into the mirror at his reflection. He had dark circles under his eyes.

"What do you think I should do?" he asked.

"Stay here." If he left now Sara would never take them seriously, and neither would Stuart or Michelle.

"For better or for worse?"

"Yes." She picked up her toothbrush and rinsed out her mouth.

"It'll complicate your life."

"My life's already complicated."

"What about your kids . . . I don't want them to become resentful."

"My kids will handle it." She turned to face him.

"I like the idea of Sara seeing us as a family," he said, pushing his hair away from his face. "And she'll have a better chance of adjusting away from Francine's house . . . won't she?"

Margo nodded.

"There are too many memories over there."

"Don't worry," Margo said softly. "We'll make it work."

He stood up and she rested her face against his flannel shirt, which felt warm and soft and reassuring.

But now Margo realized it wasn't as easy as she'd thought it would be. Andrew was overwhelmed by a sense of responsibility toward Sara. And Sara, understandably insecure, had become clinging and withdrawn. Margo thought she should see a therapist, someone to help her through the trauma of her mother's breakdown. But Andrew believed she needed only love.

They did not agree on what Sara should be told. Margo felt she should be told the truth, about everything. That it was important to learn to deal with reality.

"Since when are you an analyst?" Andrew asked angrily.

"I'm not, but you don't want Sara to grow up like B.B., do you, denying reality?"

"Sara is nothing like Francine."

"Good. Then tell her about the marriage. Tell her about Lewis."

"There's no reason for her to know about that now."

"It happened, didn't it? It's real . . ."

"It's not my place to tell her . . . it's Francine's."

"Oh, sure. And it's Francine's place to explain about the breakdown too . . . right?"

"I'll talk to her about Francine and her illness, but I don't see any reason to discuss the marriage and I'm asking you not to either. I'm not even sure, when Francine comes out of this, that the marriage will be intact."

"Is that what you're hoping?"

"I'm hoping she'll come out of it . . . that's all."

"Suppose someone else tells Sara about the marriage?"

"Who?"

"Lewis."

"I'll ask him not to."

"I don't like secrets, Andrew. Secrets always backfire."

"Just this one time," Andrew said. "Please."

"All right," Margo sighed. "All right."

She felt a growing distance between herself and Andrew, which frightened her. She missed him. Missed the closeness they had developed. Intellectually, Margo understood. Emotionally, she was having trouble. She would not allow herself to compete for Andrew's attention with a twelve-year-old. How could she possibly resent the time he needed to devote to Sara? She was his child and she had serious problems of her own. Yet, at times, Margo did feel resentful and she was ashamed.

She needed to talk to Andrew about her feelings. But right now there was so much going on that they weren't talking about anything except Sara and B.B. and what to have for dinner. They fell into bed exhausted each night. They had not made love in weeks.

"Darling . . ." her mother said over the phone, "are you sure you haven't bitten off more than you can chew?"

"I'm taking each day as it comes," Margo said.

"It's a big responsibility, another child."

"It's temporary."

"You're sure?"

"No, I'm not sure of anything."

"You have to do what's right for you, and for your children."

"I'm trying, Mother," Margo said, choking up. "The funny thing is, all I ever wanted is what you and Dad have."

"No, darling . . . you wanted more."

"Are you saying that you and Dad don't have what I think you have?"

"We have closeness and respect and love, if that's what you mean, but none of it happened overnight."

Clare told her, "You look like hell, Margo. Are you sure you're not walking around with pneumonia or something?"

"I don't think it's physical," Margo said, but she had pains in her stomach and a rash on her neck.

"I could take Sara for a while if that would help," Clare said.

"No. She belongs with Andrew . . . with us."

"Is she giving you trouble?"

"No, not at all. She keeps to herself. I'm worried about her, but Andrew thinks she's okay."

"You should get a checkup, Margo. It's not going to help if something happens to you too."

"I'll be okay," Margo said.

At the office the next day, Michael Benson said, "Is there anything I can do?" They'd been discussing the Danish Plan—designed to limit growth in the city by restricting the construction of residential units for the next five years. Michael had said, "I don't think it's going to hurt us that much. We've established a reputation for creative renovations and that's where the business is going to be." He'd paused for a minute to look at Margo and out of nowhere she had started to cry.

"That bad?" he had asked.

273

"I feel overwhelmed, Michael. I feel like I've lost control of my life."

"I warned you, didn't I? I tried to tell you about my own mistakes."

"This isn't a mistake," she said. "I love him."

"Enough for all of this?"

"I hope so."

"You know, Margo . . . you're a really fine architect . . . a really talented person. You can't toss it all away for some guy."

"I'm not tossing anything away."

Several times, before B.B.'s breakdown, Andrew had talked about tossing it all away and going to the Virgin Islands. He would start a salvage business, working when he felt like it, living the easy life. Margo would turn away, angry and frightened, when he talked that way, partly because she wasn't sure there would be room for her in his carefree island life. But more than that, she still had responsibilities—to her children, to her work, to herself. She did not want to drop out, to sleep in some bare room on a mattress on the floor. As much as she wanted to be with him, she did not want to live that way.

Other times he would be full of plans for their future. After the kids were out of school they would travel—to New Zealand, to South America, to the Orient. Maybe he would write travel books, maybe she would do architectural photo essays. She would play along with him for a while, then she would say, "I like what I'm doing now . . . you know that don't you?"

And he would hold her tightly and say, "I'm only talking maybes. Don't take it all so seriously."

* * *

Margo went to see her doctor.

"Are you tense?" he asked.

She laughed. "You might say so."

"A difficult time?"

"Yes, but I'm trying to work it out."

"Are you exercising?"

"I do Jazzercise," she said, thinking that B.B. had also done Jazzercise.

"Good," Dr. Kaplan said. "Go easy on the diet for a while . . . stick to bland foods. I'll give you a prescription for those patches of eczema. Looks like you've lost weight too."

"A few pounds . . . with the flu."

"You need rest, Margo. Are you getting enough sleep?"

"I sleep."

"A change of pace wouldn't hurt either. Are you getting out enough?"

"Come to think of it, probably not."

So, when they were invited to Early Sumner's house for dinner, Margo accepted without asking Andrew first. She knew that if she asked him, he would find an excuse not to go, not to leave Sara. But Sara seemed pleased that they were going out and invited Jennifer to spend the night.

Before the party Margo lay in the bathtub, soaping herself, thinking back to the night last fall when she had calmly made a mental list of the qualifications her steady man would have to have.

He would be divorced and have kids at least as old as hers, maybe even older. She was not interested in merging families. She had only one more year, after this one, with

275

SMART WOMEN

*kids living at home. Then it was to be her turn. She wasn't
about to give up that kind of freedom for some guy with kids.*

She laughed aloud, unable to believe she had been so naive, and not very long ago. She, who had vowed to simplify
her life, had certainly complicated it. Andrew was right
about that. She rinsed herself off and unplugged the drain,
but did not get out of the tub. She lay there watching the
water run out. Suppose B.B. did not get well? Suppose Andrew decided he should have custody of Sara? Five more
years with a child at home. A child at home changed everything. She would be forty-five when Sara graduated from
high school, almost forty-six. She began to sing, "Me and
Bobby McGee."

That song had once been her Bible. She had wanted her
freedom so desperately then. But she hadn't understood the
meaning of the lyrics. That freedom is a myth. That sharing
with another person is more important.

She stood up and reached for a towel. Tears stung her
eyes. Why couldn't life ever go smoothly? Why couldn't
you live happily ever after just for a little while?

35

MICHELLE WAS HOME ALONE, DEVOURING A BOX OF DUTCH pretzels and reading *The Bell Jar*, when someone knocked at the front door. She jumped off her bed and went to see who was there. It was Puffin. "Stuart's not home yet," Michelle told her. "I think he's at tennis practice."

"I came to see you," Puffin said.

Michelle was surprised. She and Puffin were not the best of friends.

"Can I come in?" Puffin asked.

"Sure."

Puffin followed Michelle down the hall to her room. She sat on Michelle's bed.

"Want a pretzel?" Michelle asked, passing the box.

"Thanks." Puffin took one and nibbled on it. Then she said, "Guess what . . . I'm pregnant."

"I can't believe it!" Michelle said, shocked. "How did you get pregnant?"

"You know . . ." Puffin said coyly.

"I mean," Michelle said, "weren't you using something . . . some method of birth control?"

"Well, yes, but we wanted to try it one time without a rubber, to see what it would feel like. So I picked a time I thought was safe."

"There is no safe time," Michelle said.

"I know that now."

"I thought you were on the Pill, or that you had a diaphragm."

"The Pill made me nauseous and the diaphragm's so icky. You have to . . ." She paused, lowering her voice. "You have to touch yourself to get it in and I very nearly fainted trying to pull it out."

"Does Stuart know?"

Puffin nodded.

"Well, what are you going to do about it?"

Puffin shrugged.

It was amazing, Michelle thought, watching Puffin, that Clare had produced this air-brained creature. Which proved that you never knew what you were going to get when you decided to have a kid. You tossed up the genes and took your chances. Margo and Freddy had been really lucky. She wondered what this baby of Stuart's and Puffin's might be like. She wondered if it might be anything like her. But finding out was out of the question. Puffin had to have an abortion. And it was up to Michelle to make her see that. "I don't think you're ready to have a baby, Puffin," she said.

"But I'd get ready. There's plenty of time to order the cradle and buy the clothes and all that."

"That's not what I mean. I mean you're not emotionally ready and neither is Stuart. If you two get married now it'll be a disaster. It'll be over before you're twenty." She sounded wise, she thought, but not pushy.

"You probably don't know this," Puffin said, "but I'll be eighteen in August. I'm a year older than my class. I repeated seventh grade."

"I didn't know," Michelle said, trying to figure out what that had to do with anything.

"I switched schools in seventh grade and the headmistress thought it would do me good to take the year over again. Since no one there knew me anyway it didn't really matter, although I did cry about it at the time."

"Look, if you think that was hard," Michelle said, "picture yourself at twenty, divorced, with a two-year-old kid. You and Stuart would wind up hating each other, blaming each other. It would be really bad, not just for you, but for the kid."

Tears came to Puffin's eyes. "I do remember how I felt when my parents were divorced. It was just terrible. And even now that they're back together, I hate it when they fight."

"You see?" Michelle said. "That's what I'm talking about. Teenage marriages hardly ever work."

"My parents weren't teenagers when they got married," Puffin said, walking across the room and looking out the window. "That dog, Lucy, is digging a hole in your garden."

"She likes to dig."

"What's it like, having Sara here?"

"We're surviving."

"I'm an only child. That's why I want to start young and have a bunch of my own."

"Have you thought about giving the baby up for adoption . . . I mean, if you're dead set against abortion?"

"Please don't call it a baby!" Puffin said, turning around. "Please just refer to it as my pregnancy."

"Okay," Michelle said. "Have you thought about an adoption for your pregnancy?"

"I would not be able to give up my pregnancy for adoption. Not to brag or anything, but no family could give it as much as mine. It would have trust funds from the day it was born. It would have everything. So adoption is out of the question. We're the kind who might adopt, but not give up for adoption. Do you see what I'm saying?"

"Well, then . . ." Michelle said, sighing, "it sounds as if abortion is the only answer."

"Won't you please try to talk Stuart into marrying me? We'd have plenty of money. He wouldn't have to worry about supporting me or the pregnancy. He could still go to college if he wanted to and we'd go with him."

"I can't do that."

"I guess I didn't think you would." Puffin zipped up her vest. "Will you come with me to the clinic?"

"If you want me to."

"Will you call and set up the appointment for me?"

"When do you want to go . . . tomorrow?"

"Whenever." They walked to the front door. "You know something, Michelle? I used to think you were too serious, that you never had any fun, but now I wish I was more like you. I wish that I knew all that you know."

Michelle put her arm around Puffin's shoulder and was surprised by how small she seemed. "I don't know everything," she said.

"Maybe not . . . but you know enough."

Michelle accompanied Stuart and Puffin to the clinic. Stuart had been pale and edgy that morning. He'd snapped at Sara at the breakfast table, telling her to keep her goddamned dog out of the kitchen. Sara had left the table in tears.

He did not say a word to Michelle while they sat, side by side, in the outer office of the clinic, waiting for Puffin to have her abortion. And when Puffin came out, smiling bravely, it was Michelle who hugged her first, asking if it had hurt. Puffin shook her head and held Michelle's hand. Stuart just stood there, like a zombie. Then he drove them to Puffin's house, where Michelle heated up a pot of soup. They sat with her all afternoon, watching over her as she dozed. When Clare came home they explained that Puffin had come down with a virus that was going around school.

"Not again," Clare said. "We just got over the flu."

"This one only lasts forty-eight hours," Michelle explained. "Maybe even less."

"Well, that's a relief."

That night Stuart came to Michelle's room. "Thanks for coming with us today."

"I'm glad I could help."

"You won't say anything to Mom, will you?"

"No."

"Good. Puffin wanted to tell the whole world, but I convinced her not to."

"Do you love her, Stu?"

"I thought I did, but now I don't know. The idea of spending the rest of my life with her scared the shit out of me. She had all these plans for us, like how we'd fix up our house and where we'd go on vacations."

"Do you feel bad about the baby?"

"What would I do with a baby, Michelle? I don't even know where I'm going to college."

After Stuart left Michelle thought about how, in Margo's day, you couldn't just go out and get an abortion. If you got pregnant then you had to get married. And it was that fear, that fear of pregnancy, that kept girls virgins. Except, of course, Margo had slept with this one boy, James.

Suppose Margo got pregnant now? Michelle thought. Even though she was forty, it was still possible. God, what an idea! Margo, pregnant. Would she have an abortion or would she and Andrew get all sentimental and decide to get married and have the baby? That would certainly change things. She had worried when her father had married Aliza that they might have babies too, but so far they hadn't. And Michelle was glad. She didn't think either of her parents should have more kids. They should just try to do a better job with the two they already had.

During Christmas vacation one of Freddy's friends had come over to visit. He had three screwed-up teenagers from his first marriage, but now he was married again and his new wife was pregnant. *This time I'm going to do it right*, he'd told Freddy. *I know a lot more about raising kids now. For-*

get the permissive stuff. What they need is authority.
Bullshit! Michelle thought. What they need is love.

Even if Margo and Andrew did get married there was no
guarantee that they would stay married. Look at that fight
they'd had on the night of Early Sumner's dinner party.
They had come home around one A.M., shouting. Mainly it
had been Margo doing the shouting. Andrew had just kept
repeating, "You've got it all wrong. She was just being
friendly."

"Friendly!" Margo had yelled, slamming their bedroom
door so that their voices were muffled. "She had her hand
on your thigh. You call that friendly?"

"What was I supposed to do?" Andrew asked.

"You could have removed her hand. You could have
walked away from her. For Christ's sake, Andrew, you're a
grown man. You know the difference between friendly and
flirtatious."

"I'm here with you, aren't I?" Andrew said. "Doesn't
that mean anything?"

"No . . . being here isn't enough. I need to be able to
trust you."

"I didn't fuck her. I didn't even want to."

"That's not what I'm talking about. I'm talking about
needing to trust you not to hurt me. I'm talking about needing to be able to depend on you emotionally."

So, something had happened at the party, Michelle had
thought. Somebody, probably Early Sumner, had put the
make on Andrew, and Andrew had responded, leaving
Margo feeling hurt and betrayed, not to mention jealous.

Early Sumner was old, more than fifty, but she had an interesting face. It looked carved. She was very thin and al-

ways wore black leather pants, big shirts, and amber beads, each one the size of a golf ball. She gave a lot of money to the library and the museums. Once a month she would drop by school to see who might be free to do some odd job around her house. She paid five dollars an hour. She never chose any of the girls though.

Whatever had happened Margo had been steaming. Michelle kept listening even though she was frightened.

"Men, you're all the same," Margo was shouting. "You're all babies with big egos. You're all such push-overs."

"And you're all so goddamned insecure."

"Who's insecure?"

"What do you want from me?" he asked. "Don't you know what I've been going through? Don't you know what a hard time this is?"

"It's a hard time for me too," Margo said. "Taking on the responsibility of another child and all the family problems that come with it. Not a day goes by without a phone call about either B.B.'s mother or B.B. herself. Jesus, Andrew, I'm so sick of Goldy and her stroke and B.B. and her breakdown I feel like I'm going to have one or the other myself. I've been afraid to tell you how tense I am because I know you are too. But here I am trying to help Sara feel at home and trying to think of your needs and her needs and my children's needs and my work, and my own needs have gone right down the drain . . . and yes, I'm feeling a little resentful because I needed a night out so badly and this is what I get from you!"

Michelle felt a lump rise in her throat, a lump as big as one of Early Sumner's amber beads. She wanted to run down the hall, to fling open their bedroom door, and shake them by the shoulders, yelling, *Stop this stupid fighting. Stop it right now, before you ruin everything!*

She realized then, for the first time, that she did not want Margo and Andrew to split up. She liked them together. She liked having Andrew in the house, in spite of Sara. It made her feel good. It made her feel as if she were part of a family.

"Come on, Margo . . . come on . . . I'm sorry," Andrew said, softly now, so that Michelle could barely hear him. "I just wanted to have a good time, that's all."

"I wanted to have a good time too," Margo said, crying, "but you acted as if I wasn't even there. I felt invisible . . ."

Michelle understood what Margo meant. Sometimes she felt invisible herself. And she would have to pinch herself to make sure she still existed.

A few days later, when Sara and Michelle were the only ones at home, Sara knocked on Michelle's bedroom door.

"Yeah?" Michelle called. She was still reading *The Bell Jar.*

"It's me, Sara."

"Come in . . ."

"Hi," Sara said, standing in the doorway.

"Hi."

"Could I, uh, borrow one of your, uh, Tampax?"

"Yeah, sure. They're in the bottom cupboard in my bathroom," Michelle said, without thinking. She was at this really interesting part of the book, where Esther was just getting out of the hospital. But then it suddenly dawned on her that this was Sara's first period, so she looked up and said, "First time, huh?"

Sara turned red and nodded.

"You need some help?"

Sara shrugged.

"You know how to use Tampax?"

"Jennifer showed me once."

"Well, go try and if you can't get it up call me, okay?"

"Okay."

Sara was locked in the bathroom for twenty minutes. Finally, Michelle knocked on the bathroom door. "You okay?"

"I think I got it up, but I'm not sure. It feels like it's going to fall out."

"Try again, with another one. Put some Vaseline on the tip before you shove it up."

"Where's the Vaseline?"

"In the bottom . . . where the Tampax is . . ."

"Okay, I see it."

"You want me to come in and help you?"

"That's okay. I'll try it again."

Sara came out ten minutes later. "I think it's up there this time."

"You shouldn't feel anything. It should be comfortable."

"It's pretty comfortable," Sara said. And then she smiled shyly.

Oh, she was so pathetic, Michelle thought. So young and so pathetic. "The first time I got it," Michelle told her, "I was almost fourteen and I was at this sleep-over with six other girls and I didn't want to tell any of them it was my first time so I just kept shoving Kleenex in my pants until I got home and then I told my mother and she was so excited she cried and that night we went out to dinner to celebrate."

Michelle saw the hurt come into Sara's eyes. "Oh, I'm sorry. I didn't mean to make you feel bad about your mother."

"That's okay."

"Well, if you need any more help just ask me."

"Thanks."

Michelle went up to the kitchen then and baked a chocolate cake. When the icing cooled she wrote *Congratulations, Sara* across the top.

36

Sara still had not heard from her mother, but she had talked to Dr. Arnold, her mother's doctor. Sara had been scared that once she heard Dr. Arnold's voice she wouldn't be able to think of a thing to say. So she had rehearsed her first question over and over in her mind. And then, when Dr. Arnold came on the line, Sara had said it. "Exactly when will my mother be better?"

"That's hard to say," Dr. Arnold answered, as if Sara's question was just ordinary. "She's improving, but very slowly."

"Should I keep on writing to her?" Sara asked.

"Yes," Dr. Arnold said. "Your letters mean a lot to her."

"Then how come she doesn't write to me . . . or call?"

"She's not ready to communicate, Sara."

"What does she do all day?"

"Well, she's begun to go out for walks and that's a very good sign."

"What else?"

"She watches TV."

"Mom *never* watches TV. She says it ruins your mind."

"She's watching now."

"Which shows?"

"Whatever's on in the lounge."

"Like *Happy Days* and *M*A*S*H?*"

"Sure."

"Does she laugh?"

"No," Dr. Arnold said, "she doesn't laugh."

"Will you tell her that I'm coming to see her as soon as school's over, unless she's better before then?"

"I'll tell her. And when you come down I'll introduce you to my daughter, Mimi. She's your age."

Sara did not tell Dr. Arnold that she didn't want to meet Mimi. Mimi would feel sorry for Sara, knowing that her mother had had a mental breakdown. *Mental breakdown.* That was such a weird expression. Sara imagined all these little pieces inside her mother's brain coming apart and spinning around. They would have to be put back together, like a puzzle, before her mother would be well again.

Sara thought it was good that her mother's doctor was a woman. Her mother was always saying, *Never hire a man if you can find a woman who can do the same job. Women are so much more dependable, Sara. Women take their responsibilities seriously.*

Sara found out about her own responsibilities the night they came home from the movies to find that Lucy had raided the pantry. She had dragged at least a dozen boxes of food into the dining room, hiding them under the table. She had chewed up parts of each box so that cookies, crackers, cereal, and spaghetti lay all over the floor. "Looks like Lucy had a great time tonight," Stuart said, and he and Michelle laughed.

Sara laughed with them until Margo looked at her as if she was as guilty as Lucy.

"Clean it up, Sara," Daddy said.

"But . . ." Sara began.

"No buts," Daddy said. "Lucy is your dog. You're responsible."

And so Sara cleaned up the mess by herself.

If they were a real family, like the Brady Bunch, Sara thought, everyone would have helped her. But they were just people who happened to live in the same house. They had responsibilities, but no feelings.

Sara was learning more about them every day. She understood that Margo was responsible for Stuart and Michelle, that she was responsible for Lucy, and that Daddy was responsible for her. Which got Sara to thinking that if anything happened to her father she would be all alone. Margo wouldn't want her. Margo had only taken her in and painted her room purple to please Daddy. But Margo didn't really care about her. Sara had suspected as much, but she was still disappointed to find out it was true. She heard it from Margo herself on the night that Margo and her father had had their big fight.

Jennifer had slept over and they'd gone to bed right after *Saturday Night Live*. Sara was just about asleep when she heard a door slam. At first she wasn't sure what was happening. Then she heard Margo's voice, followed by her father's. They were shouting at each other. Sara lay very still, pretending to be asleep. She hoped that Jennifer was already asleep and would not wake up, would not hear Margo and her father arguing. There was a lot of talk about loyalty and betrayal before Sara heard her own name.

"Sara!" Daddy said. "What has this got to do with her?"

"Having another child in the house means added responsibilities," Margo said. "I can't pretend that she isn't here just because she's yours."

"I can pack my bags and leave," Daddy shouted. "If that's what you want, just say so. If it's too much for you having Sara here . . ."

"Don't yell at me," Margo said. "I need to be able to be honest with you. If I can't be honest about the way I feel . . . if I can't discuss it . . ."

"Do you want me to go?" Daddy asked.

"Do you want to go?" Margo said.

"Sometimes," Daddy said. "Sometimes I want to get the hell out of here and just sail off to Bali."

How could he? Sara thought. How could he want to sail away without her? Unless he meant that he wanted to sail away *with* her. Yes, maybe that was it. Oh, that would be nice. Just the two of them, sailing off to Bali, wherever that was. She wouldn't have to go to school or anything. And she wouldn't have to share him with Margo either.

"Sometimes I wish you would just sail away," Margo said, ". . . sail right out of my life the way you sailed into it."

Sara could tell that Margo was crying.

"But then I think of life without you," Margo continued, "and I know that isn't what I really want."

"What do you want?" Daddy asked. "What the fuck do you want?"

"I want the closeness back."

Sara felt a sharp pain in her stomach. She drew her knees up to her chest.

"Sara . . ." Jennifer whispered, "are you awake?"

Sara did not answer.

Jennifer yawned noisily and rolled over in her sleeping bag.

Soon the house was quiet again and when Sara heard the familiar sounds of Margo and her father making love she covered her ears with her hands.

Ever since that night Margo and her father were lovey-dovey again. He called her Margarita, like the drink. Sara hated it when they kissed in front of her. And one time she had caught her father sliding his hand down the front of Margo's shirt. But even that wasn't as disgusting as the Polaroid pictures. Sara had found them in the middle drawer of Margo's bathroom cabinet, tucked away beneath the plastic tray that held Margo's cosmetics. Sara had been trying out Margo's lipsticks and eyeliners when she'd noticed the envelope. She'd lifted it out, turned it over, opened it, and had pulled out five Polaroid pictures, all of them of Margo wearing some dumb-looking black underwear and showing off her tits.

The pictures had made Sara feel weak and dizzy and she'd sat down on the edge of the tub with her head between her knees to keep from passing out. After a few minutes the dizzy spell passed and Sara had carried the pictures to her room. She'd hidden them in her bottom drawer, under her scrapbook. If Stuart or Michelle gave her any trouble she would show them what kind of mother they had.

Not that they'd been giving her any trouble. Stuart more or less ignored her, but Michelle had been nice once. She had baked a cake in honor of Sara's first period. And later that same night Michelle had come to her room. "What would you do if your mother got married again?" she had asked.

"I don't know," Sara said, thinking that was a weird question since her mother was in the hospital and Michelle knew it.

"Would you like it if she did?" Michelle said.

"It would depend on who she married," Sara told her.

"What about Lewis?"

"He's okay, I guess. But I doubt that my mother would marry him. I doubt that she'd marry anybody right now. What about your mother? Do you want her to get married again?"

Michelle seemed really surprised by Sara's question. "My mother?" she asked.

"Yes," Sara said.

"Well . . . I used to hate the idea of my mother remarrying, but now I don't care that much, as long as she marries someone I like."

"What about my father?" Sara asked.

"Your father is okay."

"Do you think they will . . . get married, I mean?"

"I don't know," Michelle said.

Sara wrote careful letters to her mother. She did not write anything that she thought would make her mother feel bad.

She did not even write about her first period because she knew how sad her mother would be to find out that she'd missed a really important event in Sara's life. She wondered what life would be like when her mother returned. She did not know what to expect from her mother. She was not even sure of her father anymore, except that deep down inside she did not believe that he would leave her and sail off to Bali.

Every night, before Sara got into bed, she took her mother's blue silk blouse out of her drawer and held it to her face. She forced herself to think first of something good about Mom and then something bad. Because she knew it was important to hang onto the truth.

To help her remember, Sara went home one day after school. The neighborhood was so different from Margo's. She missed the wide streets, the big old trees, and the Victorian houses. She sat on the swing on her front porch for a minute. The swing squeaked. It needed oiling. It always did after winter. Then she got up and rang the doorbell. The house sitter answered. He was a tall man with a gray beard and he had a yellow pencil tucked behind his ear. He seemed to know who she was.

It felt so strange to be home, mainly because it didn't feel like home anymore. Sara thought about throwing herself across her bed and just crying for as long as she felt like it, until her throat was sore, until she couldn't catch her breath. Instead, she took the photo album out of her mother's closet and left quickly. The house sitter told her she could come over any time, but that she should call first, to make sure he was at home.

Sara did not answer him.

That night, when her father came to her room to kiss her

goodnight, Sara was on her bed, thumbing through the photo album. Her father lay down next to her and pointed to a picture. ''I remember the day that was taken. You had just come out of the bathtub and . . .''

''What's happened to all the pictures of Bobby?'' Sara asked.

''I have some of them,'' Daddy said, ''and Grandma Goldy and Grandma Broder have some too.''

''How come Mom had to pretend that Bobby was never born?'' Sara asked.

''So she could pretend that he never died,'' Daddy answered.

37

Francine and Dr. Arnold walked along the garden path on the grounds of the hospital. "Is my mother dead yet?" Francine asked.

Dr. Arnold looked up at her. "No, she's partially paralyzed, but she's improving."

Francine nodded. "Is my daughter all right?"

"Yes." Dr. Arnold smiled at her.

"Do you know what's happened to me?"

"Do you know?"

"Sometimes I think I do and sometimes I don't."

Dr. Arnold reached over to a hibiscus bush and plucked off a flower. "I'm going to try to help you figure it out," she said, handing the flower to Francine.

Francine held it to her nose. "When I married Andrew I carried a single rose."

38

MICHELLE DECIDED NOT TO GO SKIING WITH THE FAMILY even though it was a beautiful day and she enjoyed spring skiing best. The snow would start off like icy corn, turn soft by noon, and wind up slushy. Her face would get sunburned and that night Margo would give her a combination skin cancer/aging lecture that she would ignore.

But as tempting as the idea was, the idea of spending the day alone in a quiet house appealed to her even more. Maybe she would ski next weekend, even though her frost-bitten toes still hurt in the cold. It would be her last chance before Eldora closed for the season. Andrew's parents were coming to town next weekend and Margo had already informed her that she and Stuart were expected to be at the family dinner she was planning, a sort of Passover Seder, but without the religious ceremony, since Passover would be over by then.

Margo had also made it clear that the family dinner she was planning was for family only. Not even Puffin was to be invited, which wasn't exactly breaking Stuart's heart, since he and Puffin were on the verge of breaking up. But of course, Margo didn't know that. Margo didn't know anything, not even about the abortion. Maybe some day Stuart would tell her.

Michelle decided to do some work on her World Cultures paper. She sharpened six yellow pencils and began to make an outline when the doorbell rang. She ran down the hall to the front door with Lucy at her heels. She opened the door and this gorgeous guy was standing there. He was big and blonde and suntanned and when he saw her he smiled.

"Hi . . . is Margo here?"

"No, she's not. Not now, anyway." His eyes were as blue as the sky. "Can I help you?"

"I'm Eric. I met Margo last summer in Chaco Canyon. She said if I was ever in town I should come by, so here I am." He rested one hand against the house and leaned forward. He had a hole in the left thigh of his jeans and Michelle had to resist the urge to put her finger into it.

"Well," Michelle said, "she should be home by five. You want to wait?"

"Could I?"

"Sure . . . come on in."

39

MARGO WAS NOT REALLY LISTENING TO THE CONVERSATION
between Andrew and Sara as they drove back from Eldora.
She was thinking about the hot tub, about how satisfying it
would feel to peel off her clothes and step, naked, into the
steaming water. The perfect end to an almost perfect day.
She had taken one bad spill, on a fairly easy trail, winding
up with a faceful of snow and a brief pounding in her head,
but after she'd rested for a few minutes she'd felt better. Andrew had been loving and concerned and had wiped off her
face with his bandana. The fight on the night of Early Sumner's dinner party, as painful as it had been at the time, had
cleared the air between them. They were no longer walking
on eggs. They were talking and laughing and making love
again. Sara seemed relieved too. And today, during lunch
on the slopes, Sara had been friendly. She had even laughed,

making Margo believe in the possibility of a positive relationship with her after all.

Now, as Andrew pulled the truck into their driveway Sara pointed to a motorcycle parked next to the house. "Who's here?"

"Probably one of Stuart's friends," Andrew said.

"No, Stuart's still skiing," Sara said. "He passed me on our last run and said he'd be home around six-thirty."

"Well, maybe one of Michelle's friends, then," Andrew said.

"She doesn't have any friends who ride motorcycles," Sara said.

Margo hated the idea of motorcycles. She'd known a boy in college who had been killed on a motorcycle. *Decapitated*, the headlines had said. She'd had nightmares about that boy, whose name she could no longer remember. She had forbidden her own children to ride either mopeds or motorcycles.

As soon as Andrew unlocked the front door Sara tore up the stairs, calling, "I'm dying of thirst."

"Me too," Andrew said. "You want a drink, Margarita?"

"Grapefruit juice," Margo said. "I'll get the tub going." She went to her bedroom, stripped down to her longjohns, slid open the glass doors, and stepped outside.

"Oh, Mother! I didn't expect you so soon."

Michelle was in the hot tub. Michelle, who was so modest she would not even undress in front of Margo, was naked and in the hot tub with some boy. Margo froze.

"Hey, Margo . . ." the boy called. "How're you doin'?"

Jesus Christ! It was not just some boy. It was Eric. What the fuck was he doing here? What the fuck was he doing in the hot tub with her daughter? "What are you doing?" Margo asked.

"We're soaking," Michelle answered. "What does it look like?"

"I was passing through," Eric added. "You said that any time I was . . ."

"Yes, I remember what I said," Margo caught a whiff of marijuana.

She had shared a joint with Eric last summer in Chaco Canyon, and afterwards, she had become paranoid. "Are you going to kill me?" she had asked timidly, as Eric had caressed her neck. She'd thought he was going to strangle her.

"No, baby," he had answered. "I'm going to fuck you." She had nodded, as if it were okay either way.

Now he was smoking with her daughter.

"Here's your juice, Margo," Andrew called from the bedroom.

"I'm out here," Margo called back.

Andrew joined her, took in the scene, and looked confused.

"This is Eric," Margo told him. "He was just passing through, so he decided to drop in." She could tell that Andrew still didn't get it. "Eric," she said, again. "From Chaco Canyon . . . from last summer . . ." She and Andrew had once exchanged lists of their former lovers, discussing each of their sexual encounters late into the night.

"Oh," Andrew finally said, nodding. "Eric." He handed Margo the glass of grapefruit juice.

301

"This is Andrew," Michelle said to Eric. "My mother's boyfriend."

Margo cringed at the word. It sounded so childish.

"Hey . . . how're you doin', Andrew?" Eric said. "You guys want to join us?"

"No!" Margo answered quickly.

"Could you toss us the towels?" Michelle said.

Andrew handed each of them a towel. Eric stood and stepped out of the tub first. Margo turned away.

When Michelle and Eric had disappeared into the house, Margo jumped into the hot tub, still wearing her longjohns. "Can you believe this," she said to Andrew. "Can you believe what's going on here?"

Andrew eased himself into the tub. "I think you're overreacting," he said.

"Overreacting!" She pulled off her sopping longjohns and tossed them out of the tub. "I don't like it. I don't like it at all."

"They were just soaking," Andrew reminded her. "Aren't you the one who told me that hot tubbing is not a sexual experience?"

"Sure, that's what I told you, but that doesn't mean I believe it."

Andrew laughed.

"Did he have an erection when he got out of the tub?" Margo asked.

"No."

"Good."

Eric not only stayed for dinner, he stayed overnight. "He doesn't know anyone else in town," Michelle told Margo, as she took bed linens from the hall closet. "I'm going to make up the sofabed for him."

That night Margo lay awake for hours. Michelle had been lively and flirtatious during dinner and Margo had suddenly seen her as Eric must, a very desirable young woman. Finally she got out of bed, put on her robe and slippers, and tiptoed through the darkened house, needing to convince herself that she should not worry, that Eric was asleep on the sofabed, alone.

But Eric was coming down the stairs as Margo was going up. They startled each other.

"Where are you going?" Margo asked sharply.

"To the bathroom. I have to take a piss."

"There's a toilet upstairs. Didn't Michelle show you?"

"I must have forgotten."

Eric followed Margo up the stairs and she led him to the half-bath, turning on the light. "Voilà."

"Thanks."

He was wearing only Jockey shorts and they were torn. He had a beautiful body, Margo thought, remembering the feel of his skin, the weight of him on top of her. She cleared her throat. "I'd appreciate it if you didn't go prowling around the house in the middle of the night. The dog will start barking and wake everyone and tomorrow is a school day."

"Okay." He put his hand on her shoulder and looked into her eyes. "And Margo, I want you to know I appreciate your letting me stay the night."

"Everything is different now, Eric. This is my home. These are my children. Do you get what I'm saying?"

"Sure." He took his hand away. "In the canyon you were a woman. Here you're a mother."

"That's not exactly it," Margo said, "but it's close."

"Well, if you don't mind, I've still got to piss."

She could hear him splashing into the toilet as she tiptoed back down the stairs.

The next morning, without Margo's permission, Michelle rode off to school on the back of Eric's Honda. Margo watched from the kitchen window, her stomach in knots.

When she got home from work Eric was in the driveway, working on his bike. "What are you doing here?" Margo asked.

"Michelle invited me to stay for a few days, until I can find a place of my own."

"A place of your own? Here in Boulder?"

"Yeah . . . this town has good vibes. I got a part-time job today, working on a construction crew up in Sunshine Canyon."

Margo marched into the house and went directly to Michelle's room. Michelle was humming to herself and writing in her diary. "He cannot stay in this house," Margo said. "We have enough people living here."

"But, Mother . . ."

"No, Michelle. You should have discussed it with me first."

"You can't just kick him out. At least let him stay tonight."

Margo let out a heavy sigh.

"Please, Mother . . ."

"Tonight is absolutely the last night, Michelle. Andrew's parents are coming to town on Thursday."

"I don't see what Andrew's parents have to do with Eric. They're not staying here. They're staying at the Harvest House, aren't they?"

"Listen, Michelle . . . either you are going to tell him he has to be out by morning or I am."

"He was your friend first, Mother. He came here to see you . . . remember?"

"But I didn't invite him to stay with us."

"I don't understand why you're behaving in this intensely hostile way, unless it's because we used the hot tub without your permission. Is that it?"

"That's part of it," Margo said. "And you know how I feel about motorcycles."

"You're getting to be a neurotic worrier, just like Grandma Sampson."

"That's bullshit, Michelle. And you know it."

That night, when Margo could not fall asleep, she wandered through the house again, but this time, as she passed Michelle's room, she heard muffled sounds and knew that Eric was in there. She felt a sinking feeling in the pit of her stomach. She did not know what to do. If she opened Michelle's bedroom door and demanded that Eric leave at once, Michelle would never forgive her. Besides, she had always vowed that she would respect her children's privacy.

"Margo." She spun around. Andrew was standing behind her. "Come back to bed," he whispered, taking her hand.

"He's in there with her."

"I know."

"You know?"

"From the way they've been looking at each other it was inevitable."

Margo followed Andrew back to their bedroom and climbed into bed beside him. "I can't stand the idea of it," she told him. "A girl's first lover shouldn't be someone who has slept with her mother. Michelle is such an innocent. I wanted her first sexual encounter to grow out of love."

"Desire is the next best thing," Andrew said, holding her.

"No . . . it's not the same at all. I know him, Andrew. He's just a fucking machine. He doesn't care about her."

"There's nothing you can do about it now. Try to get some sleep. Talk to Michelle tomorrow."

"Tomorrow is too late. You wouldn't be taking it so calmly if it were Sara."

"Maybe not," Andrew said. "Why did you give him your address in the first place?"

"You know how those things are. You have a nice time, you think you might want to get together again . . ."

"Was he that good?" Andrew asked.

"He's a kid."

"You just said he's a fucking machine."

"He was all right. It was pure sex, Andrew, nothing more."

"I keep picturing the two of you together. I keep thinking that if you hadn't met me, if I hadn't been here when he came to visit . . ."

"That's a whole different story. Besides, I wouldn't have been interested. You're not jealous, are you?"

306

"About as jealous as you were the night we came home from Early Sumner's."

"That jealous?"

"I think so."

On the night of Early Sumner's dinner party Margo had been blinded by sexual jealousy. She had been furious—at herself, for feeling vulnerable and insecure, at Early Sumner and other women like her, for not knowing how to relate to men except in a flirtatious way, and most of all, at Andrew, for allowing it to happen.

Oh, she hated women like Early Sumner. But she also recognized her former self in them, her married-to-Freddy self, when going to a party meant an evening of flirtations that would go nowhere but which would bring immense pleasure for a few hours—eye contact across the dinner table, a brushing of arms, of thighs, tingles followed by fantasies. She'd put out vibes in those days. *Here I am . . . come and get me . . . if you can.* She no longer put out those vibes, but other women did. And she could not stop them from coming on to Andrew.

It's your life, the voice inside her head had said that night. *You're in charge. If this is how he's going to behave and it makes you unhappy, then get rid of him.*

I don't want to get rid of him.

Then what do you want?

I want him to want me as much as I want him.

Oh ho! That old song.

Is that so unreasonable?

Depends who you ask.

So what should I do?

Tell him how you feel. See how he reacts. Maybe he'll un-

derstand. Maybe next time he'll be more aware of your feelings.

You know something . . . for once you're making sense.

Margo . . . I always make sense.

The next day, at noon, Margo drove out to the building site in Sunshine Canyon. She wandered through the new house until she found Eric. "I want to talk to you," she said.

"Sure, Margo."

"Not here. In my car."

"Be back in a few minutes," Eric told another worker, who raised his eyebrows in response. Margo knew what he was thinking, but she didn't care.

"What are you doing, Eric?" she asked, opening the car door.

"Mainly laying the floors and the patios."

"That's not what I mean. I mean, what are you doing with Michelle?"

"That's not something I'm going to talk about with you, Margo."

"She's too young for you. Too inexperienced."

"She's seventeen, isn't she?"

"Yes."

"And I'm twenty-one. That sounds just right to me."

"Damn it, Eric! I won't have you pulling any Mother-Daughter number on us."

"What's with you, Margo? Are you jealous? Is that it?"

"Jealous?"

"Yeah, that's how it looks to me. Oh, sure, you've got

yourself some guy, but he must be what . . . forty, forty-five? It's not the same, is it?''

Margo thought about smashing him in the mouth, kicking him in the balls, telling him what an immature asshole he was. But she held back her rage and said, instead, "You're so far off the wall I won't even attempt to respond."

"You're afraid I'm going to tell her . . . that's it, isn't it?"

"It would be destructive to tell her."

"Hey, look . . . I don't brag about my sexual experiences. I don't have to."

"So why, when you could have any woman in town, does it have to be Michelle?"

"I like her. She reminds me of you."

That night, after dinner, while Andrew and Stuart cleaned up the kitchen, Margo went to Michelle's room. "Honey . . . I'd like to talk to you."

"I don't have much time, Mother. Eric's coming by at eight. He found a room on Arapahoe. He wants me to see it."

"Don't you have schoolwork?"

"I already did it."

"You can't ride on the Honda at night."

"I know. We're borrowing the truck. Andrew said it was all right."

"Michelle, listen . . . there are some men who go through life taking whatever they want, without ever giving in return."

"There are women like that too."

"Maybe. But some men, like Eric, think that nothing else

matters . . . that no woman can resist them and all because of their good looks . . .''

"Good is putting it mildly, Mother . . ."

"I never thought you would be so sexist, Michelle."

"Me? You're the one who's being sexist. You're the one putting him down just because he's so good looking, without even giving him a chance, without even bothering to find out what's underneath."

"I know what's underneath."

"How . . . how do you know?"

"I sense it." She wasn't making herself clear. She wished she could come right out and say, *He slept with me, Michelle. We were lovers for a week. I know what I'm talking about.* But in this case honesty was out of the question. "Don't sleep with him, Michelle . . . please."

"My sex life is my own business."

"I don't want to see you hurt."

"Are you jealous, Mother? Is that it?"

"Jealous of what?"

"Us. Our youth. Eric says that women of your age sometimes resent their daughters' youth."

"I don't resent your youth, Michelle. I've had my own."

"Well, I'm glad to hear that, Mother." Michelle pulled a blue t-shirt out of her dresser drawer. "I've really got to get changed now. Don't worry about me . . . okay?"

"I'm trying not to."

"Remember when I was little and you used to read me that Maurice Sendak book, *Higglety Pigglety Pop?*"

"Yes . . ."

"Remember Jennie, the dog who was trying to get experience . . ."

"What about her?"

"Well, that's me, Mother."

"Michelle's after experience," Margo told Andrew later that night. They were in bed, reading.

Andrew ran his hand up her leg. "How about you and me having a little experience tonight?"

"You're not listening. You think it's all a big joke, don't you?"

"Mmm . . ." Andrew had his hand between her legs now.

"And speaking of jokes," Margo said, "our Polaroid pictures are missing. I only hope Eric didn't find them. He used our shower last Sunday."

"More likely Mrs. Herrera found them."

"If Mrs. Herrera found them she'll quit. She doesn't approve of me living with a man who's not my husband . . . . a man who used to be married to Mrs. B.B. She thinks I'm a sinner. Those pictures will prove it."

"Come here, sinner."

"You have a one-track mind."

"It's not my mind," he said, "it's this."

"Oh," Margo said, "I see." And in a minute she forgot about the pictures.

40

ANDREW'S PARENTS CAME TO TOWN ON THE DAY THAT Clare left for Miami to visit B.B. Andrew and Sara had met the Broders at the airport, had spent a few hours alone with them, then had dropped them at the Harvest House. Now Andrew was on his way back to their hotel to pick them up and bring them to the house.

Margo sat in the living room, waiting. She had dressed in southwestern style—a denim skirt, her concha belt, a brightly colored vest, boots, and silver bracelets. She waited nervously, fussing over a tray of cheeses from Essential Ingredients and a bowl of chopped liver from the New York Deli. She had picked up a tulip plant at Sturz and Copeland, which she moved from the coffee table to the dining table, then back again. She wanted the Broders to like her, to appreciate her, to see that she was just right for Andrew. Freddy's parents had accepted her, but they had never thought she was good enough for their son. No woman would have been good enough for their son, which is why their son treated women like shit.

She had had a call from Freddy that afternoon, accusing her of using his support payments to care for another child.

"That's ridiculous!" she'd told him.

"You've taken in his kid, haven't you?"

"She's living with us while her mother is in the hospital."

"The looney bin, as I understand it."

She'd held the phone to her chest and inhaled deeply. She would not allow him to throw her into a frenzy.

"Do you think it's fair, Margo," Freddy had continued, "taking in his kid at the expense of your own?"

"It's not at the expense of my own."

"You have to devote time and attention to her, don't you?"

"It's not your business, Freddy."

"Anything relating to my children is my business. And I don't want my money used to take care of his child."

"Not a penny of yours goes toward the care and feeding of Sara Broder!"

"Good. I'm glad to hear that. Now that we've got that straight, what about graduation?"

"What about it?"

"Have you booked us a room yet?"

"I sent you a list of hotels."

"I'm trying not to remind you that if you had stayed in the city Aliza and I would not have to fly out to never-never land for Stuart's graduation."

"All right," Margo said. "I'll book you a room." She no

longer blamed Freddy for his hostility regarding the distance she had put between him and the children. She had learned, from living with Andrew, what it's like to lose your children to the geographical whim of a former spouse. She had learned how it could tear a person apart and she was not sure the law should allow it under any circumstances.

If only Freddy had made the time for Stuart and Michelle when they had all lived together, if only he had made it clear that he had loved them and had not wanted to lose them. Life was full of *if onlys*.

Maybe divorce should be outlawed, Margo thought. Divorce screwed up as many lives as disease. She tried to imagine a world in which there was no divorce, a world in which she would have been forced to make some kind of life with Freddy. Probably she'd have taken a lover. More than one. Probably Freddy would have too.

Michelle came into the living room and eyed the tulip plant, the cheeses, the basket of crackers and pumpernickel bread. "It looks like you're expecting the queen, Mother."

"It does look that way, doesn't it?" Margo said, surprised at how easy it was to avoid unpleasantness. A year ago she would have become defensive at Michelle's remark and there would have been a major confrontation.

"Eric is coming over at six. We're going to an early movie."

"Don't you think you're seeing too much of Eric?"

"I don't have time for a lecture now, Mother," Michelle said, skipping down the stairs.

No, not now, Margo thought. She closed her eyes, picturing Andrew and herself on a sailboat, moving silently through the emerald green waters of the Caribbean. She could almost smell the salt air, taste the spray, feel the wind whipping through her hair. She had not been sailing since the day she and Freddy had capsized in Sag Harbor Bay, but she and Andrew often talked about a sailing trip. Maybe this summer . . . if they could get it together.

Stuart came barreling up the stairs and began to attack the food Margo had set out so carefully. "Please, Stu . . . wait until the Broders get here."

"I'm hungry now," he said, his mouth full of food

"Then take something from the kitchen."

"Jesus, you'd think Andrew's parents were more important than your own kids."

Margo clenched her teeth.

Stuart laughed and pecked her cheek. "Just a joke, Mom. No one's more important than your own kids, right?"

"Right," Margo said.

Finally, the front door opened and Margo ran down the stairs to greet Andrew's parents.

The Broders were a handsome couple, in their early seventies, both slim, silver-haired, and perfectly groomed. Nettie Broder wore a pale pink ultrasuede suit with a strand of coral around her neck. Her lipstick was bright, with a purple cast, and when she smiled Margo noticed that it had smeared onto her front teeth. In Sam Broder, Margo could see Andrew in thirty years. The same jaw, the same smile, but without the sparkle in his eyes.

Sam Broder had sold his Buick agency in Hackensack twelve years ago. He and Nettie had settled in Florida, not just because it was the place to go when you retired, but because Andrew and Francine had lived there, with the grandchildren. Now Bobby was dead and Francine had brought Sara to Boulder. So much for carefully conceived plans.

Margo wished again that she and Andrew had shared the last twenty years so that by now they would know each other so well, would love each other so deeply, that nothing could ever come between them.

Margo would have embraced the Broders, but she did not want to come on too strong. So she offered her hand and each of them shook it warmly. "Well," Margo said, "shall we go upstairs?"

"Upstairs?" Nettie asked.

"The living room," Andrew explained.

"The living room is upstairs?" Nettie said.

"Yes," Margo told her. "It's an upside-down kind of house."

"A split level?" Sam said.

"No, not exactly," Margo said.

"We looked at a house once with the living room halfway upstairs," Nettie said, "but you still had to go up another four steps to get to the bedrooms. Remember that house, Sam?"

"But that was a split," Sam said.

"Our bedrooms are on this level," Margo said.

"You don't mind sleeping on the ground floor?" Nettie asked. "You're not afraid someone will come in?"

"We're used to it."

Andrew started up the stairs and his parents followed.

"How about a glass of wine?" Margo asked, after they had settled on the sofa.

"Just club soda for me," Nettie said. She opened her purse, took out a compact and looked into the mirror. She quickly wiped the lipstick off her front teeth, then smiled awkwardly at Margo, and Margo realized that Nettie was not at ease either, in this house in which her son was living with a strange woman.

"So where's our little Sara?" Sam asked.

"She's taking a bath," Margo said. "She'll be up soon." Margo had insisted that Sara bathe before dinner. Sara had argued that she didn't need a bath, that she had taken a bath yesterday, but Andrew had backed up Margo, telling Sara, no bath no dinner at John's French Restaurant.

"Andrew tells us you have two children," Nettie said.

"Yes . . . they'll be up in a minute too."

Nettie tapped her foot nervously. Sam sipped a glass of wine.

Margo heard the sound of the motorcycle turning onto the dirt road, then Eric banging on the front door and Michelle, calling, "It's for me . . . I'll get it . . ."

"My daughter," Margo said.

Nettie and Sam nodded.

Why didn't Andrew engage them in conversation? Margo wondered. Why was he just sitting there like a lump across the room? She still wasn't used to him without his beard. She had asked him what he looked like without it so many times he had finally shaved it off, surprising her. That night in bed, in the darkness, she'd felt as if she were with a stranger.

The next morning he'd said, "Well?"

"I miss it," she'd told him.

He'd laughed. "I can grow another one in a month."

At breakfast Michelle had said, "Why, Andrew . . . you're good looking. Who would have guessed?"

"Guessed what?" Stuart had asked. He hadn't even no-ticed.

But Sara had taken one look at Andrew and had cried, "Why did you have to go and do that?" She had left the table in tears.

Now Margo wished that Andrew were sitting next to her, with his arm around her shoulder, showing his parents how close they were. But he was acting as if he hardly knew her, as if he were a visitor in her home, like his parents.

Michelle and Eric clomped up the stairs, both of them wearing hiking boots and work clothes. They looked like soldiers in the Israeli Army, Margo thought. All that was missing were the rifles slung over their shoulders.

Andrew said, "Eric, Michelle, these are my parents, Net-tie and Sam Broder."

"Hey, how's it goin', Nettie?" Eric asked, pumping An-drew's mother's hand. "How're you doin', Sam?"

"This is your son?" Nettie asked Margo.

"No, this is Eric," Margo said. She paused, searching for the right words. "A . . . family friend."

Michelle did not approach the Broders. But she did say, "Hi, glad to meet you, welcome to Boulder and all that. How do you like it so far?"

"It's so windy," Nettie said. "I never felt such wind. I could hardly catch my breath."

"Yes, it can be windy in the spring," Margo said.

"And no ocean," Sam said. "Nettie and I like to be by the ocean."

"We have mountains," Michelle said.

"What can you do with mountains?" Nettie asked.

"Climb them," Michelle said.

Eric was munching on the cheese and crackers when he noticed the bowl of chopped liver. "What's this?" he asked.

"You don't know chopped liver?" Nettie said.

"Chopped liver . . . never saw the stuff, but I'm always willing to try." He took a blob, dropped it on the center of a cracker, and wolfed it down. "Interesting," he said, brushing off his hands.

Margo felt her face stiffen into a half-smile.

"Well," Michelle said, "we really have to go. Nice to meet you Mrs. Broder, Mr. Broder . . . see you on Sunday, if not before."

Margo poured herself a glass of wine and drank it quickly, as if it were water. Then she poured another.

"Some handsome boy," Nettie said, when Eric and Michelle were gone. "Is he Jewish?"

Margo coughed on her wine. "No."

"I didn't think so, never to have seen chopped liver. You don't mind that your daughter goes out with a boy who's not Jewish?"

"Michelle's not marrying him, Nettie," Andrew said, coming to life.

Anyway, he's circumcized, Margo thought about saying.

How would you know? Nettie would ask.

I know because I fucked him, Margo would say.

Oh, my God! Sam, did you hear what she said?

Yes, Nettie. She said that she fucked him. And that's how come she knows he's circumcized.

I fucked him three or four times a day for a week.

Three or four times a day, Sam would say. *That's a lot of fucking.*

I'm feeling faint, Nettie would say.

It's probably the altitude, Margo would tell her.

"Oh, here's our little Sara," Nettie said, as Sara and Stuart came up the stairs.

"Hi Grandma . . . hi Grandpa. This is Stuart."

"Margo's Number One Son," Stuart said.

"You have more than one?" Nettie asked.

"No, that's just an expression," Margo told her.

Nettie nodded. Then she appraised Sara. "That's how you're going out to dinner . . . in dungarees?"

"Blue jeans, Grandma. In Boulder you can wear them anywhere. Look at Margo's skirt . . . same material."

"Well, if it's all right with your father . . ."

"It's fine with me," Andrew said.

"Did I miss Eric?" Sara asked. "Is he gone already?"

"They went to an early movie," Margo said.

"Oh, shit!" Sara said.

"Sara!" Sam said. "Such language."

"Sorry, Grandpa . . . I forgot you don't like me to use those words."

"What movie did my sister and The Acrobat go to see?" Stuart asked.

"He's an acrobat?" Nettie asked. "He works in a circus?"

Margo laughed.

"No, Grandma," Sara said, and she laughed too. "He can walk on his hands. That's why Stuart calls him The Acrobat."

"That's not all of it," Stuart sang.

"Stu . . ." Margo warned.

Margo wanted to like the Broders, for Andrew's sake.

320

She had known beforehand there would be questions. She had tried to prepare herself, planning to answer them honestly, in a friendly manner. But she hated having to tell them about Freddy over dinner, about a life that she no longer lived. She sensed, from their questions, they were trying to find out what problems she might bring to their son.

After dinner they dropped Sara off at Jennifer's, then drove out to the Harvest House. On the way there Sam ran his hand along the back seat of her car and asked Margo, "You like these little imports?"

"Yes, I've had my Subaru for three years."

"I had a Buick agency, you know."

"Yes, Andrew told me."

"It's very hard for a person of my age, a person who remembers everything about the War, to see young people riding around in these Japanese cars."

"The War's over, Dad," Andrew said, pulling into the Harvest House lot.

"Please, Andrew . . . I may be seventy-four, but I still know which end is up."

"I like a roomy American car," Nettie said, as they walked toward the hotel. "We have a four-door Buick, cream-colored. Light colors are best in Florida . . . they reflect the heat."

Margo nodded.

They went into the lounge and found a table in the back, away from the singles crowd, which gathered around the bar. They ordered two Irish coffees and two plain.

"We've been to see Francine," Nettie said. "I didn't want to discuss it in front of Sara, but I thought you should know."

"She didn't recognize us," Sam said.

"Of course she did," Nettie argued. "She just wouldn't talk to us."

"She twirled a rubber band around her fingers," Sam said. "The whole time we were there she twirled a rubber band around her fingers. Like a little kid."

"She was nervous," Nettie said. "She's always been high-strung."

"She looked terrible," Sam said. "Her eyes all sunken in. She used to be such a beauty."

"She will be again. All she needs is a good haircut. As soon as she gets out she'll get her looks back," Nettie said. "But her mother, Goldy . . ."

"That's another story," Sam said.

"She's aged overnight," Nettie said. "God forbid, it could happen to any of us, but Goldy is only sixty-five."

"Sixty-one," Andrew said.

"Really?" his mother asked. "That's all?"

Andrew nodded.

"She can't get the right words out," Sam said. "You can see how she's struggling. But at least she knew us."

"Francine knew us too. I don't know why you keep saying that she didn't. She just wouldn't say anything."

"It's just one tragedy after another," Sam said.

"You knew Francine, of course?" Nettie asked Margo.

"Yes," Margo said.

"It's a shame, not just for Francine, but for Sara."

"Yes," Margo said again.

During Sunday dinner, as Sam and Nettie brought Andrew up to date on their friends and who had died, who had been hospitalized, and who had been diagnosed as having this or that disease, Margo found her mind wandering. She stared out the window at the Flatirons, which were still snow covered, while in town, on the Mall, tulips and daffodils were sprouting everywhere. She could see Michelle out of the corner of her eye glancing at her watch, wondering how much longer this dinner was going to last, how many more minutes before she could be with Eric again. And Sara wasn't eating at all. She was just moving the food around on her plate and making silly faces at Stuart, who was encouraging her to misbehave in front of her grandparents.

It wasn't until after dinner that Nettie and Sam took Margo aside and Nettie said, "Do you think he really loves you or is he just trying to prove something to Francine?"

Margo felt as if she had been punched in the stomach. She could taste the turkey, the sweet potatoes, the fresh green beans working their way up to her throat. She could not bring herself to answer simply, to say, *Yes, he really loves me.* Instead, she said, "I don't know what you mean."

"He's never gotten over her," Nettie said. "When she left and took Sara with her, he fell apart. We thought he'd never come out of it."

"You never saw a boy so in love as Andrew was with Francine," Sam said. "He worshipped her."

"We don't mean to hurt your feelings," Nettie said. "He's our son and we love him, but he won't be satisfied until he gets her back. That's why he came out here."

"You're not the first and you won't be the last," Sam said, "but none of them lasts more than a year. Isn't that right, Nettie?"

"That's right. And it's all because he still wants her. So unless you're willing to be second best . . ."

Margo shook her head from side to side, denying what they were telling her, wanting to shout, *It's not true. You don't know anything about it.* But she couldn't say anything, except, "Excuse me . . ." and then she ran down the stairs, locked herself in her bathroom, and threw up into the toilet.

41

Francine was lying on a lounge chair in the garden. Her eyes were closed. She was practicing one of the relaxation techniques she had learned in *Group*. She pictured herself in a hammock tied to two coconut trees on the beach, the ocean lapping gently in the distance. She was wearing a loose white dress and her feet were bare. The sun warmed her body as the hammock swayed in the breeze. She felt peaceful.

She was expecting a visitor. She was not sure she would be able to talk today, but she was going to try. She wanted to be well. And in order to be well she had to relate to people. She had to talk to them and listen to them and even care about them.

When she opened her eyes she saw Clare walking toward her. Francine stood up and smoothed out the wraparound dress she was wearing. Clare waved, then hurried toward her. Francine stood stiffly as Clare embraced her.

"I'm so glad to see you," Clare said, releasing her, but still holding on to her hands.

Francine nodded.

"How are you?"

Francine nodded again. She poured each of them a glass of lemonade from the pitcher sitting on the white wrought iron table.

"Thanks," Clare said, pulling up a chair and sipping her drink.

Francine sat on the edge of the lounge chair. She wore two rubber bands around each wrist, like bracelets. Dr. Arnold said it was all right to use them if they made her feel more comfortable.

"How is Sara?" Francine asked, tentatively.

"She's fine," Clare said.

"You've seen her?"

"Yes," Clare said. "I try to see her at least once a week. She's singing in the school chorus and she got her first period."

"Her first period," Francine said. "I didn't know." She pulled a pink rubber band off her wrist and began to wind it around her fingers. She hoped it would not snap. She hated it when her rubber bands snapped, surprising her. She did not like surprises. Whenever a rubber band snapped she had to knot it and then it wasn't strong anymore.

"Sara sent you this," Clare said, pulling a blue envelope out of her purse.

Francine took it and put it into her pocket. It was so difficult to make conversation. It hurt her throat and her head.

"She writes to me every week, but I never write to her. I don't know what to say."

"She understands," Clare said.

Francine took a blue rubber band from her other wrist and twisted it around two of her fingers. "She lives with them, doesn't she?"

"Yes."

"Is she happy there?"

"She misses you but . . ."

"I know a joke," Francine said, interrupting. "How many psychiatrists does it take to change a light bulb?" She was supposed to wait for the other person to answer, to say, *I don't know* or *I give up*, but she never did. She always gave the answer herself. "One," she said. "But it takes a long time and the light bulb has to really want to change."

Clare laughed.

In *Group* they were learning to tell each other jokes. That was the only one she had learned so far. She did not find any of the jokes funny. She did not find anything funny. She watched a lot of TV, mainly sitcoms, trying to figure them out. Some of the patients laughed their heads off at *Laverne and Shirley* or *Three's Company*, but Francine wasn't one of them. Dr. Arnold said that her sense of humor would come back in time.

"Part of my problem is I don't find anything funny," Francine said to Clare. "Except for this. I married a man over New Year's in Hawaii. I don't remember having married him, but apparently I did. Isn't that funny . . . to have married someone and not remember? Of course, I don't have to stay married to him if I don't want to."

"You married Lewis?" Clare asked, leaning forward in her chair.

Francine wound the blue rubber band around her thumb. "Yes."

"Are you sure?"

"Yes, I'm sure. I'm not that kind of crazy."

"I'm sorry," Clare said. "It's just such a surprise. Does Sara know?"

"No one knows, except for Dr. Arnold, Lewis, and my *Group.*"

Clare finished her lemonade.

"Here's something else," Francine said. "I had a son who died in an automobile accident when he was ten. They tell me I have to learn to accept that. Do you think a person can ever learn to accept that?"

"Is all of this true, B.B.?" Clare asked, a worried expression on her face.

"Yes, it's all true. I'm learning to deal with the truth. That's why I'm here. And from now on would you call me Francine? That's my real name."

42

MICHELLE WAS IN LOVE AND NO ONE WAS GOING TO SPOIL it for her. Not Margo and her hostile attitude, not Stuart, calling Eric The Acrobat, not Andrew's knowing looks, not even her best friend, Gemini, warning Michelle that Eric was a loser. It was embarrassingly obvious that Gemini, like the other girls at school, was jealous. Only Sara understood the incredible, the amazing truth—not only did Michelle love Eric, but Eric loved Michelle.

Michelle had always known that if she waited long enough her time would come. She was glad she hadn't gone with any of those creepy boys at school, glad that she had saved herself for Eric. She would ride to the ends of the earth on the back of his Honda, her arms wrapped around his waist, the wind in her face, the helmet over her ears so that she could hear only the thump of her own heartbeat.

He waited for her every day after school, surrounded by a

group of girls who stood back in awe as Michelle approached. She would climb onto the Honda and wave goodbye, as Eric revved up the motor and sped off, whisking Michelle away to his room on Arapahoe, where he would make love to her until dinnertime. Then, he would deliver her home to her mother, her cheeks rosy, a secret smile on her face.

She had gone to the clinic for a diaphragm after their first night together. No accidents for her, like Puffin. She had questioned Eric about venereal disease since he had had so many partners, but he had sworn he was clean. He'd encouraged her to examine him. He had turned on the lights and told her to get down close to his penis and look it over carefully and she had. She had never seen a penis up close before. She had never touched one. She liked the way it sprang to life, like an inflatable toy. He had been gentle that first night, but she had been so scared she couldn't let go. It had hurt like hell. She'd felt no pleasure, except for the pleasure of the idea. She hadn't even loved him then. It wasn't until the next day that she'd loved him. And her love had grown steadily in the five weeks since they had met. Eric had changed her life. There could be no going back for her now.

And so, when he told her on May 15 at 5:28 in the afternoon that he had to be moving on, she passed out. She was in his bed at the time.

When she came to, Eric was hovering over her, fanning her face. "What'd you do that for?" he asked.

"The shock, I guess. Do you have to go so soon?"

"I have to get back home in time to find a decent summer job," he told her. "If I'm going back to school in September then I've got to go after the bucks now."

She had known from the beginning that some day he would have to leave. But she had hoped that it would not be until the end of the school year, and then, that he would ask her to come with him to Oregon for the summer, where she would get a job waiting tables in some quaint inn while he worked on a highway construction crew. They would live in a tiny room, with just a hot plate, or else in a trailer, and she would learn to sew so that she could hang curtains in the windows. In September she would come back to Boulder, finish up her final year of high school, and apply only to colleges in Oregon.

"I can come out to Portland as soon as school is over," Michelle said. "I don't have to go east this summer."

"No."

"Why?"

"Because I can't get involved with you."

"You don't call this involved?"

"I never made any promises, did I?"

"No, but . . ."

"I want you to have this," he said, reaching across to the bedside table, handing her a small cactus plant. "I want you to take care of it for me."

Michelle held the plant close, feeling its prickly spines. "If it blooms, I will bloom," she said, closing her eyes. "If it dies, I will die too."

"That's real poetic, Michelle," Eric said. "You have a definite flair for the dramatic. You ever thought of going on the stage?"

She did not remind him that she had given him the cactus plant in the first place.

* * *

She could not eat for a week. At night she would wake up suddenly, drenched in sweat, her heart pounding. She would climb out of bed and check the cactus. It was thriving. She wished she were a child again, so that she could run down the hall to her mother's room and climb into bed with her. Her mother would hold her close, until she was no longer afraid. But her childhood was over, whether or not she was ready to give it up.

"I knew from the beginning that this is how it would end," Gemini said. "I saw it in his eyes. He did not know the way of the world."

"What exactly does knowing the way of the world mean?" Michelle asked.

Gemini shook her head. "I don't know."

"What do you mean you don't know?"

"I made it up."

"You made it up?"

"Yes."

"All this time you've been telling me who knows the way of the world and who doesn't, you didn't know what you were talking about? It's not some ancient Pueblo saying?"

"No."

"But why?"

"I wanted you to think I was exotic and very wise."

"But you are!" Michelle said. "You didn't have to go and make something up for me to believe that."

"Are you angry?"

Michelle looked around her room, focused on the cactus, and said, "No . . . because even if you did make it up, it's true. Some people know the way of the world and some don't."

"But you loved him anyway," Gemini said.

"Yes."

"Even though he was no good for you."

"He gave me exactly what I wanted," Michelle said. "He gave me experience."

"But was it worth it?" Gemini asked.

Michelle's eyes filled up. "I don't know yet. If I live, then I guess so. If I die of a broken heart, then probably not."

"You're not going to die of a broken heart," Gemini said. "You're too smart for that."

"I don't think it has anything to do with being smart," Michelle said.

43

SARA COULD NOT BELIEVE THAT ERIC HAD LEFT TOWN without saying goodbye to her. And after promising to wait until she grew up, until her braces came off her teeth, after promising to be there for her first teenaged birthday, which was coming in just a few weeks. She'd had it all arranged in her mind. How Eric would sit next to her at the table, and then, after she'd blown out the candles on her cake, the way he would kiss her. She could almost feel the softness of his lips on her face. She had believed him when he'd made those promises.

Michelle had been the one to tell them that Eric was gone. She'd said it one night at the dinner table. "Eric left town. He won't be back." She'd said it in a very small voice and everyone except Stuart had stopped eating and looked up at her.

"So, The Acrobat took off," Stuart said, biting into the

skin of a baked potato, "without even so much as a goodbye. Nice guy."

Michelle shoved back her chair, stood up, and raised her glass of apple juice, as if to make a toast. Then she turned and threw it in Stuart's face. "Asshole!" she cried, running from the dining table. A moment later her bedroom door slammed.

"Jesus!" Stuart muttered, wiping off his face with his napkin.

Sara expected Margo to give Michelle hell. You didn't just throw a glass of juice in someone's face and get away with it. But instead, Margo said, "Really, Stu . . . was that necessary?"

"What?" Stuart asked. "What'd I do?"

Margo just shook her head. Then she turned to Sara's father. "I better go down and see how she's doing."

Sara opened her mouth to speak, but Daddy covered her hand with his own and she knew that she should shut up and stay out of it. After that she wasn't hungry anymore, so when no one was looking she passed the rest of her pot roast to Lucy, who sat under the table, waiting.

Every night after that Sara could hear Michelle crying herself to sleep. Probably Eric had made a lot of promises to Michelle too.

Ten days after he'd left town, two postcards arrived from Eric. Sara collected the mail from the box that afternoon and read both of them. One was addressed to Michelle. It had a picture of a beaver on the front with *Greetings from Oregon* printed above it. On the back, Eric had written:

Dear Michelle,
Just a line to say you're a great girl and that knowing you was a great pleasure. Hope to see you again some day.

Yours,
Eric

The other was addressed to Margo. It had a picture of the Columbia River on the front. On the back it said:

Dear Margo,
Thanks a lot for your hospitality while I was in Boulder. I'm sorry I didn't have a chance to say goodbye to all of you. Please tell Andrew, Stuart, and, of course, Sara, that I hope to see them again. You're a swell family.

Sincerely,
Eric

It would have been nice if he had sent a card just to her, Sara thought, but at least he had mentioned her by name.

Margo didn't seem all that interested in Eric's card, so Sara asked if she could have it.

"Yes," Margo said. "Just don't let me see it around."

Sara knew that Margo hated Eric, but she did not know why, unless all mothers hated their daughters' boyfriends. She wondered if her mother would hate Griffen Blasch, this new boy in her class who was not exactly her boyfriend, but who she secretly liked, even though he was so shy he never spoke to her.

Not that what she felt for Griffen Blasch was anything

like what she felt for Eric, but being in love with Eric was kind of like being in love with Matt Dillon or some rock star.

Sara took the postcard to her room and hid it in her bottom drawer, with the Polaroid pictures of Margo and her mother's blue silk blouse. She turned on her radio and tuned it in to KPKE Rocks the Rockies. They were playing "Love Is the Drug."

Later that night Sara walked into the bathroom and found Michelle standing over the sink, a pair of scissors in her hand. "Oh, I'm sorry," Sara said. "The door wasn't locked."

"It doesn't matter," Michelle told her.

"What are you doing?" Sara asked.

"What does it look like I'm doing?"

"It looks like you're cutting Eric's postcard into tiny pieces."

"That's exactly right," Michelle said as the pieces fell into the sink.

"But why?" Sara asked. "It was such a cute picture of a beaver."

Michelle just snorted.

The next day, after school, Sara went to Jennifer's house. They were upstairs in Jennifer's bedroom and Sara was holding Jennifer's hamsters while Jennifer cleaned out their cage. The hamsters felt soft and furry, but their feet squiggled as they tried to get away from Sara.

"Have you talked to your mother yet?" Jennifer asked, as she removed the newspaper from the bottom of the cage.

"Not yet," Sara said.

"She'll probably call for your birthday."

"Probably," Sara said. But she wasn't sure that her mother would even remember her birthday. "Margo and my father said I should have a party."

"What kind of party?" Jennifer asked. She lined the cage with clean newspaper and sprinkled cedar shavings onto it.

"A birthday party," Sara said.

"I know that," Jennifer said, taking the hamsters from her and returning them to their cage. "I mean, what kind of birthday party?"

"Whatever kind I want."

"A boy-girl party?"

"Whatever." The hamsters ran around in their wheel, making a whirring sound.

"Have a boy-girl party," Jennifer said. "I'll help you write out the invitations and we can plan it together."

"I don't know," Sara said. "My mother wouldn't want me to have a boy-girl party. She'd want me to invite six girls over for pizza and a movie, then we'd go back to my house for cake and ice cream."

"You're always thinking about what your mother would want," Jennifer said, "instead of what *you* want. You've got to start thinking for yourself, Sara. After all, it's *your* life."

Sara walked across the room and looked out the window. The sky was clear and very blue. A bunch of kids were roller skating on Mapleton.

"Listen to this . . ." Jennifer said, rattling the newspaper. "Omar says *Today is a big improvement over yesterday, particularly in connection with your love life, social activities, or various recreational pastimes. Give a party.*"

Sara turned around. "Omar says that?"

"Yes, right here," Jennifer said, tapping the paper.

"Hmmm . . ." Sara said, "maybe I will have a boy-girl party. And maybe I'll invite Griffen Blasch."

"I knew you liked him!" Jennifer said.

The baby started to cry then and Jennifer went into the nursery to get him. He was fat and adorable and Sara watched as Jennifer expertly changed his diaper.

It would be very nice to have a baby, Sara thought. A baby would need you. A baby would love you, no matter what. Now that Sara got her period she could have a baby if she wanted. If Eric came back when she was, say, eighteen and wanted to have a baby with her, she might. Then they would buy the blow-up house on Sixth, the house that was made of foam and looked like it belonged to some other planet, and she would go to C.U. and become a vet and Eric would open a motorcycle shop downtown and she would ride to her classes on the back of his Honda, the way Michelle had.

"Do you think your mother and Bruce will have another baby?" Sara asked.

"No, my mother only had this one because Bruce wanted the experience of being a father. My mother didn't need another kid. She already had the three of us. Maybe your father and Margo will have a baby. Then you'll find out what it's like when you're not an only child."

"I'm not an only child," Sara said. Jennifer passed her the baby. He grabbed a fistful of her hair.

"Stuart and Michelle don't count," Jennifer said, rubbing her hands with baby lotion. "They don't belong to either one of your parents."

"I'm not an only child," Sara said again.

"You are too, Sara."

"No. I had a brother, but he died." Sara was surprised at how easy it was to say. "He was ten. His name was Bobby."

"Baa Baa," the baby said.

PART
FOUR

44

FROM THE MOMENT MARGO TOOK HER SEAT ON THE GRASSY field of Boulder High School she choked up and could not speak. The idea of her son graduating from high school seemed not only a monumental event in his life, but in her own as well. She had kissed Stuart's freshly shaved cheek that morning, telling him how proud she was to be his mother, telling him how handsome he looked in his cap and gown.

He had flushed and said, "I feel pretty weird dressed up this way."

Out of uniform, out of his chinos and alligator shirt, he looked much younger to her, like a boy dressed in a man's costume.

The last few weeks had been so filled with the pain of her children Margo had hardly had time to deal with her own. On the day that Stuart received five college rejections he had

343

locked himself in his room and when he came out, hours later, although he had been accepted at one school and wait-listed at another, he had said, "This is the saddest day of my life since the divorce."

His remark had cut into her, bringing back all the old divorce guilt, and for a moment she could not respond. It was the first time Stuart had admitted the divorce had affected him at all.

"It'll be okay," Margo had said finally, trying to comfort him. "Believe me, Stu, it'll all work out."

"That's what you always say. That's what you told me when you and Dad split up."

"And I was right, wasn't I?" she asked. But, of course, she had no way of knowing.

"I'm a failure at eighteen," he said sadly, shaking his head.

"No," Margo told him, "that's not true. We make too much of college. It's not your whole life."

"Maybe not to you . . . but what about Dad? What'll he think?"

"He'll understand," Margo said, praying that he would.

"I got six-fifties on my Boards, I have a solid B-plus average, I play second on the tennis team. What more do they want?" He paused for a minute. "Tell me, Mom . . . tell me the truth . . . is something wrong with me?"

"No, there's absolutely nothing wrong with you."

"Then why?"

"I don't know, Stu. Probably there were just a lot of kids with even higher grades and scores. And that's what they looked at."

"Maybe I came on too strong during my interviews. But I didn't want them to see me as some hick from Colorado."

"Rejection always hurts," Margo said.

"What do you know about rejection?"

"Plenty." Let it go at that, she thought. Let him learn to deal with one kind of rejection at a time. Later he would find out that college was just the beginning.

That had been on April 15. By May 15 Stuart had settled on Penn. "It's Ivy League," he'd said, consoling himself. "And it's Dad's alma mater."

Still trying to please his father, she thought.

Freddy had been a dental student at Penn when Margo had met him, the summer following her junior year at Boston U. She had been waiting tables in Provincetown and taking painting classes during the day. He had been vacationing with two of his buddies. He had seemed so full of life to her then.

Now Freddy sat two seats away from her, at their son's graduation. He sat on the other side of Michelle and on his other side sat Aliza, dazzling in a navy Chanel suit, her hands fluttering to her head, protecting her newly blonde hair from the strong breeze, each of her long manicured fingernails painted a dusty shade of rose. Her hands did not look as if she ever washed a dish, yet Margo knew that she liked to cook.

The graduates, more than six hundred of them, began their long march—step, pause . . . step, pause . . . step, pause—to the same music as Margo had marched to at her own high school graduation. She watched for Stuart and at first sight raised her hand as if to wave, then, realizing that he would be embarrassed, lowered it. *Stand up straight*, she told him mentally. *That's it . . .*

Michelle reached out and touched Margo's arm. Margo turned to her. "He's on the wrong foot," Michelle whispered. "Isn't that just like Stu?"

Margo smiled. She had not been sure that Michelle would recover from the pain of loving, then losing Eric. But a few weeks ago when Margo had gone to Michelle's room to say goodnight, Michelle had been sitting up in bed, holding a small cactus plant to her chest.

"He never lied to me, Mother. Not once."

"Well, there's a lot to be said for honesty," Margo said.

"Do you think I'll ever get over him?" Michelle asked.

"I think you'll always remember him, honey, but eventually, when you're ready, you'll allow yourself to love again." Oh, she'd sounded so wise, so knowing. Did children ever suspect what shaky ground their parents were on when they advised and comforted them?

"Is that how it was with you, Mother?"

Did she mean after James . . . Freddy . . . Leonard?

"Yes," Margo said. "That's how it was with me."

Michelle nodded.

The graduates took their seats.

Andrew sat on Margo's left side and next to him, biting her fingernails, was Sara. Behind them, Clare, Robin, and Margo's parents. Margo was glad her parents had been able to come. She was reminded of her own grandmother's death a few months before her high school graduation.

Two endless speeches followed, one by the valedictorian and one by a Congressional hopeful, a former graduate of

346

Boulder High School. Endless speeches about going out into the world early in this decade, about the beginning of their adult lives.

Adult? Margo thought. No. Adulthood started somewhere around the age of forty.

Andrew squeezed her hand.

Margo thought back to that cold November night when, snuggled close in her bed, Andrew had first proposed the idea of living together and they had agreed to give it a try.

For how long? her mother had asked, when Margo had told her of their plans.

For as long as it works, Margo had said.

The idea of it seemed so simplistic now that Margo laughed out loud. Both Andrew and Michelle looked over at her, probably thinking she'd found something funny in the politician's speech.

Until the end of the school year, at least, they had promised each other. Well, graduation was the end of the school year, wasn't it? And tomorrow Andrew was flying to Miami . . . and Margo could not erase his parents' message from her mind.

On the morning that Andrew had been driving his parents back to the airport for their return flight to Miami, Margo had gone out to a five-acre building site in Sunshine Canyon to walk the property with Michael's clients, a couple from Cincinnati who had plenty of money, whose children were grown, and who wanted to change their lifestyles.

Michael had been in Aspen at the time, skiing with a woman he'd met through a personal ad in the *New York Re-*

view, a woman who was willing to relocate if she found the right man.

The couple from Cincinnati wanted a southwestern style house, like the ones they had seen in Santa Fe over Christmas, with white plaster walls, rough wood ceilings, and Mexican tile in the kitchens and bathrooms, plus a separate guest house for when their children came to visit.

Margo tried to concentrate on their questions, but she hadn't been able to get the Broders, and what they had said to her, out of her mind—that Andrew wouldn't be happy until he had Francine back, that Margo was just second best. With all of her problems, with all of her doubts and insecurities, which came and went, she had never thought of herself as second best and she wasn't about to start now.

When she got home from the canyon she left her muddy boots in the front hallway and went to take a hot bath. Soon she heard a thud, followed by Andrew's voice. "Goddamn it, Michelle . . . can't you ever put your things where they belong!"

"They're not *my* boots! Why do I always get blamed for everything?"

Margo wrapped herself in a towel and rushed out of the bathroom to see about the commotion. Andrew had tripped over her boots as he'd come into the house and had fallen.

"They're mine," Margo said. "I'm sorry. Are you all right?"

"Bruised my knee," Andrew said.

She helped him to his feet.

"Sorry, Michelle," Andrew said, "it's just that it hurt like hell and I was mad."

"Yeah, well . . . it could happen to anyone, I suppose."